praise for karen winters schwartz's

reis's pieces

"Karen Winters Schwartz gives us Reis. A gift. From the first page of his treacherous climb up through the forest, feet planted on the firm ground of reality and in the terrifying quicksand of delusions, I was transported. His story is all too real and one anyone can identify with. I related to his terrors, loneliness, elation, and love. And yet, as far as I know, I am not psychotic."

—Xavier Amador, PhD
bestselling author of *I Am Not Sick, I Don't Need Help!*

"In *Reis's Pieces*, Karen Winters Schwartz once again shows the human side of mental illness. How refreshing to find a novel with real-life characters affected by schizophrenia—a likeable young man struggling to accept his illness and its effect on his life, and the emotional journeys of the people who love him. This highly readable story helps us take one more step away from stigma and toward understanding and possibility, with a thought-provoking touch of enlightenment along the way."

—Randye Kaye, bestselling author of *Ben Behind His Voices: One Family's Journey from the Chaos of Schizophrenia to Hope*

"Karen Winters Schwartz's compassionate novel *Reis's Pieces* gives us a close encounter with what it would be like to suddenly lose everything—to be blindsided by the onset of schizophrenia. By alternating back and forth between Reis Welling's past life as a young botany professor who's just been granted tenure at Cornell and his present life as a lonely man whose mental illness has broken his connections to his career, his family, his friends, and the woman he loved, Schwartz intensifies the pain of Reis's losses. By working in multiple points of view, we hear the past and present voices of not only Reis, but also of all the people who have been and are part of his worlds. Because of all these views, we come to understand the complicated sides of all the stories and the step-by-step progress that is possible."

—Ginnah Howard, author of *Night Navigation*

"The image of the black crow ready to pounce on the fledgling plant captures the way mental illness descends on young, talented Reis and almost destroys him. By artfully shifting the timeframe from the past to the present, Winters Schwartz helps the reader to gain a sense of how insidious the onset of schizophrenia can be and how much of the person's life is slowly eaten away by 'the crow.' While this is fiction, it depicts a reality that is painfully true in numerous families, not all of whom have the love and ability to remain faithful. More than just engaging the reader, hopefully *Reis's Pieces* will enable readers to have more insight into this illness, which is so misunderstood and stigmatized."

—Nancy Kehoe, RSCJ, PhD, bestselling author of *Wrestling with Our Inner Angels: Faith, Mental Illness, and the Journey to Wholeness*

"This novel is a learning experience for readers. It portrays relationships affected by the onset of schizophrenia and choices that must be made in order to find a road to recovery. Free will confronts life-changing events, and no outcome is certain."

—Michael J. Fitzpatrick
MSW Executive Director, NAMI National

"Karen Winters Schwartz takes the reader on a heartfelt, enlightening journey in *Reis's Pieces*, an honest and highly entertaining novel that intelligently addresses the devastation and despair that the unexpected onset of schizophrenia can have on an otherwise bright and wonderful person, as well as on his loved ones. As she did in her previous novel, *Where Are the Cocoa Puffs?*, Karen paints the humanistic side of mental illness with a genuine and accessible brush of empathy."

—Alan Gettis, PhD, bestselling author of *It's All Part of the Dance: Finding Happiness in an Upside Down World*

"*Reis's Pieces* is a literary present to all who want to better understand the complexities and cruelties connected with schizophrenia. While helping to dissolve typical misconceptions and stigmas associated with the disease, *Reis's Pieces* provides a dynamic and engaging storyline, drawing the reader deep into protagonist Reis's past and present life, craftily showcasing his tumult into mental illness and a life forever altered."

—Joseph J. Luciani, PhD, bestselling author of *Self-Coaching: The Powerful Program to Beat Anxiety & Depression*

"Karen Winters Schwartz has captured the trauma, tragedy, fear, and courage of living with schizophrenia. The beauty of Karen's work is her empathic treatment of the illness as seen from the perspectives of parent, lover, colleague, mental health professionals, and, most sensitively, of the bearer. Her saga is beautifully and compellingly written, drawing us willingly along the painful, sometimes comic, and heroic paths each character walks. Karen clearly understands."

—Bill Cross, PhD, LMFT
psychotherapist and professor emeritus of psychology

"*Reis's Pieces* is an insightful and uncompromising work. Karen Winters Schwartz presents what's sure to be an enduring benchmark novel on mental illness, more specifically the misunderstood intricacies of schizophrenia and those afflicted. A must-read for anyone touched by mental illness or working in that arena."

—Allen Klein, bestselling author of *Learning to Laugh When You Feel Like Crying: Embracing Life After Loss*

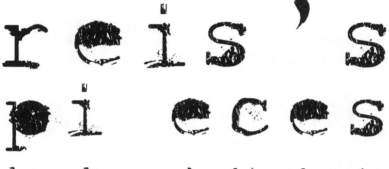

reis's pieces

love, loss, and schizophrenia

Also by Karen Winters Schwartz:

Where Are the Cocoa Puffs? A Family's Journey Through Bipolar Disorder

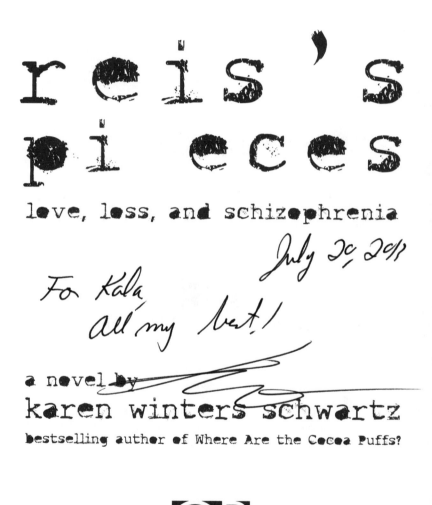

reis's pieces

love, loss, and schizophrenia

July 20, 2011

For Kala,
All my best!

a novel by
karen winters schwartz

bestselling author of Where Are the Cocoa Puffs?

GOODMAN BECK PUBLISHING

GOODMAN BECK PUBLISHING

PO Box 253
Norwood, NJ 07648
goodmanbeck.com

ISBN 978-1-936636-08-2

Library of Congress Control Number: 2012934826

Printed in the United States of America

10 9 8 7 6 5 4 3 2 1

For all who are suffering in deafening silence.
Be heard.

"But, say you, surely there is nothing easier than for me to imagine trees, for instance, in a park and nobody by to perceive them. The objects of sense exist only when they are perceived; the trees therefore are in the garden no longer than while there is somebody by to perceive them."

—George Berkeley

one

Reis was dreaming of the forest. He was reaching upward, his hand wrapping around a tree root, his foot finding that perfect step in the earth. He felt his muscles tighten in an almost sexual way as he ascended toward the brilliant fall blue of the sky—his body straining in pleasure, each advance a rush, a wholeness. Each part doing what was necessary—a perfect amalgamation of man and mountain so that when he woke only a few yards from the summit of his dreams, he felt initially euphoric, stretched his arms above his head, and yawned. His eyes then focused on the dullness of the ceiling. Feeling the sticky sensation of the sheets against his back, his head started to ache. The nauseous odor of mildew hit him each time he took a breath, while the incessant sound of Albany traffic assaulted his ears. He closed his eyes and tried, unsuccessfully, to draw himself back into the dream, into that sensation of perfect control. He rolled over on his side and drew his legs toward his chest, glad that he was alone—glad that he could roll up like a child and not be judged. And, if he chose to, glad that he could cry, or even weep, with no one there to hear that tree fall in that forest.

t wo

He slipped into the park when the sun was just a pink promise and only the most ardent of birds were contemplating their morning serenade. He moved silently through the trees, seeking solitude among the calming foliage, where he could hide himself and spend the day fighting demons or worshiping the gentle swaying of green against a too blue sky.

By noon, the city park in Albany was crowded, as it often was on Saturdays in the early summer. The winters, so harsh, were something to survive in this part of New York State. The summers, fast and glorious, could not be ignored. As much time as possible must be spent outside or one risks being overcome with both guilt and the knowledge that in the short time it takes a bird to go from a tiny egg to a wobbly airborne creature, summer will be gone. The ball fields were full of children too tiny to hold a bat without listing forward and men too old to hold a bat without risking injury. Big dogs, little dogs could be seen from every point of view. Would-be scholars lazed under trees, engrossed in the literary world. Frisbees flew and kites flapped wildly—but refused to rise in the gentle breeze of summer—as children ran. A chestnut-haired young woman and small brown dog walked briskly along the ball fields. Her right arm was extended forward as the dog pulled eagerly at his lead, choking in his enthusiasm. They made their way to the end of the first ball field before the woman stopped and suddenly turned to her left. No one took notice as they disappeared amid the dark green leaves of the tiny forest that bordered the park.

No one, that is, besides Reis Welling, who was safely shielded by a canopy of young summer leaves. He watched from his place of refuge as the girl bent down to take her dog off his lead. The dog fidgeted with barely containable anticipation, making her task more challenging than desired. Once free, the dog—a short, fuzzy dog of no particular breeding—sprang away, running from tree to tree, his nose consistently to the ground. The girl's brisk steps turned into a slow amble. The sight of some unseen victim evoked an urgent bark from the dog. The dog sprinted after it, kicking up leaves as he ran. His efforts to secure the creature, which turned out to be a squirrel, failed as it scampered up the nearest tree—a tree not all that far from where Reis resided. Reis pressed his back against the trunk and held his breath as he watched the squirrel wind its way up the nearby trunk. Failure in no way diminished the dog's enthusiasm, seeming instead to ramp it up a notch. Barking, he leapt upon the trunk, his tail wagging in a tight, frenzied circle. It was only a moment before the dog bounded onward, unfettered and eager for his next victim.

Reis let out a slow breath as the girl, watching her dog's antics with motherly approval, approached along the dirt path that wound its way into the thick wooded area. The warm sun filtered through the leaves—gems of light across the forest floor. The girl's image danced in and out of the gems, her hair shimmering, disappearing behind the green, then reappearing. Amongst the gently blowing breeze and waving leaves, her image was gone once again, only to reappear closer. She passed below, small and quite alone, engulfed by the cool, soft wildness of this tiny ecosystem. The surrounding trees muffled the sounds of the children who played in the ball field behind him, enough so that it was relatively silent other than the soft shuffle of her presence. The sound of her feet padding gently against the earth—reminiscent of a carefree doe—was soothing to his unease, and he could almost believe that he was far away from the children who screamed, the cars that honked, and the baseball bat that let off a sharp crack with each accurate swing. He felt the sudden pleasure of wild, mossy solitude, closed his eyes, and swayed.

Suddenly the dog's sharp barking crashed through the woods, shattering the soft silence. Reis almost felt the tree quiver with the dog's assault, his tiny paws banging against the trunk, his tiny, dark canine eyes pinned on him. He'd been discovered, unsheathed, naked in a sea otherwise clothed. His heart took a little leap and then beat steadily against his chest as he watched the girl take heed and step a little closer to investigate.

The barking subsided as she joined the dog, its paws still on the trunk, its gaze skyward.

"What do you see, Max?" she asked. "Is it something bigger and meaner than a squirrel?" She laughed. "Something you could really sink your teeth in?" The dog glanced at his owner, his worried-dog look apparent even from this distance. His eyebrows quivered with concern before he returned his gaze upward, his eyes finding Reis. An uncertain growl issued from his throat, his tail grew stiff and upright, and the hairs on his back rose in a slightly crooked line along his spine. Reis watched as the girl's smile slipped away and a twinge of apprehension crept onto her face. Reis pressed further into the trunk, the rough bark digging through the thin cloth of his T-shirt. She slowly lifted her eyes from her dog, slipping her gaze his way. Squinting from the brightness of the sun overhead, she brought her hand to her forehead.

He heard, quite clearly, the gasp, and watched as her feet staggered several steps away from the tree. He heard the dog's growl deepen and saw the girl's hand sweep up and to her throat as she quickly scanned the woods. In the moment it took her to decide if she should hail a hello or simply walk away—or perhaps run as if her life depended on it—Reis was swinging away from the trunk, letting his body descend with a sudden rustle of leaves. He landed on the forest floor with a gentle thud. Hunt or be hunted. And there he was, standing so close that he could smell the sweet brush of perfume mingling with the subtle odor of human fear. The dog—as harmless as he looked, relieved to find that it was just a human being he'd been aurally assaulting—sniffed at Reis's bare feet and began to wag his tail.

There was a moment of total silence as their eyes locked, her mouth slightly agape. The dog gently placed his front paws on Reis's legs, stretching so that they almost reached the fray of Reis's shorts. Reis and the girl both broke their gaze and looked down toward the dog.

"Your dog must have thought I was a pretty-funny-looking squirrel," he said, his eyes never leaving the indentations of each claw against the skin of his thigh. When he was met by silence, he glanced up and saw her mouth open to respond, but no words came out. "I've frightened you," he said, his eyes rising upward. "Most people never see me." His eyes swept the foliage with fondness. "I suppose it might seem odd to you, but it's really peaceful up there."

He shifted his feet a bit, his eyes returning to the dog. He heard the girl exhale, caught a brief childhood whiff of Wrigley's gum, crouched down, and ruffled the fur on the dog's head.

"It doesn't seem *that* odd," she said, her voice a squeak that almost made him laugh.

He smiled up at her then. It was a slow, cautious smile that took a moment to find a home on his face, but once it did—the sensation of his upper lip pressing against the tops of his teeth—he did indeed laugh. She was absolutely, breathtakingly amazing, and the only conceivable response was laughter. She smiled tentatively back, then laughed as well. As she shut her eyes with apparent relief, he rose, and when they reopened he was standing before her, looking down at her green eyes and the way her dark chestnut bangs stuck up at a strange angle. Remembering the way one of her front teeth stuck out slightly, marginally larger than the other, he wanted to hear and see that odd little laugh again. He watched as her face turned red with embarrassment.

She brushed away the sound of her laughter as if it had never occurred, brushed at her bangs, and said, "I used to practically live in trees...when I was a kid. Kids always like to climb trees." Her voice picked up steam as she spoke, losing that squeak and turning into notes. "And really, shouldn't trees hold the same appeal to an adult as to a child? And yet...very few adults climb trees...." She nervously brushed again at her bangs and knitted her brow in quick thought. "Adulthood is just not a good reason to stay out of trees, now is it? Unless, of course, you're really old. Then it might not be so safe. I mean, you could fall or something. Break a hip." She laughed again, and he smiled. "But if you're, you know, still young and in good shape...and I guess you are...." She paused for an awkward second, caught his look, and shut her mouth, the redness returning to her face.

"*Quercus velutina,*" he stated, his hand coming up stiffly toward the tree he'd been sitting in. "Black oak. It's approximately seventy-two years old. There are exactly two hundred and fifty-one mature trees in these woods. They consist mostly of three varieties of maple, two of oak, black walnut, cotton wood, and three varieties of pine." He stopped, making sure he had her full attention. "I've climbed seventy-two of them...so far. This black oak is the best. Pine, of course, you should not climb. Too soft. No one climbs trees on Christmas, anyway."

She cocked her head, suppressed a laugh, and gave him a half-smile. He narrowed his eyes and cocked his head in the opposite direction as she said, "Well, I'd say you certainly know your trees. Did you study them in school?"

"I was a botany major. Phytogeography was my specialty."

"Phytogeography?"

"The study of plant distribution," he answered, not even trying to hide his impatience. Then he smiled an apology and added, "It's not a word you hear every day."

"No...no, it's not. And what do you do as a phytogeographist? Work in a tree nursery?"

At this, he laughed—a laugh that tickled his gut in an overwhelming burst of patronizing joy, which made him laugh again. He saw a rush of irritation pass her face, so he offered, "I used to teach."

"Used to?"

He quickly saw his error but saw no way out other than to say with absolute finality, "Now I work at the library." He squatted on the ground and resumed patting the dog, whose tongue and tail exploded into action. "Nice dog," he said. He did not bother tilting his face away from the onslaught, so when he briefly glanced up at her and smiled, the dog slapped a wet one across his teeth. Before the girl could respond, he was back on his feet, looking away into the woods. "Well, anyway, I'm sorry for frightening you."

He turned, pushed the underbrush aside, and stepped into its thickness with hardly a sound. Already feeling the relief of cover, he did not turn around until he was sure he was enveloped in vegetation. When he did, he could just make her out through the leaves, staring toward his retreat, her little dog also looking his way, his little brown tail beating the wind.

th ree

Kelly Adams smiled at Brian as he talked. He looked especially good tonight, his face brushed with a fresh tan of summer and wind, his blue eyes vivid in their intensity. The waiter came bearing food, and Kelly was forced to turn her attention to the large, leafy concoction that was set down before her. They were sitting at their favorite table, next to the window where they could watch the local traffic and the people as they walked along the street. The restaurant was small and slightly unkempt. The plastic red-checkered tablecloths were ripped and soiled. The lighting was dim, which helped hide the wear on the black and white linoleum floor. Dusty plastic plants hung from the ceiling in bright red baskets. Faded photos of the Italian countryside graced the walls. It was not the ambiance that brought them there but strictly the wonderful food that Mario created in his kitchen. Brian chatted about his day while he attacked his salad, wielding large piles of speared lettuce about in his enthusiasm. As always on Saturdays, he'd worked from eight until one at the law firm where he recently made partner, claiming that he worked most efficiently in the evening and on weekends, when there was less staff around. Then he'd gone to Lake George and crewed with some friends in the weekly regatta. "I wish you'd been there, Kelly. You should've seen us turn that last marker, trailing by three lengths. Suddenly, whoosh! We hit the wind just right and sailed to victory!"

Kelly would've liked to have been there, but she couldn't recall having been asked. Brian had his life well compartmentalized, and one compartment did not necessarily blend into the next. There was the work compartment, the play compartment, the friend compartment, and the sex compartment. It was obvious which one she fell into. Would there ever be a commitment compartment? A marriage and kid compartment? Kelly stabbed a cherry tomato a bit too aggressively—without the necessary finesse—and it popped out of the bowl in violent protest. She watched as it thudded along the greasy tablecloth, and she allowed a tiny sigh to escape from her lips. Brian impaled it neatly with his fork and laughed as he popped it into his mouth. Kelly chose, as she watched the merriment on his face, not to join that laughter.

Then she felt guilty. She was feeling broody and bitchy for no good reason. She was only twenty-six. There was plenty of time for him to settle down—for him to want a family. Kelly returned her attention to her food. She did not want to be *that* woman who was waiting miserably for more.

"So what did you do today, gorgeous?" Brian asked. She looked up from her salad. He smiled and squeezed her leg beneath the table.

"Oh, I didn't do much." She shrugged with boredom. "It was such a beautiful day that I read on the patio for a while. Ran some errands. Then Max and I took a long walk in the park." She sighed, stifled a yawn. And why, exactly, would Brian want to marry her? "Oh!" Her voice brightened. "There was one interesting thing that happened in the park." She proceeded to tell him about the tree man.

"Kelly." He pointed a breadstick at her and shook his dark hair in mild disapproval. "I really don't like the idea of you talking to nuts in the park. There are a lot of really strange people in this world." She started to protest, but he raised his hand to silence her. "I know you'll talk to anyone who'll stand still, but one of these days you're going to get yourself into trouble! Normal grown men don't go around climbing trees and frightening people. Don't you ever stop to think?" He looked at her squarely now, waiting for her to admit her offense.

"First of all," Kelly fired back, "don't be poking your goddamn breadstick at me!" Brian leaned away from the words, sinking back into his chair. Encouraged—momentarily—by his retreat, her voice rose with her anger. "And don't you dare try to tell me who I can and can't talk to while you're out sailing with your fucking friends!" She paused, her anger squelched by the shocking violence of her words. *Fucking*: a word that almost never left her lips, and yet she'd just flung it into the room. She glanced at the woman a few tables over who had paused mid-drink to look her way. She slid down in her chair. "And...and third of all," she all but whispered, "this man was harmless. A child could see that. I was never in any danger."

"Well," Brian said. He put the breadstick in his mouth, bit down hard, and crossed his arms over his chest. "I stand corrected."

Kelly looked away from his angry condemnation and swirled her wine until small red flows escaped over the rim of the glass, skillfully captured with her tongue. Her eyes drifted to the window, and they both watched silently as an odd assortment of pedestrians strolled past. A very large man walked by, dressed in the shortest shorts Kelly had ever seen on a male; the pale edges of his derrière shamelessly snuck out from the bottom. He was arm in arm with a tiny, green-haired woman who was beaming up at him with great affection. Kelly smiled and almost said something to Brian, but she quickly remembered he didn't enjoy stranger studies as much as she did. The waitress brought their food, and Kelly eased the steaming, creamy bowties onto her fork and took a tentative bite. She chewed with appreciation. Even a fight with Brian couldn't diminish the pleasure of Mario's food. She scooted her fork back onto her plate and captured three of the chewy, wondrous morsels. She opened her mouth wide in anticipation.

"How's your pasta?" Brian asked brightly.

Kelly withdrew the fork, still laden, and closed her mouth. She rested the fork gently on her plate. "Let's not do that."

"Do what?" asked Brian, with a sigh.

"The obligatory culinary chitchat."

He pursed his lips and knitted his brow. "Fine."

They ate in silence, later shook their heads to the offer of dessert, and before the waitress had a chance to bring the check, Brian threw a couple of twenties on the table and stood up to leave. Kelly gulped down the remainder of her wine and contemplated the twenties. A glass of wine, a beer, two simple pasta dishes.... Yes, it was enough.

Kelly leaned toward Brian as they walked from the restaurant. She pressed her shoulder against his—an olive branch of a gesture, and Brian responded by slipping his hand out of his pants pocket and tap dancing his fingers up her back. She laughed, as this finger dance always made her laugh, and then his hand, with a grand jeté, was on her shoulder, where it drew her in. "Sorry," he said. "I would have invited you to go sailing, but it's not my boat. Richard takes his sailing very seriously."

"Oh! I know." She sighed into his shoulder. "Just ignore me. I'm just premenstrual or something. Practicing my bitch imitation and doing a superb job, if I don't say so myself. I'm the one that should be sorry," she stated.

"And, are you?"

She glanced at him in confusion.

"Sorry?" he added.

She shrugged her shoulders slyly and laughed.

Brian always stayed over on Saturdays, and although this Saturday was to be no different, when Kelly pulled back the covers to her bed and slipped in next to him, she still felt the awkwardness. So when he scooted toward her side of the bed and slid his hand along her waist toward her hip, she almost said, *Let's not do this. Please, not the obligatory sex.* But even as she kept her words to herself, he must have felt their weight, because he scooted closer, kissed her lightly, and said, "Goodnight, Kelly." Within moments, he was softly snoring.

Sunday morning, Kelly was the first to stir into consciousness. She rolled over and watched him as he slept. His face was peaceful and calm, his lips slightly apart as he breathed easily. His hair, ruffled now, fell gently on his forehead. Brian shifted slightly in his sleep; a small smile crossed his face. Kelly sighed and felt her lips curl up in a smile. Over three years of loving this man and she was still overcome by his beauty—his love of life. Even in his sleep the joy of life seeped from his pores. And isn't that what she loved the most—what she needed and drew from him—the pure, unfettered joy of life?

His blue eyes were suddenly open. "Hey, gorgeous," he whispered sleepily. His arm stretched forward, his finger lightly touching her forehead and brushing away an unruly strand of hair from her face. It lingered there, then his hand pushed gently into her hair and down her cheek to her shoulder, and then lower, until it found her breast. She closed her eyes to the sensation of his fingers gently investigating the intricacies of her nipple, and when the sensation became too much to bear, she pulled him to her. They made love with no thoughts of angry words over leafy greens or incriminations with breadsticks.

f●ur

As Reis left his apartment that Sunday, the city streets of Albany were a sing-song of idle activity: pointless street lights—red to green to yellow to red; ignored *walk* indicators; small black kids scattered across the sidewalks—their mothers almost not watching from front steps; teenagers smoking on corners; a stray dog barking for no apparent reason—maybe at the rattle of an empty beer can shifted by a breeze; an elderly white couple negotiating the uneven sidewalk; a thin yellow cat slipping into an alley; the sudden assault of a passing car, its muffler hanging by a wire coat hanger—notes blasting out through open windows; a hostile glance as Reis interrupted a small financial transaction on the next block; a homeless man still sleeping under a stoop—his mouth open to the early afternoon sun. And the closer Reis came to the center of town, the quieter it became, as if the buildings overpowered and became a force of their own. They took on an almost surreal existence that pressed down on Reis, making him walk faster through the streets until he was almost running—but not wishing to run, lest he bring attention to himself. It was with great relief that Reis hit the other side of downtown, turned the corner, and made his way up Elm. He entered into the cool interior of the city branch library—his heart slowing to a steady beat—paused, and breathed in the odor of paper, mild mildew, aging carpeting, and old cups of coffee, which was somehow soothing.

Lanie looked up from her spot behind the desk and smiled. Reis was moved to do likewise; he knew that for one more day everything would be okay.

five

Monday morning, Kelly sat staring at her computer screen. Although she had no window within sight in her tiny office, she could hear the rain banging on the metal roof above her head, and in her mind she could see the cool dark grey of the day. She rubbed at her eyes and could not seem to muster an iota of creativity or her usual enthusiasm for her work. Normally, she savored the hours of solitude. Just she and her beloved computer, working together, working out program bugs, creating new computer games—her fingers flying across the keyboard, her mind focused on the task. But today fit every cliché of a Monday.

She punched a few keys in frustration. "What's wrong with this damn thing?" And then she stroked them gently. "I'm sorry." She leaned toward the lettered, black squares and whispered her words of apology. "I'm sorry, baby," she repeated, leaving her fingers softly on the keys. Then she leaned back and shut her eyes. Who was this man, and why could she not seem to erase him from her mind? This man whose clothing was slightly soiled, mossy, and tree-like. This man whose light hazel-brown hair fell haphazardly around his forehead and ears, causing her to resist the urge to brush it off his face. This man whose gaze was now fixed into her brain like some sort of unquenchable want.

She just couldn't stop thinking about this man, the movie of their encounter a loop in her mind. She once had a favorite tree—a large pine. She had climbed to its very top, in spite of its apparent *soft wood*. There, slowly swaying back and forth in the wind, so many catastrophic, preteen problems were contemplated and often solved. And she could smell the pine—hear the sound of the wind pushing through the branches, her long dark hair flowing with the breeze....

Kelly jumped and opened her eyes to the sound of a sharp knock on the walls of her workspace. She ran her hands through the now-much-shorter tresses, brushed the hair away from her face, and smiled up at Phil.

"Sorry, Sleeping Beauty," he said. "Hate to disturb your little rest, but you did ask me for these." Phil's red hair was pulled back in a ponytail, the distinct odor of weed wafted through the room as he set the papers on her desk.

"Ants!" She sat up with alertness. "They're fascinating creatures. And there's that cute ant movie. Kids love ants."

"I used to incinerate them with my magnifying glass—pull a couple legs off and watch them run in circles."

"You're a cruel man."

Phil shrugged and turned from the room. As he sauntered off, Kelly turned back to her monitor. The screensaver had turned on, and a tiny replica of Max ran up and down the screen. Her sound system was turned down, causing his tiny little yaps to sound as if he were very far away.

That night Kelly was unsuccessful in her attempt to fall asleep. The night was hot, and her sheets felt damp against her skin. She restlessly tossed them off. Lying spread eagle on her back, she stared at the dark shadows the pale moonlight cast across her ceiling. Her double bed felt king-sized, and she left it, walking across her bedroom to the window. She peered down at the dark street below. Nothing much was happening outside her walls either. She picked up her cell phone, brought up Brian's number, almost hit send, and then put the phone down with a sigh. Then she picked it back up, closed her eyes, and hit call. He answered on the third ring. She could hear the TV—a ballgame—in the background. "Hi, Brian. How's it going?"

"Hey, what's up?"

"I was hoping maybe you could stop by. A little sleepover." She hesitated, twisting a strand of her hair in a tight little knot as she talked. "I guess I'm feeling a little lonely."

"A lonely woman! There's nothing I love more than a lonely woman." His laughter came through the phone.

"So you'll come over?" she said, dropping her hair in surprise.

"Ah, well, I'm kinda hunkered down here, Kelly. I've got this early breakfast meeting…."

"It's okay," she said softly, retrieving the strand of hair. "No biggie."

"Hey, come on. Don't be like that. It's what, nearly eleven?"

She closed her eyes, wishing like hell she'd never made the call.

"Hey, let's meet for lunch tomorrow. Okay?" he said.

"Sure. Yeah. That would be great."

They chatted for a while like lovers do, and by the time they hung up the phone, she was feeling a little better—a little less alone.

It wasn't like she ever had a lot of friends…like she wasn't used to being alone. Painfully shy as a young girl, depressed and graceless as an adolescent, she'd been that strange, awkward girl in high school—the one who made everyone else feel better about themselves. The one who bore the brunt of teenage cruelty—teased or painfully ignored by the boys, rudely snubbed by the girls. Then, in college, when she'd unexpectedly blossomed into a desired creature, she'd been freaked out by and untrusting of the sudden onslaught of male advances. So she'd gone to school, done her work, hid behind baggy sweats and hoodies, and stupidly endured the heartbreak from college men who only wanted the pleasure of her body. She had withdrawn further until, miraculously, she eventually made a few friends—a small and steady group of computer nerds from the University of Albany. The four of them had latched onto each other's neuroses during their final college years, shed the unbearable scars of high school, and found themselves in each other. But she'd stayed in Albany, while they'd moved on—all of them gone now, on to bigger and better things: Joe and Lesley in Silicon Valley, Missy in New York City.

It was really Phil's doing—why she was still there. He'd taught one of her last computer classes at UAlbany. Maybe it was his crazy red hair that had originally attracted her, or the sleepy way he accepted every aspect of life, but their short and rather awkward romantic tryst was replaced with something firm and dependable—a nice paycheck, a decent friend, and a job she loved. Then, suddenly—and quite astonishingly—there was Brian, an amazing man, right-out-of-a-storybook gorgeous. He seemed to want her—and only her.

They'd met by the dirty, smelly porcelain of a man's urinal—

something that would be fun to tell her children someday. Kelly was twenty-three and had bravely offered to take Mattie, her not quite four-year-old nephew, to the county fair. She watched with horror as Mattie clutched his tiny penis through the folds of his pants. "I really have to pee!" he exclaimed, bouncing from one foot to the next as Kelly looked up at the endless line of women and small children waiting for the women's bathroom.

"Come on," she said, freeing one of the little boy's hands and leading him to the men's room. She interrupted only one person, an old man dressed in thick, tan work pants splashed green with cow manure, which he zipped up when he saw her, proceeding to leave without washing his hands. It was then, as Kelly struggled with Mattie's stuck zipper, that Brian walked in, well dressed—a dark suit, a silky red tie—looking oddly out of place. Mattie was in tears, and Kelly was squatting down close to the boy's crotch and pulling with all she had. Dumbfounded, Brian stared down on her, his hands on his well-attired hips. The zipper finally gave way, and the little boy was—thank God—free to saddle up to the urinal. Kelly looked up at Brian and said in response to the incredulous look on his face, "He really had to go!"

"Well, so do I!" was Brian's answer.

Mattie sighed with contentment as a fine, yellow stream cascaded into the urinal. Kelly stood up and held her ground. "And who's stopping you?" She looked down to the fine, tight weave of Armani. "Is your zipper stuck too?"

Brian laughed and would later reveal that he'd wanted to say, *Would you like to find out?* He thought better of it and saved the line for another time—a time when Kelly found out that he believed, in only the most rudimentary of ways, that vegetables grew from the earth and meat came from animals. He was at the fair only for a client, and he was not, in any way, agriculturally inclined.

And so it had started and continued with this man—this man who Kelly could hardly believe had given her a second look, much less fallen in love with her. And here she was, over three years later, not in Silicon Valley, nor in a flat in SoHo, but in Albany, New York, living her life as millions of others lived their life—always, and unreasonably, wishing for more.

s ix

Five years had passed since Reis Welling first set foot on the Cornell campus of Ithaca, New York. With cockiness, he'd walked toward the botany building, where he was to pound out the final details of his new faculty appointment. He was twenty-three and had managed to graduate twice at the top of his class—first from Yale, with a bachelor's in biology, and most recently from Berkeley, with a doctorate in botany. Starting college at the age of barely sixteen had left little time for the usual teenage experiences. Learning had always been the priority, but maybe now, he thought, as he walked toward the campus, he could relax a bit and enjoy life's other pleasures.

Reis stopped and took in the beauty of Cornell. He stood atop a hill on campus—a soft summer breeze blowing through his hair—and looked down at the sparkling blue waters of Cayuga Lake framed by soft green hills. Sailboats, tiny from this distance, skimmed across its surface. White lines grew and spread apart as motorboats cruised across the water. The size of the lake was left to one's imagination as the waters extended north and then disappeared around the bend of the hills. He turned from the lake and admired the rich variation of the Cornell landscaping, the way the light stone buildings of the university contrasted against the blue sky, and how they nestled into the gently rolling hills as if they belonged and had always been there. He savored the quintessence of knowledge that permeated the air—all the minds reaching for ideas like tendrils of ivy. Yes, he could grow to love the place.

When he was done, his faculty position secured, Reis drove the four hours to his parents' house in the new Saab they'd given him for graduation, singing loudly and not caring that he was out of tune. He banged on the car's steering wheel with his right hand. The windows were open, his left arm out the window, his hand tapping the car's roof, his hair blowing with enthusiasm. This was his moment—what he'd wanted for as long as he could remember. He'd stopped at other universities during the long drive home from California. He'd stopped at all the national forests along the way. He'd spent days backpacking deep into the woods, sleeping under the stars. He'd collected plant and soil samples, with the intention of continuing his research when he found a faculty position. There had been many fine universities along the way, and he'd received several offers. But, Cornell.... Well, Cornell was his dream.

Reis drove up the long driveway bordered by tall cedars that led to his boyhood home. He could see the house sprawled across the lawn. As always, when he'd been away for a while, Reis was shocked by the enormous size of the house. In spite of its size—framed by large, stately oaks that cast cool shade across the extensive lawn, deep ivy growing along the dark stone walls, forming crazy green frames around each of its large windows—the house was warm and welcoming. Although Reis could not see the river, he pictured its brown, churning movement; when he opened the door of his car and took in a breath, he could smell and hear the movement of its waters heading toward the Tappan Zee.

"It's Reis! Walter! He's home!" his mother, Martha, called as she walked from the front steps. Then, with a few more steps, she was there to embrace him. "I'm so happy you're home! We didn't know if you'd make it today."

"Reis." His father smiled as he walked from the house. He shook his son's hand and then hugged him against his chest. "How was the drive?"

"Great. The car's wonderful!"

"So, come on in. We'll unpack the car later. You must be starved," his mother said. "I've cooked all your favorites. You just come in and tell me what you want."

"You're right. I *am* starved." Reis put his arm loosely around his mother's shoulder as they headed for the house. As they entered the large foyer he released his mother, stopped, and took it all in. Blue, green, and red light filtered down in thin shafts from the stained glass window high above, giving the entranceway a magical appearance. He looked directly ahead through the French doors, which opened up into a large sitting room, and then through the large windows overlooking a green lawn with informal gardens. Down further: the dynamic view of the Hudson River.

The house had been built in the late eighteen hundreds when soirées and banquets were all the rage. To accommodate these guests, two coatrooms with small bathrooms stood to the right and left as you walked in. To the right stood a large staircase of black marble with a dark mahogany railing that twisted around as it rose to the open second floor. Reis had spent many a rainy afternoon sliding down that rail and scampering back up the stairs to do it again. He walked past the coatrooms, past the staircase, and into the sitting room, savoring the view. Turning to his parents, a boyish grin on his face, he said, "God, it's good to be home."

Later, as they sat down to an early dinner, Reis told them about Cornell. "Oh, honey! That's wonderful!" his mother said, pressing her hands together and beaming with pride.

"Well, I guess if you must teach, Cornell's the place to do it," joked his father. It was no secret that Walter had hoped Reis would somehow enter the business world. Any true disappointment had long been resolved and replaced by good-hearted ribbing about each other's chosen professions.

"Oh hush, Walter." His mother reached out and squeezed Reis's arm. "I can't believe after all these years you're finally coming home. Just a few hours away."

"I've missed you both too."

Reis smiled at his mother. It did feel good to be home, if only for a short while, but the three of them in this absurdly large house seemed a little sad. He fought the urge to leave the table and see if his old tree fort that he and his father had built one summer was still there. Nailed between the split trunks of an old sugar maple, it was large enough—when he was a boy—for Reis to lie in the middle, on his back, with his legs and arms spread out just as far as they would go. Even so, he still could not touch the sides. It might take two boys, stretched out side by side, their fingers almost touching, before the outside walls could be reached. There had been a boy or two, but no one Reis felt brave enough with to suggest such a thing. Could he, alone, touch those sides now?

If he missed that little boy or his nonexistent siblings to lie with in his tree house, it wasn't something he ever dwelled on. A baby brother or sister had almost happened. But then there was the evening his father had rushed his mother to the hospital—the neighbor coming over, making him cookies and talking nonsense. "Where's my mom?" he'd asked over and over again, but his four-year-old mind would not accept the answer. And when she came back looking like someone other than his mother, there were no other children to help fill up the massive structure of his boyhood home.

Reis spent many hours alone—in the woods, in his tree house, swallowed up in a book on his father's big chair in the library. His mother worried, always dragging some poor sucker of a child over to play with her hermit of a son. There was an unsettling fact that would not change: Reis was happier after his playmates had gone home, when he was alone and free to tramp around the woods behind the house, or when he was alone and lost in a book. But there was also another fact: he did not necessarily want to be happier alone.

He'd rolled in the mud and splashed in the shallows of the river, scaled up trees and hopped on one foot atop fallen logs, tracked and studied forest creatures, collected plants, and gathered small trinkets. He'd come home with ruffled hair and muddied hands, ripped clothing and a smile, to the smell of hot cookies, proudly bearing such treasures as fossils, nuts, leafy plants, mushrooms, bones, dried frogs, and half-rotten carcasses of many an unfortunate small animal. "Put that thing down, and wash your hands," his mother would say. Then, with the cookies safe in his belly, he'd find the perfect spot in his room for his new treasure.

When the collection began to overflow from his room, his mother suggested he start a museum of sorts in the large attic of the house. Shelves were built along the walls, and several free-standing displays were erected for the most priceless of findings. Reis categorized each specimen into plant, animal, or mineral. He carefully labeled all he could identify, and for those he could not, he made up elaborate scientific names like *Brownish vulgaris fungus*, *Pteridophyta laceyish jade*, or *Adiantum platypus face*. His mother had never removed anything from the museum, and it remained as he had left it.

That night, after his parents had gone to bed, Reis went up to the attic. He slowly moved around the room, picking up each small fossil or bone. He smiled as he remembered those many hours of exploring. He picked up a shell of an eastern box turtle—one of his finest pieces. He could still remember exactly where he'd found it. When he got to the plant section, he read the carefully printed names on each sample. Some were pressed in wax paper, others dried or preserved behind Saran Wrap. He marveled at how many he'd correctly labeled and how much his knowledge had increased. He could name each plant, its class, and its family. He knew whether it grew only in the New York area or throughout the country, what kind of soil it preferred, and even which plants it liked best as neighbors—facts most people couldn't care less about, but facts that he savored. He sat down upon the dusty floor of the attic, turtle shell still in hand, and carefully wiped at the scutes of the shell with the bottom of his T-shirt until time slipped away.

The next morning the three of them sat at the kitchen table, a simple breakfast of cereal and coffee before them. Martha, still in her light summer robe, sipped her coffee and glanced through the gardening section of the local paper. Reis was giving his full attention to his Rice Chex when Walter looked up from the *Wall*

Street Journal and said, "I was considering taking the end of next week off. I thought you and I might spend a few days in the Adirondacks."

Reis looked up, his spoon suspended near his mouth, dripping milk. "Sounds great, Dad."

Walter tilted his chin toward his chest so that he could better see his son over his reading glasses, then smiled. "It'll give me one more chance to knock some good business sense into you before you attack the real world."

The edges of Reis's mouth curved upward. "The real world? Dad, everyone knows academia is not the real world." He emptied the spoon into his mouth and chewed.

Wednesday evening they packed the car for an early morning departure.

"You sure you won't join us, Mom?" Reis called toward his mother as he threw his backpack in the trunk of the car.

Martha looked up from the small flower garden she was weeding next to the garage. "Heavens no! You two men go and do some of that heavy male bonding that seems to be so popular these days."

Reis left the car and joined his mother on the ground. He grasped the blades of a small crabgrass plant and teased its roots from the ground. "You used to go hiking with us," he said, leaning companionably toward her. "When I was a boy."

His mother sent him a soft smile. "Reis. Look at me. Do I look like I could still drag my body up a mountain?"

Reis did look at his mother, and it was true: she'd aged. Her waist was no longer the curves of his childhood, her hair was highlighted with grey, and her pleasant face was softer than it used to be. She'd never been the athlete his father was, but some of his fondest childhood memories were the three of them around a campfire. "There is nothing more peaceful than the smell of a campfire and the rustle of the leaves," he coaxed.

"Trimming my roses and sleeping until nine is all the peace I need, thank you." She brushed her hair out of her eyes with her garden glove, leaving a smudge across her forehead.

He smiled gently. It may have been his father who'd given him the ability and desire to climb that highest mountain, but it was his mother who'd cultivated his love of botany, who'd caused him to pause from his next step upward…and be awed. "Then we'll try not to wake you when we leave at four," Reis said, brushing at his mother's forehead. "You have a little dirt there."

se ven

Reis stood between the shelves in the library, staring absently into the rows of books. He glanced down at the copy of *Moby Dick* that he held in his left hand. Someone seeing him in that moment might have thought Reis was deeply pondering Captain Ahab's descent into madness, yet Reis had never even read the book. He'd never taken the time to read many novels, as there were so many other ways to spend time, so many facts to absorb, and so many sources from which to obtain those facts.

Here he was, holding this book, in a library in a city he never would have chosen to hold a book in. But here he was, working here, in this library, which was, as it turned out, reasonably acceptable. When it was suggested he might work here, well...he'd felt both insulted and frightened by the possibility, but he'd gone along with it. What real choice had he had? What were his other options? He couldn't remember now. Memory—a bizarre and funny thing.... The point was, he'd picked this place to be close to.... Close to what? Books? Learning? His apartment? No, the apartment had come later. Certainly not other people—although his coworkers were pleasant enough. As irritating as he found their occasionally patronizing tones, he felt they accepted him and let him do his job without too much interference. He'd been here how long now? Had it been three months already? Three months, two months, one....

Reis refocused on the book in his hand with a start and contemplated it for a moment. "Moby Dick," he mumbled. "FIC 820." As he turned from the row of books and searched for the book's home, he stopped short and narrowed his eyes in disbelief as his gaze rested on the nearby table. He blinked, not trusting what he saw. But there she was: that woman—the woman from the park. Had he told her where he worked? As he struggled to remember, she suddenly looked up and saw him. He felt a sudden panic and hid the book behind his back.

She smiled his way, and his eyes took in the details of her face. Her smooth skin was slightly tanned with just a hint of freckles on her nose and cheeks. Her lips were soft and perfectly shaped— sweet summer raspberries on a fine china plate. Her chestnut hair shimmered in the light, alive as it fell gently to her shoulders. A deep, natural beauty, a river flowing in the sun...the first sun of morning. How she must look first thing in the morning...her hair all tousled with flowing beauty. "Hi," she said, a bit timidly. "Do you remember me? We met in the park."

"Of course." He felt himself smile. How odd that those muscles used for smiling still functioned automatically.

"I'm just doing a little research for my job," she continued, indicating the books spread out in front of her. "I usually go to the main branch, but I just thought today that I'd, well—" She stopped and laughed. Reis didn't move a muscle, *Moby Dick* still safely hidden behind his back. She drew a quick breath and fumbled on. "I…also…I…I really just wanted to see you again."

She might as well have hit him, for his reaction was that of shock—almost panic. He glanced around for somewhere to go. What was she after? What did she want?

"I'm sorry," she said quickly. She stood up and came toward him with a troubled look. "I didn't mean to embarrass you." Reis took a step back, but she reached out and touched him lightly on his arm as she spoke. "I'm not usually this bold."

Her touch was hardly more than a tap, but he felt her heat surge through him, forcing him to be reasonable. "I'm not embarrassed." He smiled. "Only a lunatic would be anything but flattered."

Reis closed his eyes for a long second and rubbed his forehead gently. He never should have opened his mouth, but it was too late; the words had already escaped and were flowing through the room, bouncing off the walls, striking the ceiling, falling back down, and coming to rest in too many ears. He glanced around, his eyes darting from one coworker to the next.

"Hey, Reis," Lanie called from the desk. "It's five minutes after five."

Mitchell looked up from his computer monitor. "It's after five, and Reis's still here?" he teased.

Reis looked at his coworkers and then at his watch. "I have to go. I'm late."

"Late? Where do you have to go?"

With exasperation, he looked at this woman he did not know. "It's after five. I work until five, then I go home."

"Just home?"

"It's Tuesday, isn't it?"

"Yes."

"Tuesday after work I go home. If it were Wednesday, I'd go walk in the park. Thursdays I eat dinner at Tony's." He stopped. Why was he telling her this?

"You have a regular schedule, huh?" she asked with a slight and patronizing smile.

"Yes, of course." He narrowed his eyes. "Schedules are very important." He turned his back to her and went to gather up his things.

"Yes.... Yes." She was following him now. "But what about spontaneity? It's supposed to rain tomorrow. How about a walk in the park today? It's another lovely day."

He stopped short and turned to her. "Today?" He studied his shoes suspiciously. "With you?" He glanced up.

She nodded with a nervous smile.

Reis looked at her directly now. His eyes narrowed in thought. It was obvious that she wanted him to say yes. What was she after? What did she want? Then he suddenly understood. It was so obvious; he was embarrassed by his initial confusion. But the question remained: who'd sent her? Dr. Benson? His mother? Maybe the hospital. Perhaps they'd all conspired together. She was, most likely, a social worker or a nurse. It was imperative that he find out—imperative that he protect himself.

"Go ahead, Reis," said Mitchell. "Get a little crazy." Lanie smiled from her place at the desk. Mitchell laughed gently. Reis gave his coworkers a hostile glance. Yes, they were all in on it—listening, talking about him constantly, reminding him at every moment how totally worthless he really was. If only they'd stop with all their negativity, perhaps he could rise above.... Above.... He looked up toward the ceiling.

She followed his gaze upward. "We don't have to. I just thought—"

"No." Reis forced his eyes back to this girl and smiled his best smile. "We could go. Especially if it's going to rain tomorrow." He tipped his head formally and shot her his grin. "I'll just get my things." He walked as normally as possible to the desk and collected a large rumpled paper bag and a stack of books. He nodded a curt goodbye to his coworkers before walking back toward the girl. "Shall we?" he smiled slightly as he indicated the door. She looked at him, uncertain. His smile widened with reassurance. She smiled back and took a step toward the door. He reached it first and opened it for her. The heat of the day streamed in, enveloping him like a damp mitten. He paused, letting her exit first. She stepped through the door, turned slightly back toward him, and waited. Blinking into the brightness, he stood beside her on the steps of the library, the door closing behind them with a harsh click. He hesitated just a beat too long before he gestured with his hands that they should perhaps walk.

"So, what kind of work do you do?" he casually asked her as they reached the last step.

She stopped and hesitated, her eyes searching the street, then coming back to him nervously. He stopped with her and set his face to a gentle waiting—as if the next word out of her mouth were the only thing in the world he longed for.

"I work at Disc Com Corporation," she finally answered. She gave him a strained smile and glanced back to the street.

"Tell me about what you do," he said softly.

She turned his way, swallowed, and answered, "We develop all sorts of computer software. My job's to come up with new ideas and make them work. I do mostly kids games."

Reis studied her face, the depth of her eyes. His fine-tuned powers of intuition could detect lies better than any machine. The trick was in the irises, which always told the truth. The pupils you could not trust—dark…too dark…. "What are you researching then?" he asked, trying to hide any trace of suspicion in his voice.

"Well," she said more brightly, her voice relaxing, "this may sound crazy to you, but I've got this idea for a video game that takes you inside an ant colony. The player is perhaps a visiting ant who's searching the ant tunnels for signs of a long-lost relative or something." She laughed at this but continued. "I haven't got it all straight in my head yet. The main point of the game is to locate something or someone. In order to get there, the player must answer questions and find clues about ant life. You know, what they eat, how they build their homes, communicate with each other. The possibilities are endless."

Reis smiled. Her voice was amazing—musical notes streaming through the air. He started walking slowly toward the street, and she followed. "So anyway," she smiled back, "I'm trying to learn as much about ants as I can, so I know what I'm doing. I know I could do almost all of this on the computer at work, but sometimes I just like to get out and, you know, touch my research."

"That's what keeps the library alive: hard copy," he stated. Reis began to relax. She seemed so honest and sincere. He certainly must be vigilant, but blatant paranoia was unnecessary.

Heading toward the main entrance, they walked along the sidewalk that bordered the park. The soft padding sound of their feet against the sidewalk seemed amplified, pushing back the sounds of the city streets. There was just a soft sigh of a breeze, licking gently at the fine layer of sweat that had formed across Reis's forehead. He brought his fingers to his head, lifted his thick hair off the nape of his neck, and closed his eyes with a sigh.

"How long have you been working at the library?" she asked.

He opened his eyes at the words but let them settle in before answering. "Three months," he finally said. "Not long at all." And then it was necessary to add, "I certainly don't plan to work there forever, of course."

"Do you think you'll teach again?"

Her words stopped him mid-step. She stopped one step ahead and turned her face to him with anticipation. It surprised Reis that she seemed to remember everything he'd told her on their first meeting, especially since it all seemed a bit fuzzy to him.

"I hope to. Someday," he answered. "You know what? I'm hungry all of a sudden. How would you like to grab a sandwich and eat by the pond?"

"Okay," she shrugged. They'd not moved from their spot on the sidewalk, and she looked at him for a moment, her smile warming to a pleasant salutation. "You know," she said, "we've never been properly introduced." She extended her hand. "My name is Kelly Adams."

"Reis Welling." He shook her hand, feeling strangely relaxed, and extraordinarily normal.

eight

As always, Reis arrived at Dr. Benson's office five minutes before his appointment. "Good afternoon, Dr. Welling," Sue, the receptionist, called as he entered the waiting area. He nodded to her and sat in the chair furthest from the front door and furthest from the receptionist desk.

"Is the doctor running on time?" he asked, not meeting her eyes.

With a slight smile, Sue answered his weekly question with a *yes*.

"Good. Glad to hear it." Reis sat back and studied the room for any changes. The same three paintings hung on the cream-colored walls. One was of a covered bridge situated over a gently flowing stream. The second was a landscape of soft, green rolling hills dotted with farmhouses, barns, and fencing. If Reis looked very closely from where he sat, he could just make out the tiny cows and horses upon the hillsides. The third was Reis's favorite.

It was of a small child sitting in a large field of grass and daisies. The wind blew in such a way that the details of her small round face were lost in the tangle of her auburn hair.

He noticed the frame was slightly crooked, walked over, and carefully adjusted it. He sat back down and took his weekly inventory of Dr. Benson's magazines: *Good Housekeeping, Time, Harper's Bazaar, Field & Stream*—they were all there. Reis never read them, but he took pleasure in knowing they were there, in case Dr. Benson was ever running late.

A small blonde woman of about fifty walked in from the back offices. She stopped briefly at the reception desk before she walked quickly out the door. She and Reis did not acknowledge one another as she stepped past.

"The doctor is ready for you now," Sue said.

Dr. Benson stood up from his large walnut desk and came around from behind it. He smiled as he shook Reis's hand and indicated, with a slight tilt of his head, the soft leather chair that sat to one side of his desk. Reis went to the chair he'd come to know. As he sat, he felt the coolness of the leather against the back of his lower thighs and was comforted as he ran his hands along the smoothness of the armrests. Dr. Benson sat with a comfortable sigh in his own chair, which he must have spent hours of his life in, and Reis imagined that the doctor must know each curve and lump as one might come to know a woman...familiar...soothing....

They sat, semi-facing one another, and Dr. Benson tapped his pen gently against the ever-increasing paperwork that adorned his desk. "How are you, Reis?" He was in his mid-thirties and not at all the image that comes to mind when one thinks of a psychiatrist. The first time he'd seen Dr. Benson all those many months ago, Reese had wondered why an accountant had come to visit him. Then he'd gotten to know his kindness and his gentle personality, and with time, Reis had stopped looking for a calculator hidden somewhere in Dr. Benson's pockets. He'd grown to trust him as much, if not more, than he could trust himself. But trust was something that should be regularly scrutinized.

As Reis studied his favorite ripple of darkness that threaded through the leather of the right armrest, he said, "I've met a woman." He glanced up quickly, catching the subtle rise of Dr. Benson's eyebrows.

"Really? Tell me about her."

"Well, it was really rather odd." Reis returned his attention to the armrest and watched the movement of his index finger as he traced the darkness. "I saw her the first time in the park. I actually frightened her." Reis paused, smiling slightly as he looked up and waited for Dr. Benson's reaction.

"Frightened her?" the doctor asked, without concern. He was leaning comfortably against the back of his chair as if nothing could disturb him.

Reis's smile broadened. "She was just a bit startled when she saw me up in a tree."

The doctor laughed. "Ah, climbing trees again, are you?"

"Of course." Reis grew serious. "We talked briefly, then I left. I never thought I'd see her again. But a few days later, she shows up at the library." Reis paused and narrowed his eyes at Dr. Benson. "Don't you think that's odd?" He leaned forward in his chair.

"Did you tell her you worked there?"

"I don't remember." He waved his hand dismissively. "She said she wanted to see me again. Don't you think that's very odd?"

"No...not really. She—"

"It occurred to me," Reis interrupted, "that perhaps she might have been sent there." He sat back smugly and looked at Dr. Benson.

"Sent there? By whom? For what purpose?"

Reis paused before he answered. The doctor's face was a mask of indifference. He was damn good at the game. Reis would have to be direct. "It occurred to me," Reis said carefully, avoiding accusatory intonation, "that perhaps you, or someone from the hospital, sent her."

"Why would we do that, Reis?" asked Dr. Benson, sitting forward and resting his arms on the desk.

A puff of impatient air flew from Reis's mouth. "To spy on me, obviously!" he shot back, anger spilling from him. "You people are always trying to get information of some kind or another!" He shook his head. He must try to stay calm. He'd promised himself he'd be calm. He trapped his shaking hands in his armpits and felt the wetness there.

Dr. Benson sat back again. A barely discernible sigh escaped his lips. "I assure you, Reis, she was not sent there by me or anyone from the hospital. You may believe that people desire information from you, but it's simply not the case. Everyone who knows you, including me, wants only to help you, in any way needed, so that you will continue to get better. Spying on you I would not consider helpful."

"Stop telling me what I may believe! I know what I believe! I know there is a strong desire for information. You cannot deny this."

"I'm sorry," said Dr. Benson. "Poor choice of words.... I only meant to assure you that this woman was not sent by me, or anyone affiliated with this hospital."

Reis looked at him a moment, trying to decide if he was lying. "It just seemed so odd to me that she should show up there. What other possible reason would she have for wanting to see me?"

"Reis," Dr. Benson said, "whether you realize this or not, you're a very attractive man."

Reis looked at him. "And your point?"

"Has it occurred to you," Dr. Benson added, "that she might have liked you…been attracted to you?"

Reis thought for some time before he spoke. Looking out the window behind the doctor's desk, he watched the puffy white clouds floating past. "I don't know. I guess I hadn't thought of it that way," he said, calmer now, seriously considering what Dr. Benson had said. "We had dinner together in the park." Reis shifted his gaze back to the doctor. "Even for a spy, she was very nice—beautiful."

"Did you make plans to see her again?" the doctor asked as he sat back further in his chair.

"No, of course not." Reis shifted his gaze from the doctor and back to the arm of the chair. "One shouldn't encourage such things," he said softly. His eyes shifted to the cloth of his shorts and found a small thread worth pulling on. "Say she isn't a spy after all. Well, then, certainly no one needs to get messed up in my life. Can you imagine anyone wishing a relationship with someone who's certifiably insane?" The thread gave way and dangled limply between Reis's thumb and forefinger. He looked back at Dr. Benson, his voice getting louder. "I certainly can't."

Dr. Benson nodded slightly and thought for a moment before asking, "How are you doing? Are you still hearing the voices?"

"Yes, at times. They didn't like her at all. They had lots of nasty advice to give me."

"But you didn't listen to them," Dr. Benson stated.

"No. History will show that they do not always give the best advice." Reis smiled ironically.

Dr. Benson leaned even further back and rested his right foot

on his left knee. He brought his hands together under his chin before adding, "Don't exclude the possibility of a relationship, Reis.
You are a young man with a lot to offer. You are improving every
time I see you. I truly believe that, with time, your life will fall
into normalcy."

Reis rolled his eyes. "Who defines a normal life?"

"Friendships and family are extremely important."

"Has my mother been talking to you again?"

"We talk. She'd like to see you."

"Thanks for the great advice, Doc," he said, shifting in his
chair. "I believe our time is almost up."

"No, not yet," Dr. Benson said, glancing at the clock. "How
are your medications? Have you been taking them every day? Perhaps we should increase the Seroquel."

"I'm fine. No increases. I'm hunky-dory. Taking all my meds
like a good boy." He was losing his patience with this man.

"You're still having some auditory hallucinations," Dr. Benson said softy.

"I am fine! You're trying to turn me into a drugged-up zom-
bie!" Reis closed his eyes. He must not yell. He must not let this
man get to him.

Dr. Benson waited.

Reis sighed. "I don't know.... The drug levels are fine." He
forced his voice to be calm again. Something positive must be said
in order to placate the doctor. He pondered for a moment. "You're
right about my mother. I should see her."

"Do you want to call her? Have her come here?"

"Well...you know...*should* is not the same as *will*. And *want*
is not the same as *need*. And sometimes it all gets mixed up, and
there are causalities."

Dr. Benson sat back and frowned slightly.

"Tell her I'm fine, will you? Tell her I stack books faster than anyone who's ever worked at a library." He involuntarily rubbed his shaky fingers through his hair.

"I think she'd rather hear that from you."

"Just tell her for me. Okay?" He looked at Dr. Benson. "Please?"

"Okay, Reis. I'll tell her. But you don't need to go through this alone."

"I'm not alone, Doc." He smiled a bit. "I've got you. I can bitch to you all I want. You just listen politely and take all my money. It's a perfect relationship—like a prostitute with a john. We both come out feeling better: me having relieved myself on you, and you able to make that next payment on your Mercedes."

Dr. Benson laughed. "I have to tell you that I've been called many things, but so far you're the first to call me a prostitute."

"No offense intended."

"None taken." He smiled at Reis. "And it's not a Mercedes; it's a Porsche."

n ine

There was the faint glow of daylight's approach as Reis pulled out of the driveway of his childhood home and turned onto the main road that followed the Hudson River north toward the Adirondack Park. He held a steaming cup of coffee in one hand, sipping it gently as he steered with the other. His father sat to his right, nursing his own hot brew while perusing the maps that lay across his lap.

"So where're we heading?" Reis asked.

"Let's see…. What are you in the mood for?"

"How about Owl Head Mountain?" Reis said, not looking from the road.

Walter turned from the maps. "Owl Head Mountain?" He made a face. "That's for small kids and parents with babies on their backs."

"Well, you know, Dad." Reis tilted his head toward his father. "You're getting up there. You wouldn't want to stress the old ticker."

"I can still hike circles around you, my boy!" his father answered with mock irritation. He returned to the maps, tracing his finger along the page. "How about Mount Marcy from Elk Lake?"

Reis brought the travel mug to his lips and shook his head. "Dad, I'm not even up for that."

"Okay. Let's compromise. Haystack, via Phelps Trail?"

Reis scrunched up his face in quick thought and nodded. "Kudos to the old man to my right!"

"Smartass!"

As long as Reis could remember, they had always enjoyed making their final plans in the car, a fact that irritated Martha to no end. "Every good hiker leaves an itinerary with a loved one. You both know that!" she complained. "What if something happens and you don't come back? How am I supposed to know where to begin to look?"

And even when Reis was a very small boy, his standard answer was always, "The highest mountain, Mom. And always at the top!" Then he'd laugh, his father would grin, and his mother would moan.

They reached the Garden trailhead at seven that morning and signed in on the hiking log. There were only a few cars in the parking area, which pretty much guaranteed they'd reach the summit alone; it was unlikely anyone would pass them on the trail. After a quick inventory of their gear, they locked the car and hoisted on their packs. The day promised to be hot with only slight humidity. There was a breeze that they hoped would be enough to keep the black flies to a minimum but not so strong as to blow up a storm.

"Shall we?" Walter smiled at Reis and then glanced toward the gently ascending trail, which quickly disappeared behind the cover of surrounding trees.

"Let's do it!"

The two men hiked with a definite purpose, keeping talk to a minimum, as was their habit. The only conversation consisted of occasionally pointing out an interesting plant or animal. When the sun reached the eleven o'clock position, they stopped for an early lunch. They were almost halfway up the mountain, the easiest part behind them.

Reis sat down on a small log and watched his father take a long drink from his water bottle. "How you holding up, old man?"

"Better than you, by the looks of you."

They were both wet with sweat, the humidity having greatly increased. Black flies swarmed around their heads. Small red welts covered Reis's neck and face. "Are you kidding? I'm doing great. I live for this shit!" Reis looked about in pleasure. They were surrounded by old-growth forest—massive eastern hemlocks, paper birch, American beech, bigtooth aspen, and sugar maple. Impressive buttresses of moss-covered roots snaked across the ground. The slow decomposition of standing and fallen snags mingled with the living trees. Outcrops of metamorphic rocks dotted the landscape. The air was heavy with the odor of the earth—of moisture and rot and growth—and bustling with the sounds of life: the soft fluttering of birds, the distant call of a crow, the humming of insects, the soft shuffling of squirrels forging through last fall's leaves....

"It is great out here," his father agreed as he scanned the forest. He sat heavily on his own log and rested the back of his head against a tree. "This is when I truly feel at peace, out here with God's creations surrounding us." Walter closed his eyes with fatigue.

"You know, Dad, there's one thing I've never understood."

Reis removed his sandwich from his pack before looking up and continuing. Walter's eyes opened lazily. "You have such a love of nature—probably every bit as strong as mine. I just can't imagine going to that city every day and doing the work you do. How can you stand it?"

Walter opened his eyes further, sat up a bit, and looked fondly at his son. "Well, Reis, the city is not so different than this forest. They're both filled with life-and-death struggles. They both present challenges. Not every man could make it up this mountain, and very few men can make it on Wall Street, especially in today's market. I've managed to conquer both," he said with a smile.

Reis contemplated his father for a moment. "So you do it for the thrill of victory?" His words were laced with friendly incredulousness.

"Something like that. I believe you have a more pure love of nature than I."

Reis scanned the forest with his hands. "You see all this as something to be overcome?"

"That's right," said his father.

Reis took a bite of his sandwich, his forehead creased in thought.

"You find that disturbing?" Walter asked.

Reis narrowed his eyes at his father. The truth was: he did. He found it quite disturbing. "I see this forest as a part of me, an extension of myself—of all of us. It's hard to explain. It's as if my soul lives among the rocks and the trees. The only time I truly feel whole is out here."

Walter stared softly at his son, and if the words *the only time I feel truly whole* elicited any sort of fear, Walter did not let on. After a moment he nodded his head slowly, as if in understanding, both men knowing that there was no understanding. They were quiet for a time, absorbed in their own thoughts as they ate their lunch. Walter shifted his legs and looked up through the breaks in the canopy at the thickening clouds. "Do you know how very proud I am of you, son?" said Walter.

Reis followed his father's gaze to the sky. "Yes. I believe I do." His head came down and he met his father's gaze. "I imagine it's very close to how I feel about you."

They looked intensely at each other for a moment before Walter looked away. "Well," he said, crumpling up the wrapping from his sandwich and tossing it into his pack, "if we're both done pouring our guts out all over the forest floor, I'd like to get up this damn hill before nightfall."

It was late in the evening when they finally reached the crest of the mountain. The sky glowed with the pinkish blue hues of sunset, leaving them little time to contemplate the incredible views the summit offered. The going had been very slow. A little past the halfway point, the trees had thinned, and the soft forest floor was replaced by hard rock. The wind increased in intensity, and as dark gray clouds appeared from the west, they negotiated the rocky footing. Daylight slipped away as a storm rolled in. Lightening decorated the skies with large spidery streaks, and rain pounded the ground with fierce determination. Sheets of water, encouraged by the wind, forced the men to stop. They sat miserably under a small ledge until the rain slowed to a fine, spitting drizzle. With grumpy wetness they picked their way among the slippery rocks, needing both hands and feet for the slow ascent. An hour later the rain stopped, and the sun burst out with renewed intensity. Their wet clothing began to steam in the heat, sending fine white wisps toward the heavens as they plodded along. They went on this way in silent, determined misery for almost an hour before Walter stopped suddenly and moaned. Reis went a few feet further before he stopped and turned toward his father with a questioning look.

"Okay," said Walter, with a second moan. "I admit it. I'm old! Let's stop and rest a bit."

Reis flashed a smile of victory at his father. "I could, of course, go on like this for hours. But for your sake, I'll gladly stop."

They removed their wet clothing and laid it out to dry. After a small snack and drink, Walter said, "That little grassy patch looks pretty inviting."

"Go ahead. We've got all the time in the world."

While his father slept in the sun, Reis rested nearby but did not sleep. He let his body relax totally as he absorbed the warmth from the sun and the strength from the earth below.

That evening, as night closed in, they made camp halfway down the mountain and ate a dinner of reconstituted stew and dried fruit. "Not quite Mom's cooking, but damn satisfying after a day like today," said Reis as he took a large bite of the stew.

"What's the matter? You tired?" his father asked with a smile.

"Yes. I am," admitted Reis. He stretched his legs closer to the fire. "It's a good tired, though."

"I'm not so sure mine's so good," said Walter as he rubbed his calves. He sat back and sipped his coffee. "You know, son. I envy you. By the time I was your age your mom and I were married, and you were a baby. I'd already made enough money in the stock market to buy our house. I was so busy trying to succeed that I never really enjoyed my youth." He paused for a moment, staring at the fire as he collected his thoughts. Walter's gaze shifted back to his son. "Your mother and I have never been sure sending you away to school so young was the best thing for you."

"It was," said Reis. He threw a small stick into the flames. "I was bored to death in high school."

They watched as the stick quickly caught on fire, crinkling in on itself as if in pain. "Be that as it may," his father continued, "it must have been hard to make friends, being so much younger. I know you've worked very hard at your studies, but I hope you've taken time out for some fun too."

Reis smiled. "By *fun,* do you mean women, Dad?"

Walter glanced at Reis with the slightest of grins. "Well, it's not as if you've ever talked about any girlfriends." Walter's eyes slipped back to the fire. "At twenty-three, I'd hate to think you're still a virgin."

Reis, unruffled by his father's bluntness, added, "Or gay."

Walter looked up. His eyebrows rose as he said, "Don't even joke about that, Reis."

Reis looked away from his father's gaze. "Who says I'm joking?" he said quietly.

Walter gave his son a hard look. Reis watched as the momentary panic crossed his father's face. Reis waited as long as he could, but then merriment took over his face. Within seconds he was doubled over with laughter.

His father rolled his eyes and shook his head. "That's not funny, Reis. And even if you were gay, I could learn to accept it."

This statement brought another burst of laughter from Reis. "Oh! Right, Dad! I forgot what an extreme left-winged liberal you are." Reis wiped the tears from his eyes, taking a moment to gain control over his amusement before continuing. "Getting back to your original concern.... You're right, I have spent most of my adolescent and adult life deep in my studies, but let me assure you, I've taken time out for *fun.*"

"You know, the only reason I bring it up is, as I said before, you've never mentioned any girlfriends to your mom or me."

"There just haven't been any worth talking about, Dad. You

were lucky. You met Mom when you were young, and you've built a life together. That's not always easy."

"You're right; I *am* lucky. When I met your mother, I met my soulmate. She fulfills me." He smiled. "Like the forest fulfills you."

The fire crackled loudly, and the wind shifted. Reis leaned away from the sting of the smoke. Walter stretched out his arms and yawned loudly. "I think I'll hit the sack. We've got an early start tomorrow if we want to reach the Garden at a decent hour."

"Night, Dad."

Reis sat up long into the night, nursing the coals and listening carefully to the nocturnal state around him. He closed his eyes and allowed his mind and soul to mingle with the forest. He could sense each raccoon as it shuffled across the forest floor. He felt both the terror of a small mouse as it was snatched by an owl and the satisfaction of the owl as it swallowed it whole. He heard the sad sigh of the trees as they soaked up the acid rain. He felt the nervousness of a rabbit as it foraged for food, along with the intensity of a fox searching for prey. His father had been right about the life-and-death struggle, but Reis could never feel the need to conquer that which he loved so. His only goal was to join it—in its attempt for survival.

t en

Reis waited until the two young punks left the Albany Capital Mart before he stepped inside. The door jingled behind him as it closed, but being used to that by now, he didn't cringe. Recognizing Reis as a regular, the young man behind the counter didn't look up again from his *Rolling Stone* magazine. Reis glanced at the big fish-eye mirrors—first at the one in the right-hand corner and then at the one on the left—noted the cameras, and looked away. He pulled his baseball cap down a bit lower and grabbed a shopping basket, holding it slightly away from his body so as not to let it bang into his legs.

The aisles were narrow and void of other shoppers, the lighting harsh, the music, as always, bad. Mr. Rolling Stone, who always worked the third shift, must have had access to the sound system, but it was not the old rock and roll one would have hoped for when seeing the young man perched fixedly over his magazine with his perfect Beatle-imitation haircut—a mixture of Paul and

Ringo. No, the auditory assault was tinny, teeth-gritting, home-grown techno, which initially had almost been enough to cause Reis to walk the extra five blocks to Lee's Mart. But he was used to it by now.

He made his way to the dairy section and grabbed a half gallon of 1% milk and a square of extra sharp cheddar. He contemplated and then rejected strawberry yogurt, instead choosing blueberry. He checked his surroundings before turning into the next aisle, which housed the breads. He was hoping they'd gotten in that four-grain loaf with currants he liked toasted with a little butter each morning; he'd been forced to eat cold cereal for the last four mornings. He laughed loudly when he saw it—louder than he'd intended to laugh—and looked up toward the register to see if he'd disturbed Mr. Rolling Stone. Nope. Not even close. It would take Steven Tyler screaming through his harmonica to get a reaction out of this kid. Reis had the heavy loaf securely in his basket and was heading toward the canned goods when he heard the jingle through the techno. He looked up to see a Steven-Tyler-equivalent group of young girls come stumbling into the store. Mr. Rolling Stone looked up from his magazine as the four girls, dressed in slinky halter tops and short skirts, made their way to the line of coolers on the right side of the store.

"'What the fuck?' I said to him," said the tallest of the three. The others laughed. "So then he says to me, 'Listen, bitch.'" They'd made their way to the cooler and were studying the beer.

"What kind?"

"So he says to me, 'Listen, bitch.'"

"Bud Light?"

"Busch is on sale."

"So he *says* to me! Listen! Bitch!"

Reis glanced at the cameras and then at Mr. Rolling Stone.

He eased his way back toward the dairy section. Mr. Rolling Stone was watching the girls, but Reis couldn't read his face. Reis glanced again at the cameras, their red eyes blinking away. Would the elucidation of this moment be altered by a soundless black and white?

The shortest girl—the one with the bright yellow halter top that was noticeably struggling to contain her overgrown tits—then opened the cooler and pulled out the twelve pack of Busch, turned toward her friend, and said, "Listen, bitch!" They all collapsed into laughter, leaning on one another as they made their way toward Mr. Rolling Stone, who was narrowing his eyes. Reis slid behind a standing display of Ding Dongs and Ho Hos and leaned in toward the Twinkies. He felt his breath coming faster, his heart rate increasing with the same tinny note that pulsated through the store. Mr. Rolling Stone shook his head at the ID the girls offered.

"Are you fucking kidding me?" one of them barked. The note suddenly changed from a C-sharp to a D-flat, the rhythm shifting, Mr. Rolling Stone rolling his eyes, the door jingling open, Mr. Rolling Stone and Reis both taking in the do-rags and the saunter of this newest group, Mr. Rolling Stone's eyes then finding Reis's in the madness of the music, the cameras still rolling. Mr. Rolling Stone narrowed his eyes in accusation, letting the *Rolling Stone* magazine fall fully from his grasp. Reis's breath was now coming out in short, little bursts, the bread weighing down his basket, the basket pressing against his knee. Too much to handle, he dropped the entire thing, shoved his way through this newest group of late-night shoppers, and pushed the jingling door open, exiting the place breadless and milkless, without cheese or blueberry yogurt.

eleven

Reis sat with his back against a tree. He stretched his legs out lazily and smiled as the young woman with a backwards baseball cap over her short blonde hair screamed, "Get it!" in a way that was incredulous—considering her pleasing exterior. It was Doug Majors, a fellow faculty member from the Cornell Botany Department—who must have been near seventy—whom she was screaming at, and Reis watched in amazement as he somehow managed to bop the volleyball up into the air. The blonde leapt after it, sending it flying over the net. The ball fell hard between two opponents. "All right! Way to go, team!" she exclaimed. She double palmed Doug Majors as he stumbled back in her enthusiasm.

Reis turned to Mike Green, who sat a few feet away. "Who is that?" After three years at Cornell, Mike was one of the few department members Reis could actually classify as a friend. Mike was a good ten years older than Reis, but he looked much younger than his years, with his thick flop of dark hair and the perpetual smile that defined his face. The most welcoming of the faculty, he'd been the first to shake Reis's hand during his initial interview. He'd taken Reis under his tenured wing and shown him how to survive the ropes of academic research in a place as competitive as Cornell. He'd refused to allow Reis to withdraw into the quiet solitude of research, teaching, and writing. Dinners with Mike and his wife—with the enjoyment of watching their two young children be children—were Reis's primary social activity. And this was fine by Reis. His first three years at Cornell had been everything he'd hoped they'd be. His research was going even better than he'd assumed it would; his tenure track lay straight and smooth and well within his reach. The teaching was wonderful, and his writing filled any possible lonely hours of solitude. But Mike was persistent, and this was the first time Reis had allowed himself to be, if not exactly dragged, at least prodded into attending a faculty event—the annual Cornell Fall Faculty Picnic.

"Ellen Sachs," Mike answered. "Finished her doctorate in genetics here this spring and just joined the biology department. Strictly a researcher. I'm not sure what she's working on." They watched her dive after a ball, unfazed by her impact with the earth. "She's quite a pistol, isn't she?"

"I'd say so." Reis smiled. "I'm glad I sat this game out. I'm afraid she'd hit me if I missed the ball."

Mike laughed. "Strong competitive spirit. She's really very nice. I'll introduce you when they're done."

"Hey, Ellen!" Mike called out when the game broke off. She came over with a smile. "I'd like you to meet Reis Welling. He joined the botany department a few years ago."

"Hi!" she said, extending her hand down to him.

He reached up and shook it, saying, "Good game," with a

smile.

"I'm afraid I'm used to a slightly different caliber of play," she said apologetically as she sat down with them. "I used to play in college. I shouldn't play at places like this." Ellen leaned toward them and whispered, "I think I kinda piss people off."

Reis sat up from the tree and leaned forward also. "I think you might be right," he whispered back.

"I promise," she raised her right hand, "I will terrorize no one else today." Ellen sat back and turned her baseball cap the other way. Her eyes lingered pleasantly on Reis. He met her gaze with equal pleasure before she looked away and flicked an ant off her leg. "So, Reis…. Reis. That's an interesting name…."

"My great grandfather's name. A very proper English gentleman," he said in his best English accent, causing her to laugh loudly.

"Oh. I see," she said, matching his snooty English drawl. They both laughed. "Well, *Reis*, are you from the Ithaca area?"

"I prefer *Sir Reis* or just *Lord*, but no. I grew up just north of New York City. Before I came here I spent the last few years out west, going to grad school at Berkeley. This part of the state is all new to me."

"You grew up in Ithaca, didn't you, Ellen?" Mike asked.

She smiled at Mike. "Yes. All my family's still here." Her gaze returned to Reis. "How do you like it here so far?"

"I love the campus and Ithaca itself." He sat back against the trunk, shifting his weight into the roots of the tree. "I haven't had much of a chance to explore the surrounding area, though."

Ellen's eyes flashed with a sudden idea. "Hey, do you like to hike? I'm planning to hike Sunday with some friends. Maybe you'd like to come."

"Actually," Reis said, with an easy smile, "I love to hike."

She matched his smile. "Great. Then it's set." Her face turned to Mike. "How about you, Mike? Can I entice you to leave the city limits?"

"No, thanks." Mike's eyes went to Reis's with a collaborative grin. "I think Reis will do just fine on his own."

Sunday morning, Reis walked into the old diner. When he didn't see Ellen, he had a moment of panicky doubt. Was this the right place? Perhaps she'd changed her mind. It was, of course, possible he was simply the first to arrive. As he stood there trying to decide if he should just make himself at home at a table somewhere, he felt a soft squeeze on his upper arm. "Good morning, Reis," Ellen said. "We're over here." He smiled in salutation, shifted his light daypack to his other arm, and straightened out his jacket. "Come on. I'll introduce you to Sandy." She turned from him, and he hesitated just a moment before following her to a table partially hidden behind a partition. "Sandy, this is Reis—the guy I told you about." Ellen turned to Reis. "Sandy's in the music department at Ithaca College."

Sandy was a small, stocky woman who appeared to be in her early thirties. She smiled warmly up at Reis, extending her hand and pulling him into a chair with her greeting. "Oh my God, Ellen! This man is gorgeous!"

Reis laughed with embarrassment.

"Settle down, Sandy. I found him first." Ellen sat down on Reis's right.

"Yes, but will you respect him in the morning?" She leaned toward him. "Trust me, handsome. She's a bitch. You'll get nothing but respect from me." Sandy tugged playfully at the collar of Reis's jacket, then ducked as Ellen threw a packet of creamer.

Reis grinned stupidly as the women laughed. What the hell

had he gotten himself into?

It wasn't long before the rest of the small hiking group started showing up. Ellen took control of all the introductions. First there was Mary and Tim. Mary was tall and thin with thick brown hair that fell slightly past her shoulders. Her husband, Tim, was also tall and athletic with sandy blonde hair and a full beard. Their looks seemed to complement each other, and the combination was striking. Bob, the last to arrive, was the oldest of the group. He had a kind, ruddy face with large, mischievous brown eyes. He was just short of being plump and about a foot shorter than Reis.

Reis watched with amazement as the group bantered and joked. Apparently, his presence did not detract from the general merriment of the group—or their obvious intimacy. As he took his first sips of coffee, Reis allowed himself to relax. It was, after all, nothing more and nothing less than a walk in the woods.

They all piled into Bob's van and drove the short distance to a place they called Farmer Brown's. Farmer Brown's consisted of several hundred acres of dense, hilly forest, containing the typical rocky, moss-covered gorges of Ithaca. The group had standing permission from the owner to hike on the land, and there were at least half a dozen creeks and small waterfalls nestled within the terrain, whose waters eventually found their way down and into Cayuga Lake.

Bob parked the car in a farm lane, near dried stalks of corn, and shut off the engine. The early October morning was still chilly, and a thin layer of dew sat shimmering on a cut field of alfalfa that lay before a hillside. Covering the incline, the trees were quickly reaching their peak color—bright oranges, reds, and yellows stood out boldly. The group made their way over the damp field and onto the leaves of the forest floor. It wasn't long before they began to strip off their coats as the sun rose warmly in the sky and their bodies warmed from exertion. By noon they'd covered a significant distance, having scaled down various gorges and having explored several falls. They settled in near a small pool of a waterfall to eat their lunch.

"So have you done a lot of hiking?" Bob asked Reis as the six of them put their light packs on the ground and searched for the most comfortable spot among the flat, smooth rock.

"I've hiked all my life," Reis answered, settling in on a relatively dry rock. Ellen sat to his right on her own perfect stone, and Tim stretched out to his left. "My father's really into hiking and started me young," Reis continued. He pulled out a sandwich and several apples from his pack. He rolled the apples gently toward the center of the group. "Help yourselves," he offered.

"Ah, that's wonderful!" said Bob, who was sitting across from Reis. He plucked up one of the apples and added, "We are so very much in need of another man in this group. I often feel so all alone."

"What about Tim?" asked Mary, who violently shook her husband's arm. "What do you think he is?"

"Tim?" Bob took a large bite of apple, sending a spray of juice Mary's way. "Oh, he's way too pussy whipped by you, dear." Bob smiled widely toward Mary, tiny pieces of apple pressed in his teeth. "Any resemblance he may have once had to a man has long been beaten out of him."

"Bob's the comedian of the group," Tim told Reis, with a smile. He reached into a bag of raisins and popped a large handful into his mouth, then offered the bag to Reis. "He's just jealous because I have sex on a regular basis."

Reis laughed and accepted the bag.

"Bob has sex on a regular basis too," added Sandy, putting her right arm around Bob's shoulder and patting his belly with her left. "He just happens to be alone when he has it."

"Hey, narcissistic sex is not merely satisfying but extremely safe," was Bob's answer to their laughter. When their amusement had quieted down, Bob turned to Reis. "Ellen told me you were at Berkeley. There must be some great hiking out there."

"It's beautiful, yes. But of all the places I've hiked, there's nothing like the Adirondack Mountains."

"We usually get up there a few times a year," said Sandy. Then she laughed and addressed the group. "Remember that winter trip two years ago?"

"The one where your butt froze to your sleeping bag?"

"That's right!" said Bob, pointing at Mary in agreement. "She couldn't get out of her bag. We had to pry it off of her!"

"My butt's never been the same," she said sadly.

"That's the trip your toes got frostbite, wasn't it, Tim?" Ellen asked.

"It was *my* toes," said Mary. "It was Tim who sucked on them to warm them up."

"Yuk!" was the overall remark.

"Hey, I love her toes!" said Tim as he gave her foot a squeeze.

Ellen made a face at Reis. "I hope you don't think my friends are totally weird."

"What?" said Bob, with a sly smile. "Are we supposed to be on our best behavior for your new friend, Ellen?" He turned to Reis. "You better watch it, Reis. I think Ellen likes you. If she gets her hooks in you, it's all over."

"Shut up, Bob!" Ellen warned.

Reis laughed. "I could think of worse fates."

The four friends exchanged looks.

"Oh dear, I believe my warning has come too late."

That evening, Reis held the large pizza box in front of him as Ellen leaned over, set the six pack of beer down on her front porch, and searched through her pack for the keys to the old house she rented. He just couldn't help himself—he enjoyed the view.

The house was an easy walk from campus. It'd been converted into apartments long ago, Ellen explained as she rifled through the bag. Several years ago she'd been fortunate enough to snatch up the first floor. She smiled up at him and jingled the keys. "Success!" She struggled briefly with the old lock before the door swung open with a creak, revealing the charm of the hardwood floors, high ceilings, and curved doorways that only a truly old home could possess.

"Wow! This is a great place," exclaimed Reis. He followed her through the large living room and into the kitchen. "I've just got a room in the top of a very old house on the other side of campus."

"I was very lucky to get this," Ellen said as she put the beer on the table.

Reis set the pizza near the beer and walked to the window above the old, chipped white sink. "You even have a garden out back."

"Oh, yes. I love my garden." She put a couple of plates and a large stack of napkins next to the pizza. "Beer?" she asked. Reis accepted the bottle she handed him. He twisted off the cap, and it foamed up with excitement. He quickly leaned over the sink and tried to capture it with his lips. "Whoa!" she laughed. "It's a geyser. Of course, this time of year most of the flowers are gone and the vegetables harvested." Reis wiped at his mouth and shook his wet fingers over the sink.

They sat down—the pizza box between them—at the old, round oak table, which pretty much filled her kitchen. "You have a great group of friends," Reis said. He selected a slice of pizza, first for Ellen, then for himself; the strands of cheese stretched from the box as he brought it to his plate.

"Thanks. I grew up with most of them," Ellen answered as she took a small bite from her piece. "Mary and Tim went to high school with me. They dated and then lived together for years. They finally got married last year. They both have really great jobs, working long hours. I'm not sure if they'll have any kids or not, but that's why we figured they got married."

Reis nodded and took a bite of the pizza. It was hotter than he expected, and a small glob of tomato sauce squeezed out and dribbled down his chin. He reached quickly for a napkin. Apparently, he was going to wear more of his food than eat it. Why hadn't he suggested something easier to negotiate, such as canapés?

"Tim's an architect, and Mary's a lawyer," Ellen continued, either unfazed or unaware of his culinary trials. "I've known Bob for almost as long. We were both in the same hiking club in college. Sandy: we met on a hiking trail a few years ago." Ellen wrapped a strand of cheese around her finger and sucked it free with her mouth. "She somehow just fit right into the group. We've been taking hiking trips together ever since. We have a few other people who come sporadically, especially on long trips." She licked at her greasy fingers and smiled at him. "I'm sure you'll meet them soon."

Reis stopped chewing and looked at her. He pushed the food to one side of his mouth with his tongue and managed to say, "That would be great." He took another bite and considered the prospect. Was he now part of the group? It wasn't like he'd never had any friends; it was just that it took up so much time…and it was work—the socializing, the maintenance of some sort of expectation…. He concentrated on his chewing for a few moments before asking, "What does Bob do for a living?"

"He's an OB/GYN," she said with a grin.

"Really? I never would have guessed that he was a doctor. Do you go to him?"

She laughed. "God no! That's a very scary thought. He's got a great reputation, though. He has one of the biggest practices in town."

When they were done eating and the beer bottles stood erect and empty in a short little line across the table, Reis said, "Show me your garden before the sun sets."

Ellen's garden was a small courtyard surrounded by a tall cedar fence. Every inch of it was filled with vegetation. Fall flowers—bright yellows and oranges—formed a beautiful border. Large squash plants and late tomatoes still had fruit ripening on the vine. She handed him a green bean, gently brushing his fingers and lingering there before bringing her own bean to her mouth. His eyes squinted in pleasure as he watched the slender green tip disappear between her lips. He followed her movement with his own, and she smiled. She turned away, and he slowly munched on the bean as she led him through her garden. Golden-red light streamed down from the quickly setting sun, and Reis watched the shimmering light flicker across Ellen's hair as she moved among her plants. She passed her hand gently across the seeds of a naked sunflower and smiled over her shoulder. "Do you see my Brussels sprouts?" she said proudly. She stopped at the large green plant, squatted to the ground, and carefully pulled back the waxy green leaves. She smiled up at him. Reis knelt by her, and they both peered under the leaves at the small, hard balls lined up along the stalk.

"*Brassica oleracea*," he whispered in her ear. "And they're beautiful." She turned her face toward him. The fading light gave her cheeks a soft, rosy glow and painted her hair with pink, shiny strands, which he brought his fingers to. He drew her toward him, tasting the beer and the pizza and not caring that she was tasting something similar. He gently rolled her to the soft soil of the garden, pausing above her and searching her face with his eyes. He could see the intensity of the sunset reflected in her eyes, and framed by that reflection was the tiny silhouette of his head. The image disappeared with a blink. She reached up and pulled his face to hers. And then she was tugging off her clothes, throwing her shirt across the Brussels sprout plant, snapping free her bra, removing her underwear.... Reis was quickly moved to do likewise. Within moments, they were naked. Their bodies—pale against the earth—came together with the ardent urgency of youth. The union was as intense as it was brief.

"My God," said Ellen as Reis lay down beside her and looked up at the fiery sky. "That was the most incredible thirty seconds I've ever experienced in my life!"

Reis turned to her with a smile and kissed her neck. "Hey! It was at least a minute and a half. Otherwise, I totally agree."

"Do you think the neighbors saw?" She giggled as she reached for her T-shirt.

"I don't think anyone saw us," Reis said seriously as he struggled to get his foot through his right pant leg.

"How can you be so sure?" She slipped the shirt over her head, not bothering to replace her bra.

Reis stopped fighting with his pants and sat very still. "Listen," he said. "Do you hear anything?"

Ellen followed his lead and listened carefully for a moment. "No.... Why?"

"Surely," he shot her a grin, "if anyone had seen, they'd be applauding."

tw elve

"Hey," she asked suddenly. "Are you gay?"

"What? No." Reis stopped in the middle of the path. "Do I act gay?"

"No, rather morose, in fact." Kelly laughed, then quickly frowned. "So, it's me. You find me repulsive."

Reis scrunched up his face in disbelief. "What? I—"

"Well, it doesn't matter." She jumped up and snapped a dead twig off an overhanging branch. "I have a boyfriend." She leaned his way and added, "*He* doesn't find me repulsive."

Reis was dumbstruck; he had no idea how to respond. He barely knew this girl. She'd shown up again at the library a week ago and now today, so this was the third time she'd joined him on his after-work walk in the park. Today she'd met him as he left the building—sitting on the steps, with her dog in tow. Last week it had been just her.

She'd just walked in, three weeks after her first visit to the library, and sat herself down at that very same table. He'd seen her before she'd spotted him, and his mild surprise quickly turned to pleasure as he watched her chew the eraser on her pencil. After considering Dr. Benson's remarks, he'd pretty much given up on his spy theory; it really didn't make any sense. He might have been insane, but he certainly wasn't crazy. If this beautiful young woman wanted to befriend him, what possible harm could it do? So he'd approached the table, leaned against a chair, and said, "More research?"

She'd looked up from her work and smiled at him. "Always."

"How's your ant project going?"

"Oh, that. I had to scrap it. Turns out something very similar had already been done."

"That's too bad. It sounded interesting."

"Oh, I have lots of interesting ideas." And then she'd smiled up at him, and he just couldn't refuse her desire to join him on his Wednesday stroll through the park.

And now here he was, on a path in the middle of a woods in a city park in Albany, New York, looking at this strange, beautiful girl who was accusing him of either finding her repulsive or being gay, but then telling him, in almost the same breath, about her boyfriend. "I should hope he doesn't find you repulsive."

Then she began to walk again, so he followed. "You know, Reis," she said, breaking the twig in tiny, little pieces and dropping them to the earth, "it seems as if I do all the talking. In fact, it seems I never shut up."

And it was true: she talked constantly—a trait he found most endearing. She talked long hours about herself, her job, and things that happened to her as a child, chattering pleasantly as they walked through the woods, sat among the branches of a tree, or ate a simple dinner by the pond. He knew that she grew up about an hour north and that her parents were still there, still married and happy with one another for the most part. Her father's obsession with fishing, perhaps, was the main source of contention. He knew she had an older sister in the area, six years her senior, and that although the two of them had never been terribly close, Kelly loved her niece and nephew and made an effort to see them regularly. He knew she'd broken her arm falling from her bike when she was five and that she had split her sister's lip open with a rock when she was seven, laughing as she told him that her sister was being an unreasonable thirteen-year-old. But now, when she looked at the small scar adorning her sister's lip, she was still burdened by guilt. He knew she loved her job and her ideas—the rush of conception and the satisfaction of completion.

While resting against a tree or staring at the ripples of the pond, Reis would close his eyes and gather her words. He was calmed by the way her voice rose into a laugh and the way it dropped into a whisper. He preferred to listen and not talk, and certainly, he did not wish to talk about himself. And she, up to now, had had no problems with that arrangement.

"I like to hear you talk," he told her. "You have a great voice."

Her eyebrows lifted a bit in surprise, and he smiled at her then. "Well thanks.... I think." She paused a moment before continuing. "We've known each other for weeks now. You know most of my life story, yet I know practically nothing about you. Let's see.... What do I know about you?" She looked up at the branches of the trees. "You work at the library. You used to teach. You're not gay. Whether or not you find me repulsive is still in question." She turned her face to him. "It's not like I haven't tried, you know. You have a way of evading my nosiness."

He laughed.

"Come on. Give me something." She shrugged. "Where'd you

grow up? Where'd you go to school? Why are you working in a library when it's pretty damn obvious that you're pretty darn smart?"

He narrowed his eyes. "There's not much to tell."

"Oh, but I think there is!" She stopped walking and placed herself squarely in front of him. Max paused from his spot up ahead and trotted back to them. "Why are you so sad?" she demanded.

What? he thought, exasperated, but managed not to say it this time. "Do you always just say whatever pops into your head?" he asked, shifting his face into his best boyish charm.

"There you go again." She narrowed her eyes at him. "Evading my questions! You know…" she continued, her voice dropping to a whisper, "I just want to help you."

Well, this was really just too much. She'd crossed the line and was stepping into places she just didn't belong. Reis shifted his weight on his feet. "What makes you think I need your help?"

"I don't know. I just sense it. You're struggling with something. I just don't know what. I'd just like to help." She sighed gently and lightly touched his arm. "I want to be your friend."

Reis frowned and attempted to put an end to this ridiculous conversation by sliding past her and continuing up the path.

"Reis," Kelly pleaded gently, blocking his route of escape with her body. "Talk to me."

Reis closed his eyes and sighed. He felt the subtle sensation of anger, mixed up with the predictable panic. "Kelly," he said quietly, forcing his voice into normalcy, "you *are* my friend. Hell, you're the only friend I have. I'm sorry if you feel I shut you out. And I certainly don't find you repulsive. It's just that…I guess…I have nothing to share right now."

He watched her face fall from stubborn determination to

shame. She looked away. "No, I'm sorry. I have no right to pry into your life."

They walked on in silence, and Reis felt the day slipping away, the surrounding woods growing dark and foreign. Crickets, eager for the night, began to chirp, and the distant, low rumble of a bullfrog joined the chorus. "I grew up living by water." She stopped at his words, and he stopped as well. "On the Hudson River about forty-five minutes from the city. When I was little I'd sit for hours watching the water roll by." She tilted her head ever so slightly, the details of her face fading with the light. "I remember how excited I'd get when the big tankers floated by. I'd leap up and down on the shore, yelling, 'Come get me. Take me for a ride.'"

"Did your father work in New York City?"

"Yes. He worked long hours in that city." Reis took a few steps and sat on a bench at the edge of the path. She sat down also, so close that he could feel her thigh tickle the hairs on his. Max lay down on the ground between them and rested his head on one of Reis's feet. "He took the train," he continued. "Each day." The sudden, bright light of a firefly flew by his head, and he paused until it glowed again a few yards away. Kelly leaned a tiny bit his way, and he could feel the full weight of her existence. "A stockbroker. Long train rides never bother stockbrokers. Coming home late into the night.... So many hours on that train. All those buildings.... I could never understand why he loved all those buildings." He finished with a sigh.

"Did it bother you?" she whispered. "Growing up without your dad around much?"

"Oh, I don't know. I just remember what a great man he was and how much I loved him." He turned to her and let the sadness settle in. "He died...about a year and a half ago."

"I'm so sorry."

"So am I."

thir teen

Reis settled into the leather chair and sighed at the doctor. "I feel like I'm being tested."

"Tested?" asked Dr. Benson.

"Well, more like a child, really...or a criminal. Like my life isn't my own."

Dr. Benson frowned, then nodded and waited.

"It's like, now that I'm part of this system, there's no way out. So many people looking after my welfare.... It's rather insulting." Reis stood up and began to pace. "It's not like I committed a crime against society. I'm not a criminal." He stopped and appealed to Dr. Benson. "Why do I feel like I'm trapped? No longer able to man my own life?"

Dr. Benson leaned forward, rested an elbow on his knee, and placed his chin in his hand. "Reis, the system's there for you. As you said, to look after your welfare. As long as you're not a danger to yourself or anyone else, you're free to walk away."

Reis sat back down in the chair and ran his fingers through his hair. He tried to stop the gasp of sorrow that escaped from his mouth, but he just couldn't. He rubbed his fingers into his eyes and looked at Dr. Benson. "But don't you see? Don't you understand? I have nowhere to go."

fourteen

"Martha," Walter said as he watched his wife scrub the floor of the foyer on her hands and knees, "the way you're acting, you'd think Reis were bringing home Hillary Clinton."

"I hope Ellen's a bit younger than Senator Clinton," said Martha, not looking up from her work. "You need to get the ladder and clean this ceiling."

"Martha, please. No one's going to look at the damn ceiling!"

"It's full of cobwebs, and the stained glass window is filthy," she stated.

"Really—no one's going to notice."

Martha sat down on the floor and peered up at her husband. "This is the first girl your son has ever brought home. Who knows, it may be the last one. The *least* you could do is clean the ceiling."

Walter shook his head and mumbled as he headed for the garage to get the ladder. "Maybe we should just buy a bigger house. Lord knows we want to impress this girl."

"What if your parents don't like me?" Ellen asked as they drove to Reis's boyhood home on Wednesday evening. She bit her bottom lip and gave him an anxious look.

He turned his eyes from the road and smiled. "That's not possible." His eyes went back to the road as he negotiated a slight curve.

"Well, what if I don't like them?"

He shrugged. "We'll leave immediately! No turkey! No pumpkin pie! We'll simply leave."

"No, no," she laughed. "Even if your parents are just awful people, I can't leave without at least one piece of pie."

"Okay. Pie. Whipped cream. Then we're out of there!"

Ellen was silent for a while. She looked out the window into the darkness, catching glimpses into lit windows of homes they passed along the way. "Are we almost there?" she asked.

"Why? Do you have to go to the bathroom again?" he teased.

"I can't help it. I'm nervous."

Reis placed a hand on her thigh. "El, I know you think my parents are gods of some sort...after all, they produced me." He grinned her way in the darkness; she could see the quick flash of his teeth in the light of the dash. "But really, they're just normal human beings."

Ellen rolled her eyes at him. She sat in silence and tried to calm herself. Why was she so nervous? She'd had other boyfriends—a lot of other boyfriends—and had met a lot of other parents. It was no big deal. Reis wasn't even the first man she'd lived with. She'd lived with Mark for the last two years of undergrad, and there was the short and greatly flawed time she'd lived with Scott.... But things had happened so fast with Reis. Now he was living in her home, sharing her life—and it was wonderful. He was all she'd ever wanted: driven, successful, gentle, and sexy. She knew how much he loved her, yet it still amazed her that she was the first and only love of his life.

Was that the problem? His lack of intimate relationships? The fact that she knew—that he'd told her—she was the first and only woman he'd ever brought home to meet his family? And what exactly did that mean? And did it really matter? She turned to him in the darkness of the car and leaned across the gearshift. His arm came out and pulled her toward him. She kissed his neck.

"You know, I love you," she stated.

He kissed the top of her head.

"That's as it should be, considering that I love you too."

It was a short while later when Reis slowed down and turned down the long lane that led to his boyhood home. "Are we here?" asked Ellen, suddenly alert.

"Uh-huh."

Ellen leaned forward and searched for the house through the dark row of cedars. She could see nothing but dark silhouettes of trees against the faint light coming from the house. As they turned into the bend of the driveway, a large expanse of brightly lit windows came into view. "What are all those windows up ahead?" she asked.

"They could be windows to my parents' house."

"All of them?"

"That's right," he said, without looking at her.

"Jesus Christ! Why didn't you tell me your parents live in a fucking mansion?"

"Ellen, dear, please don't say *fuck* in front of my parents," he said.

"Oh, shut up! I can't believe you didn't warn me!"

Reis grinned slightly. "I didn't want to make you nervous."

"Oh good! It's much better that I'm in total shock. I feel just like what's-her-name in *Love Story*."

"*Love Story?*"

"You know! That old movie! Ryan O'Neal. Ali MacGraw. He takes her home to meet Mr. and Mrs. Rich and Snobby."

"Right...."

"Jenny. That was it. They hated her," Ellen mumbled, barely audible. Reis stopped the car in front of the house and turned off the engine. He reached over and gently squeezed her knee. "I think I'm going to be sick," moaned Ellen.

"Come on. It's going to be fine. I promise." They stepped out of the car. Reis came around to her side of the car just as the front door of the house opened. Reis grabbed her arm and said, "Look out! Here they come!"

"Cut it out, Reis," Ellen whispered, gently extricating herself from his grasp.

"You made it," called his father from the steps. Reis pulled their bag from the car and put his hand on Ellen's shoulder as they walked toward the house.

"Mom, Dad, this is Ellen," he said proudly. Reis's parents beamed at her, and she smiled back with only a hint of nervousness.

"Ellen," his mother said, grasping her hand, "we are so glad to finally meet you. Come in. It's cold out here."

"It's good to meet you too." Ellen smiled at Mrs. Welling, enjoying the warmth of her hand and the sincerity on her pleasant face. Reis's father was quickly taking her hand, and it was Reis's eyes she met and an older Reis's face who smiled her way as he squeezed her hand.

She was being pulled into the house, her eyes growing wide as she scanned the room, her mouth slightly ajar. "Jesus," she whispered, then grew red with embarrassment.

"Yes. It's a bit over the top, isn't it?" said Walter. "I got it for a song, many years ago."

"It must've been one hell of a tune," came out of her mouth. She was relieved when they all laughed. She whistled vaguely between her teeth, her eyes following the beauty of the wood trim of the foyer, coming to rest on the ceiling. "Wow! What a great ceiling! Is that a stained glass window?"

"Yes." Martha jabbed Walter in the ribs. "It's stained glass."

"Ouch!" Walter rubbed at his side and met his son's questioning look. "You don't want to know."

"Let's just hope the sun is out tomorrow," continued Martha as she collected their coats and turned from the foyer. "That's when it's truly lovely."

Walter made everyone drinks in the library, and they snacked on thin slices of pound cake. The wood crackled gently in the fireplace, and Ellen's body eased into the soft leather of the couch, the warmth of Reis's hand on her thigh and the mellow sensation of alcohol slipping through her veins. By the time Martha went to bed, Ellen was immersed in calm contentment. Reis, Ellen, and Walter spent another hour deeply discussing the problems inherent in research funding. When Walter finally stretched his arms and stood up to go to bed, he said, "I assume you two are old enough to get yourselves to bed?"

"Yes, Dad, I believe we can handle it. Thanks for asking, though." Reis grinned at Ellen and her face grew warm with embarrassment.

After Walter left, Reis turned to Ellen and asked, "Well, what do you think of my family?"

"They're wonderful," she beamed. "And I think they even liked me!"

Reis wiped imaginary sweat off his brow. "Whew! What a relief! You know what this means, don't you?" She shook her head. "We can stay! *Two* pieces of pie and late night turkey sandwiches tomorrow."

It was on Christmas day that Reis met Ellen's family. They spent the day at her parents' old brick house in Trumansburg, which was on a tree-lined, snow-covered street. Fireplaces blazed in both the living room and dining room; even the kitchen had an old wood stove. The place was hot and smoky and filled with the pleasant smells of cooking and an abundance of noise. Ellen had three sisters and two brothers. All were married with, what seemed to Reis to be, dozens of children. Reis had never seen so many gifts or experienced the volume of noise so many excited children can make. By the time they got into Ellen's car to drive home, his head was spinning from the pure madness of the day.

"How'd you like my family?" Ellen asked as they drove back toward Ithaca in her old red Honda Civic.

Reis was stretched out in the passenger's side, trying to find some relief for his uncomfortably full stomach and his aching head.

He turned lazily toward her and opened his eyes. "They were great. There are, however, a lot of them. I wish they'd worn name tags."

Ellen laughed. "All religious affiliations aside, my family seems to have serious issues with birth control."

"You're lucky to have such a large family. You must have had a blast growing up." Ellen made a face, but Reis continued. "I wonder sometimes what it would have been like—how I might have been different—if I had a lot of siblings...or even one for that matter."

"I think you're perfect—just the way you are."

He stretched out his arm and squeezed Ellen's thigh. "I wouldn't mind having my own little tribe of kids."

"Really?" She looked at him and then back to the road. "I'd be perfectly happy not to have even one."

Reis's hand suddenly felt awkward on her thigh. Not knowing if he should remove it or tighten his fingers again, he just left it there, like a dead thing. "You don't want any kids?"

Ellen shrugged. "I don't know. Not something I've ever planned. Not sure I'm quite the mothering type." Ellen reached for the radio and turned the music up a bit. Dave Matthews Band's "Crash" was playing, and the notes filled the car. "I love this song," she said, turning to him and smiling. "It's exactly what I'd like to do: crash into you." Then she turned back to the road and sang loudly with Dave, but she changed the words to *when you come into me....*

Midway through the spring semester, Reis was in his office working on his latest grant proposal when Mike Green knocked on the frame of his open door. Reis looked up from his laptop and smiled. "Hi, Mike. How's it going?"

"It's going fine." Mike leaned a moment on the doorframe, a soft grin easing onto his face. "But from what I hear, it's going great for you." Reis gave him a quizzical look, and Mike's smile widened. He stepped into the room and sat casually on the arm of one of Reis's chairs. "You just got your grant approved, didn't you?" said Mike.

"Oh, that. Yes. It's not a great deal of money. Just enough to fund my field research this summer."

"True, it's not that large, but it's your third one this school year." Mike let himself slide into the seat of the chair. "How many publications have you had since coming to Cornell?"

"Oh, I don't know." Reis leaned back into his own chair. It was pretty obvious that this was not just a quick *How you doing?* visit, so he closed his laptop and let the sentence he was about to write slip from his mind. He closed his eyes in thought, then answered, "Ten or so, including the book. I'm waiting to hear on two other journal articles."

Mike shook his head in amazement. "My first few years were a nightmare. It was all I could do to get through my teaching syllabus."

Reis shrugged his shoulders. "I like to write," he stated simply.

Mike smiled at his younger colleague but didn't say anything else. Reis smiled back and waited. "Well?" said Reis, after a long moment.

"Well, what?" said Mike, still with a goofy smile.

"Oh, for God's sake, Mike. You better just tell me whatever it is you're smiling about before you bust a gut or something."

"Okay, okay." Mike sat a little deeper in the chair before saying, "Rumor has it that the powers that be are very impressed." He paused, letting Reis contemplate this, before adding, "I wouldn't be at all surprised if you're asked to submit your evaluation for tenure soon."

"Tenure?" Even as he heard himself repeat the word, his mind could not quite wrap around it. "Really?"

Mike shrugged. "I wouldn't say it if it weren't true."

"But I'm just barely into my fourth year." Reis's confusion deepened. Was he missing something here? Was this some kind of sick joke? He'd just gone through his midterm review. Sure, it had gone well, but he still had a good three years to prove his worth.

"The department likes what it sees. Why wait and risk losing you to some other institution."

Reis's smile became more private. "Imagine. Tenured...."

When Reis got home, Ellen was sitting by the fire—no book or paper on her lap—staring distantly into the flames. Reis, in his own excitement, did not quite acknowledge this irregularity. "You'll never guess what Mike told me today," he said before she'd turned from the flames. He paused, and she turned her head and looked up at him expectantly. "He thinks I should put in for early tenure evaluation. He seemed certain I'll be offered tenure this fall," he continued with a grin.

"That's just great." Her words fell flatly to the floor; there was no smile on her face.

His face fell. He looked toward the floor and back to her face. "You don't seem very happy for me."

"I'm sorry," she sighed. "Really, it's great." She looked at him darkly, an uncomfortable surge flowing through the room. "You know," she continued, "I've been here longer than you, getting my degrees, busting my ass, and I've never even heard the word tenure. Hell, I've never even been given a pat on the back for a job well done."

"Ellen, what are you talking about? We're not in competition. We're not even in the same department. You're not even in a tenure-track position."

"Oh, well...thank you for reminding me of that! Everything's always come easy for you, hasn't it?" She stood up and angrily threw a log on the fire. The embers broke apart from the impact and flew into the air. One lone ember sat dying on the tiles in front of the hearth. She turned to him and glared.

What was that he saw in her eyes? He had to look away. He sunk down on the couch. "I've worked for everything I have," he said. He watched as the ember turned black and harmless.

"Oh right!" She waved her arms at him as she spoke. "All

your parents' money certainly helped! Sending you to all the best schools. I was strictly a scholarship kid. I bet you never had to slop pepperoni on pizzas so you could stay in school!"

"I don't get it." He glanced her way and then back to the flames. "Where's all this coming from? What's wrong?"

She looked at him with exasperation. "Don't you ever get mad? I'm being a total bitch, and all you do is ask me what's wrong!"

Reis sighed and met her gaze. "If you want someone to fight with, I'm sorry; I won't oblige. If you want to tell me what's wrong, I'll be glad to listen. Otherwise...." He stood up. "I think I'll go back to my office."

Ellen sat back on the couch and put her head in her hands. "I'm sorry. I just get so frustrated." She looked at him with tears in her eyes. "I have no right to take it out on you." She lifted her hand toward him, and he took one quick step and folded her fingers into his. "I had a major setback in my research today. Almost a whole year's work for naught."

Reis felt the weight of her words and understood what it meant. He squeezed her fingers and sat next to her on the couch. He took both her hands and pulled them into his chest. "Maybe it's not as bad as you think."

"Oh, but it is. All the statistical mumbo jumbo in the world won't help. The numbers just aren't there!"

He pulled her close and held her for a long time, knowing there was nothing he could say. After awhile, she said softly into his shirt, "I'm truly sorry for all those terrible things I said. I'll be the first one to congratulate you when you get your tenure this fall."

fif teen

Kelly and Reis sat on a grassy hillside on the edge of the park and watched the sun slip away. All the awkwardness of the previous week was gone. The hesitation and doubts she'd wrestled with all week had also slipped away. Now, as they sat watching the amazing spectacle of the sunset—the soft glow of companionship easing away loneliness—she was glad that she'd decided to come. Reis was relaxed and almost chatty—so interested in her work and willing to share vague vignettes of his life—to the point where she was slowly piecing together his past. They'd been talking together for several hours and had only now fallen into a comfortable silence as they watched the sky slowly change into an assortment of colors. Max was quiet too, lying between them, his head gently resting on Reis's knee. He sighed with canine contentment, Reis's hand resting gently on his head. Kelly eased further into the hillside and watched as the sun's rays weakened into golden redness. This was, she realized—with just a twinge of unease—the highlight of her week.

The day soon turned sharply colder, and as the sun slipped out of sight, Kelly wrapped her arms around her legs. She shivered slightly, a cool breeze climbing up the hill. "Fall will be here before long," Reis stated in response to the breeze. "I'd really like to go to the Adirondacks before the weather cools." He looked up a bit sadly at the darkening sky as if he expected to see snow. He did not look her way as he said, "Maybe you'd like to go with me?"

"The Adirondacks? I haven't been up there in years."

"We could just do a day hike," he said, turning his face to hers. Kelly watched his face turn from gentle longing to the beautiful anticipation of a child. "I know some really incredible small mountains."

"When would you want to do this?"

"How about Saturday? We'd get an early start. Make a day of it."

Did she want to take this relationship outside of this park? "This Saturday?" She kept her voice light and upbeat—hiding her hesitation—not wishing to see his face change to something less beautiful.

"Sure! Do you have plans?"

"No...not really."

Would Brian want to do something? He was trying. The Saturday after their fight, they'd spent the afternoon together, shopping at the local farmer's market, a fun stroll in the park, a picnic supper at an outdoor concert, amazing wine-buzzed sex.... The following week he'd been out of town but called her daily. Then, on Saturday, he was right back into the routine of their romance. He: late for their dinner plans. She: so hungry that she'd eaten cereal and refused to go out. He: sweetly and sexily wooing his way back in, slipping his fingers along her spine, laughing at her disgruntlement, breathing words into her ears—"You know, gorgeous, how much I love you"—tingling the back of her neck with his tongue.... Kelly shivered at the thought.

She turned to Reis and shrugged. "Okay. Why not?"

His lips turned up to a smile. "Great!" He leaned back and peered toward the sunset with a happy sigh. He softly bit his bottom lip with boyish pleasure, the sunset reflecting in his eyes. She watched as his face suddenly dropped to despair. "Oh wait. I have no car!" He brought his hands to his temples, pressing his fingers into his skin.

"It's okay, Reis," she said, touching his shoulder lightly. "We can take mine."

There was a quick intake of his breath as he looked her way. "What? Take your what?"

"My car," she answered patiently. "To the Adirondacks."

"Oh, yes. Of course. Saturday, right?"

s ix teen

"Where the hell is my car?" Reis demanded as he entered Dr. Benson's office on Thursday at his usual time. His hair was rumpled, his clothes freshly slept in, his face rough with a stubby layer of brown.

"Your car?" Dr. Benson did not extend his hand in salutation.

"Yes! My God!" Reis said with patronizing impatience. "What the fuck is wrong with you? Yes! My car! I haven't seen it since I left the hospital."

Dr. Benson sat on the edge of his desk, shoving away a small paper pile with his hip and carefully watching as Reis paced back and forth in front of his desk. "Where did you have it last, Reis?" he asked slowly.

"I don't know. I don't know, damn it! Would I be asking if I *knew*?"

"Reis, you need to calm down. Let me assure you, I do not have it. I have my Porsche, remember?" He smiled at Reis. Reis ignored his joke and continued to pace. "Sit down, please, and let's think about this." Reis stopped walking and stared miserably at the doctor. "Please, Reis," Dr. Benson said, indicating the chair.

Reis sat down reluctantly, angrily. "Do I look like a child?"

The doctor shifted from his desk and settled into his chair. "No, you do not look like a child." Dr. Benson waited until Reis's angry glare subsided. Reis sat back with an impatient sigh, and Dr. Benson nodded his head slightly and softly said, "Think about the last time you drove it. Where were you going?"

"I don't know!" Reis ran his fingers through his hair in frustration. "It's immoral. Stealing a man's car, his life.... My father picked it out himself! And to what end—this thievery?"

"Let's, just for a moment, assume your car wasn't stolen," Dr. Benson said slowly. "Wasn't the last time you drove it when you left Ellen's apartment?" He paused a moment, then continued. "Weren't you on your way up north to the Adirondack Mountains?" He stopped, letting his words sink in.

Reis pushed both hands into his hair and squeezed. Dr. Benson waited patiently. "Yes. Yes. Okay. I remember now," Reis said after a long moment. He looked up at the doctor, his anxiety only slightly lessened. "But what happened to it?"

"I can only assume your mother has it now. I can ask her, if you'd like."

"Will you? Will you do it today?"

"I can call her right now," said Dr. Benson, indicating his phone on his desk.

"No!" said Reis, looking at the phone. "Do it later, then call me at home."

"I will, Reis. I'll call you tonight."

"You know, I love that car. My father picked it out. How could it not cross my mind in all these months?" Reis looked at

Dr. Benson in confusion.

"Reis, you've had a great amount to deal with. I don't think you should let forgetting about your car concern you."

"How many other things have I forgotten? How do I know significant things aren't missing? Chunks and pieces. Boulders of knowledge. Can one live without knowledge? Stolen away...life... knowledge...cars.... I'm left with just a shell. I used to *know* things! It was all right here," he held out the palm of his hand and slapped it sharply with his other. "All right here! Ellen, car, knowledge. Mountains of knowledge. I was a fucking wonder boy!"

"It's very true. You've lost a lot. It's not right...or fair. And yet..." Dr. Benson waved his hands in acquiescence, "here we are—in the mode of recovery."

Reis was quiet for a while before stating, "And yet, here we are." He leaned back in his chair, closed his eyes, and began to visibly relax. The doctor waited. Dr. Benson was considering the mound of paperwork on his desk when Reis finally opened his eyes and sat forward. "Kelly and I are going hiking Saturday. That's why I needed my car. I guess we'll take hers," he said matter-of-factly, staring blankly at a spot on the wall behind the doctor's head.

"To the Adirondacks?" The corners of Dr. Benson's mouth turned down a notch.

"Yes." Reis met and then flicked away from Dr. Benson's gaze. "I know what you're thinking, but I'll be fine. I haven't been back up there since...since I was released from the hospital. I really think I'm ready."

"You seem a bit out of sorts today. Take an extra hundred-milligram Seroquel tonight. I think you'll sleep better. You still have some Ativan? Take it if you need to."

"Yes, yes. Whatever."

"Are you sure you want to do this trip with Kelly?"

"Oh yes." Reis sat up straighter and looked back with forced confidence at the doctor. "You're right, of course. Today's a bad day. It's the car thing, you know," he said with a dismissive wave of his hand. "Once you call and tell me where it is, I'll be fine."

Dr. Benson nodded his head and thought for a moment before he said, "You and Kelly seem to be getting close."

"We've become friends," Reis stated impatiently. He fidgeted uncomfortably in his chair and began to inspect his fingernails.

"Have you told her about your illness?" Dr. Benson asked carefully.

Reis did not answer right away. He pushed on his cuticles and said, "No. She wouldn't understand. How could anyone?"

"I think there are a lot of people who would understand."

Reis looked up and laughed. "Oh! I think there are many more who wouldn't." He met Dr. Benson's eyes and shook his head in disbelief.

"You're afraid she wouldn't want to see you again if she knew."

He puffed out an exasperated sigh. "Wouldn't you be? Hell, the only reason you talk to me is because it's your livelihood."

"That's not totally true, Reis. I've come to think quite highly of you. It's my hope that no matter where your life takes you, we can continue our friendship."

"Even if that's true, Doc—and I truly doubt that it is—the word schizophrenia does not frighten you the way it does a lay person."

Dr. Benson nodded in agreement. "You're right...about the word...wrong about our friendship. Don't get mixed up in the word—the label. It doesn't even matter what you call it; it's not even a word you need to use. You are more than capable of friendship. Don't underestimate Kelly's feelings for you. She must have some sense that something's not quite right, and yet she continues to spend time with you. Perhaps, if she had a sense of what you're dealing with—knowing a little bit of what's gone on—it would be better than the unknown."

Reis shook his head again. "I'm afraid I've allowed myself to care a great deal about her. I'm not sure how I would handle it if she reacted badly. I just can't deal with that now. I'll tell her when I feel there's a reason for her to know. Ellen never understood. She grew to hate me."

"Ellen never knew what she was dealing with."

"Yes." Reis brought his head down to his hands and sighed deeply. "And neither did I…back then."

seventeen

One point six million acres of forest preserve and he was right in the middle of it. Reis turned slowly and took it all in with a slow and easy smile. His eyes met those of his three graduate students, and they looked back with the same sense of wonder and enthusiasm. Yes, he'd picked his field research assistants well, and he had no doubt that the weeks spent here in the Adirondack Mountains at Cornell's research facility would provide the data that he was after.

Jim Cooper pulled the baseball cap from his head and scratched at the few fine strands of blonde hair that still clung to his scalp. He then moved down to his chin and gave his thin, wispy beard a good going-over. He grinned over at Reis and laughed. "Black flies—you just gotta love 'em." Jim was twenty-nine and just pages away from finishing his doctorate, but when Reis had asked him if he'd like to join his team, Jim had jumped at the opportunity to lay his thesis aside and spend the summer outdoors.

"They're bloodsucking motherfuckers," said Kim, slapping at her neck and then laughing. Kim was a small, stocky woman with bright red hair and an abundance of freckles. She had a lot of hiking experience, a sharp wit, and an easygoing personality, which Reis knew would help maintain the equilibrium as they worked. Both women of his team, Kim and Holly, were new additions to the botany department, just starting out on their quest for a PhD. Reis was their advisor, and he'd managed to land just enough funding to bring them along.

Holly, the third member of his team, was twenty-two with long dark hair that, with just the slightest twist of her neck, she could magically flip up and back over her shoulder. And she did this just then, a fan of dark hair spreading through the warm summer air. Her dark, almond-shaped eyes turned his way as a smile raised her already high cheek bones. Reis took in her exotic beauty—as it was quite impossible to overlook—made all the more beautiful pressed against the wildness of the forest. And although his lips met her smile, his eyes did not linger on her beauty but turned away; he was totally sated by the vast expanse of greens and browns, the multitude of shapes of blue against the green, and the patches of sunshine that filtered to the ground.

The facility consisted of several laboratories, an eating cabin, and half a dozen sleeping cabins. Much of their time would be spent deep in the forest and not in the luxury of this place. This was to be their base camp—where they would return after days or weeks in the woods, to compile and test the soil, plant, and water samples they'd collected.

It wasn't very many days until they'd settled into the camp and into their work, much as Reis expected they would. The long hours of the day were spent deep in the forest, collecting, charting, and photographing. Their packs grew heavy with samples as each day wore on, sweat flowing in gentle streams along the declines of their faces and sliding around the red welts of black fly bites. And on those especially hot days when it became too much to bear, they flung their packs to the ground, covered those packs with articles of clothing, and flung their naked bodies into one of the many tiny pools of comfort that dotted the mountain terrain. The warm summer evenings were for resting by the fire, drinking beer when at camp, or smoking the more portable weed when in the field—talking, playing cards, and taking midnight skinny dips in the cool blue lakes of the Adirondacks.

Reis watched—and sometimes joined—the evening activities, but more often than not, he'd read quietly by the fire or write letters to Ellen in his tent or in his cabin. Holly tended to break away from the other two and join Reis as he relaxed by the fire, entering into long hours of conversations about ecology or general botany. And if she sat too close or laughed too easily at his jokes, it was nothing he wasn't used to—nothing he couldn't handle.

The days grew longer and the forest sizzled under the summer sun, and Reis felt the full weight of Ellen's absence. It had been his hope that Ellen could spend some time with him in these woods, taking time away from her lab and meeting him on the weekends. But this summer, as she played catch up with her research, she could not afford the time off. Perhaps it was his imagination, but on those rare occasions he'd managed to get through to her on the phone, she seemed distant and self-absorbed. He knew she was busy, but was there not even time to answer his emails? And now, the Monday of the fourth week into his field research, she'd finally promised to come for the weekend.

As the week dragged by, the joy of discovery and the pleasure of the forest slipped away from Reis. At night his assistants' antics

were especially irritating as they drank and smoked and laughed—
the shafts of light from the fire insulting his retinas, their voices an
insult to his ears. When it became intolerable, he left the campsite
and took slow, thoughtful walks in the dark woods. It was only
then, with the quiet darkness of the forest surrounding him, that
he felt at ease—the distance between himself and Ellen a less significant thing. Long after the fire had turned to lazy, glowing coals
and his assistants were snug in their sleeping bags, he'd slip back
into camp, and when the first shrill notes of morning filled the
forest, he'd be there—still awake, in the safety of his tent.

On Friday, as shadows lengthened and the trees blended into
the darkness, the four of them hiked back to the base. As they
entered the grounds of the camp, Reis's tired eyes strained in the
dimness in search of Ellen. There was a soft kick to his chest—
a tightening, a pain—and then he found her leaning casually
against the rail of the open porch of his cabin, her foot resting
on the boards, her head tilted in waiting, her lips curving up in
unabashed pleasure. He closed his eyes in relief and broke away
from the others. In a moment there was the weight of her arms,
the smell of her hair, the taste of her skin. "Ellen." The word came
out like a sob, and he sucked in his emotion and turned toward
his team. "You've all met Ellen."

"Sure we have," said Jim. "How are you?" They all smiled and
nodded greetings.

"I'm doing fine." She smiled back, reaching out and slipping
her hand into Reis's. He smiled her way and tightened his fingers
around hers. "It's you all that look beat," she continued.

"It's been a long week," Reis said, turning his attention back
to his team. "Let's take the weekend off." He indicated the packs
full of samples. "We'll meet in the lab Monday morning to start
rifling through this stuff." They nodded in agreement and trudged

off toward their cabins.

Reis gave Ellen a wicked grin as he ushered her into his cabin. Barely getting the door shut, Ellen playfully wrestled him out of his shirt and onto the bed, then began unzipping his shorts and pulling them from his body. "Wouldn't you like me to take a shower first?" he asked, running his fingers through her hair. He helped her pull her shirt from her body, her breasts falling free before she shimmed her shorts down her legs.

"Nuh-uh," she whispered, slipping between his legs, running her tongue through his dark, coarse hair and then up further to his lower abdomen. "I love it when you smell like the forest."

He reached for her and pulled her to him. She kissed his forehead, his cheeks, his lips.... He closed his eyes to the intensity of her touch, her smell, her taste…. The sensation of her skin pressed against his, and he slipped into her wetness—her movement easing into his. It was all too much—almost more than he could bear. He pushed hard into her body, and then his words were dripping out of his mouth. "I've really missed you these last few weeks." Her answer to his words: a soft moan.

Sunday afternoon he leaned too heavily against Ellen's car. "I wish you could stay a few more days."

"I do too." She looked up at him through the open window, the blue intensity of her eyes sawing at his senses, the lie as intense as the blue. "But I really need to get back. It's only a few more weeks, then you'll be home, and with any luck, I'll be back on track."

He pushed his body from the car, took a step back, and nodded slowly. "Then I'll see you in three weeks."

"I love you," she called as she backed the car around and drove away.

He watched the shrinking car until it was indistinguishable from the forest in which she'd left him.

The days eased into weeks. The subtle shift of the sun in the sky and the shortening of the days pushed against Reis as he mourned the loss of each and every second of sunlight. There was an urgency and a desperation—something very significant slipping away. It was quite impossible to sleep, other than quick catnaps here and there. Their last trip into the woods in the far northern reaches of the park—the last great push to collect the truth, to understand the mysteries, to get at the answers—was all too imperative. While the others slept, the dark forest whispered seductively in his ears, and he moved amongst its shadows—coming close, grasping at the fleeting, teasing truth.

In the brightness of daylight it was easy to move among his mortal companions, not allowing them to see how close the answers really were. It was not that they were unworthy of the truth but just that they were simply unready—not quite up to his level of understanding. So he kept up the pretense, gently pushing them in their tasks, their bags heavy with the sundries of the forest, the days slipping away until it was done and over—his final evening with these woods.

Jim sat up with Reis after Kim and Holly had gone to sleep, lazily poking a long stick through the fire as they watched the embers fall apart, sending shimmering ashes toward the sky. Reis felt his anxiety rising, heard the forest whisper, longed to leave the fire and walk through its seduction. They were silent by the fire. Jim: quiet and respectful. Could he also hear the forest call? Then the silence was sliced through by his words. "You seem a little out of it these last few days, Reis. Everything okay?"

Reis flinched. After a moment, he offered, "I haven't been

sleeping too well." He paused. "I don't know why. I normally sleep like a log." A log shifted and crackled with fire.

"You must be stressed about your tenure review. Don't they make their decision soon?"

"I should find out within the month," Reis said flatly. The log broke in the middle and complained loudly as it collapsed into the ashes. Starry embers floated skyward.

"That would be…" Jim started, "right there…" The sky was clear. "…keep me awake." Stars blinked down at him. "Though you…" A soft kiss of a wind. "…they'd be insane…" The invasion of smoke. "…grant you tenure, until it's official…." He leaned back to the sting of tears. "Slight nagging doubt." His eyes made a soft, squishy sound when he rubbed them. "Real pain. The less you sleep, the more anxious you get about not sleeping." His tongue slipped, the moisture spreading across his lips. "The more anxious you are…" The quick flash of teeth. "…to sleep, you know?" His mouth came to a stop, waiting for an answer.

Reis had no idea how to respond. He forced his mind to attention—forced a response. "I'll just be glad to get home," were words that seemed safe.

"This has been a great summer for me, Reis. To think I could have spent it sitting in front of my computer, pounding out my thesis. Thanks again for giving me the opportunity to work with you. It's been an invaluable experience. I know Kim and Holly feel the same way."

"I appreciate your saying so," Reis mumbled in reply. "You guys have been great too." He compelled his voice to show enthusiasm, but he still came off edgy. He rubbed his eyes and ran his fingers through his hair.

"Well," said Jim as he readied to get up. "Try to get some sleep."

Reis braced himself and did not tense away from the friendly squeeze Jim placed on his shoulder as he got to his feet. A soft sigh blew through Reis's lips, and Jim disappeared into his tent. Minutes ticked off, and when enough destruction of time had occurred, Reis got up and walked through the woods, the relief almost immediate. The moon was close to full and rising quickly, dressing the forest with a honey glow. He made it through the short distance to the small bluff that overlooked the valley below—his relief now complete.

He stood and studied the outlines of the trees in the valley, their leaves shimmering with moonlight as a summer wind blew. The silver fish of ponds glistened as they dotted the landscape. Lowering himself to the ground, he closed his eyes to the fish and took in a deep breath of air, his body relaxing into the night as he reached for the connection—the connection of his mind and soul to the forest. But the connection fizzled away and was lost. The power of the earth was outside of his grasp—his own thoughts scattered by the wind. As he struggled to draw them back, the smallest of sounds reached his ears, and he turned. Holly was standing very close. Her white nightshirt glowed in the moonlight, her black hair—wings of a bird—flowed around her. He blinked—twice—but she did not go away.

"Dr. Welling?" she said quietly and sat down next to him. "I heard you and Jim talking. I couldn't sleep either. Are you okay?"

"I'm fine, Holly." Her face was very close to his—her hair licking at his cheek in the breeze.

"If there is anything I could do to help…." Her almond-shaped eyes searched his face, then the sudden pressure of her hand on his thigh. His thigh muscles recoiled on their own accord, her lips suddenly pressing against his, her tongue slipping neatly between his teeth. His body responded to the warm wetness of her tongue—the soft sensation of her lips—his arms sliding around her, his hands feeling the bare skin beneath the thin white shirt. Her moan softened the night air, and her body shifted closer to his. A burst of wind and her hair—shiny black fingers of a bird—whipped around him, beating against his skin. His hands moved to her shoulders and felt the hard sensation of her fragile bones. He shoved her roughly to the ground, falling with her so that his face was just above hers, the softness of her body beneath him.

"Is this how you would help me, Holly?" he hissed angrily into her face. "Is this what you want?" He pushed his hips into hers. "For me to fuck you right out here, in the middle of the woods?" His arms tensed, sending her shoulders tightly against the ground—her face twisting in pain. "When you know damn well I love Ellen!" He gave her just a little shake to emphasize his point. "Not to mention the university doesn't look too kindly on the faculty fucking the students!"

She shook her head slightly, her eyes filling with tears. His vision suddenly focused, and he saw the soft brown of eyes looking back in fear. "Jesus," he whispered, letting her go. "What the hell am I doing?" His anger was gone with the beat of a wing. He sat next to her, put his head in his hands, and squeezed. Holly lay crying silently next to him. A stunned moment passed before he said, "Holly, I am so sorry."

"No," she replied through her tears, "it's not your fault." She got up awkwardly. "I never should've come out here like this. You've been nothing but professional with me. I had no right to throw myself at you."

"Even so, I had no business hurting you," he said, his voice straining with emotion.

"You didn't. I'm fine."

She left him there. He heard her feet shuffling through the forest floor, heard an owl cry, saw the moon shifting overhead, and watched as the night slipped into day.

eighteen

Kelly arrived a bit early on Saturday morning to pick up Reis. She leaned toward her steering wheel and peered up through her windshield at the surrounding buildings. He'd told her he'd meet her at the corner of James and Manner Street at seven. It was six forty-five. She parked the car along the curb and told Max that she'd be back in just a few minutes. She stepped out of the car and took a better look at the buildings. The gray stone structure across the street was a bank. On the opposite corner sat what looked to be strictly an office building. Behind her, down the block a bit, was an old brick building with a faded green awning stretching out from its double glass doors, the deteriorating words *Manner Apartments* painted on the canvas. She turned that way and stepped through the unlocked doors.

The sort of place people lived only to keep a roof over their heads, the apartment building was typical of many inner-city dwellings. The gray walls of the small foyer were only slightly soiled, and although the place was clean and kept up, it held no warmth, no plastic plants of welcoming, no sense of human comfort. She stepped to the wall of tiny metal mailbox fronts and scanned the names. It took only a moment to find it: *R. Welling*, typed neatly behind the little plastic square. *Apt 3G* was typed next to the lettering.

She considered the narrow staircase, took a step its way, grasped the handrail, and stared up into the gloom. Then she shrugged—what the hell—and walked up the dark flights of stairs that led to Reis's third-floor apartment. She knocked tentatively on his door and jumped as it was opened abruptly.

"Kelly!" he said in surprise.

"I'm a bit early. I hope you don't mind that I came up."

"Umm, sure.... No problem.... I'm almost ready." He disappeared back into his apartment, leaving the door partially opened.

Kelly tilted her head through the small opening, straining to fulfill her curiosity. "Should I come in?" she called.

"Sure," came his answer from somewhere inside.

She walked into the apartment, closed the door softly behind her, and waited a moment for her eyes to adjust. The single window was shaded with a dirty roll-down scroll; the only light in the room was from the vertical slats of light that streamed in around the window shade and the faint glow of a bulb in the kitchen ceiling.

"I'll only be a minute," he called from what she assumed was the bedroom. Kelly scanned the small room. There was absolutely no doubt he was a bachelor. Other than one of those old-style, padded office chairs on wheels, a desk with a small lamp on it, and the piles of papers and stacks of books that lay scattered about on the floor and desk, the space was bare. There were no rugs, no couch, no TV, no photos, no pictures on the walls. There was a small kitchen off to the right with an old, round, white refrigerator and tiny white stove, but no eating table. The faded blue kitchen counters were bare—wiped clean. Not even a coffeepot or toaster was visible from her vantage point. She stepped closer to the desk, careful not to tread on the carpet of books and papers. She read the titles as she tiptoed around the space. Most were various botany texts and scientific publications. The author of a loose publication caught her eye, and she bent down to retrieve it from the floor. The title read *The Phytogeography of the Northeast Forests and its Relationship to Environmental Pollutants.* Under the title was printed *Reis M. Welling, PhD.* Kelly glanced at the doorway where Reis had disappeared, then quickly flipped to the last page. In the lower corner was printed *Reis M. Welling, PhD, Department of Botany, Cornell University, Ithaca, New York.* She'd assumed he'd taught high school or junior high. It certainly never occurred to her that he was a professor—at Cornell, no less. She leaned over and carefully set the paper down. She studied it momentarily, nestled atop similar publications. She straightened back up and jumped slightly.

Reis was standing in the doorway of his bedroom, his head tilted her way, his mouth tilted toward a smile. He had on khaki shorts and a simple crew neck shirt. He wore hiking boots with ragg wool socks and had a backpack slung over his shoulder.

She smiled. "You look like you just stepped out of an L.L.Bean catalog."

His smile widened. "You look like you're going shopping at the mall."

Kelly glanced down at her white shorts, light blue knit short-sleeve blouse, and white canvas shoes. "What's wrong with what I'm wearing?" she responded defensively.

"Nothing! Not a thing. You look great." His eyes crinkled in amusement. "Let me just get my other pack from the kitchen, and we can go."

"Your other pack?"

"Sure. We want to eat at some point today, don't we?" He went to the kitchen and grabbed a pack off the floor.

"If that's food, then what's in the other one?"

"Oh, just some hiking gear. Emergency stuff."

They walked through the door. Reis set one of the packs on the floor of the hallway and carefully locked the door to his apartment, checking the knob twice to make sure it could not be opened.

"I see.... Emergency stuff, huh?" Kelly said. She watched him check the door one last time. If someone were to break in, what exactly would they steal? As they made their way down the stairs, she said, "I'm beginning to realize that this trip may be a little different than our walks in the park."

Reis laughed. "I certainly hope so." Somewhere toward the last flight of steps, he asked, "So...when's the last time you went hiking?"

"Hiking? Oh. Well…I must have hiked at some point in my life." She thought for a moment before saying, "What exactly is the difference between walking and hiking, anyway?"

"Good question. I think, in order to officially hike," he glanced at her shoes, "one must wear hiking boots."

"Fine." She puffed out a little blast of air, sending a spray of her dark bangs into the air. "You hike. I'll walk."

When they reached the car, Kelly asked him if he wanted to drive.

"No. You drive. It's your car. Hi, Max," Reis said as he got into the passenger side of the car. Max's body wagged in delight. Reis scratched the dog's fuzzy head. "Besides," he told her as she got behind the wheel, "I want to look at my maps."

"Maps? Don't you know where we're going?" Kelly started the car and pulled out into traffic.

He gave her a sly grin. "I've got to find a mountain trail suitable for white shorts."

"Oh, you're just hilarious."

Reis's smile widened before he spread the maps across his lap, his face constricting into concentration. He began to study them intensely. Kelly glanced at him from time to time as she drove. He seemed totally absorbed in his maps. She kept thinking about the discovery she'd made back at his apartment. There were so many questions she wanted to ask—so many missing pieces. She knew the likelihood of getting answers was slim. She hadn't missed the look in his eyes as he'd stood by his bedroom; it was not a look of one willing to have his life scrutinized.

He was, however, in an extraordinarily good mood. She glanced his way again. He seemed almost relaxed as he hummed to the radio, his fingers drumming against his maps. Kelly admired his profile, his hair falling slightly into his eyes. She resisted the urge to brush it gently aside.

Her mind then turned to Brian. What was he doing now while she was driving off with this man she barely knew? He'd be on his way to the office, surely—gearing up to work on some found-out criminal's defense, figuring out some angle, always assuming that even the guilty ones would take advantage of a second chance. You had to admire that—the almost childlike belief in the goodness of man. Or was it simply the challenge—putting goodness and hope in a place they had no right to be? And while he was defending the world, she was treading down this slippery path toward the Adirondack Forest.

She'd told Brian she was going hiking, of course. She'd told him, in the simplest of ways, about Reis—about their friendship. The fact that Reis was the man she'd met in the tree, the fact that she'd stalked this man down, the fact that she looked forward to each Wednesday.... It just didn't seem necessary to reveal those facts. And if she liked the way Reis smiled or the way his hair flew about in the light breeze from the car window...well, that too was best kept in the recesses of her mind. Best not to think of it at all. She turned the radio up, just a touch, and turned her attention to the road.

Reis picked a small mountain near the High Peaks Region of the Adirondack Park. It was an easy hike but still provided a spectacular view, he told her as he pointed. "See that hill straight ahead? That's the one we're going to."

"That one?" She squinted through the windshield. She glanced at him and pointed to the tall, green mound of earth. "You want to climb to the top of that?"

"That's the general idea. It's not as bad as it looks. The trail is winding—gradual." Kelly gave him an *Are you out of your mind?* glance, and he laughed gently. "Really! I can carry you up there if I have to."

Her eyebrows rose at the thought, then a smile. "I'm sure you could...and you might just have to."

They parked the car at the small pull-off by the trailhead. Max flew from the car, smelling the ground with pleasure and lifting his leg on every possible outcropping. Kelly stood by the car and watched as Reis checked the organization of his packs. He fished out a couple of light hiking caps and wiped them with bug repellent. "Helps keep the bugs out of your eyes," he said as he plopped one on his head and offered the other one to her. She set it on her head, a bit unwillingly, carefully slipping the strands of her hair around the fabric, making sure nothing was sticking up in some laughable fashion. She pulled her cell phone out of her purse and checked for a signal.

"Will this work out here?" she asked.

Reis shrugged. "I don't believe in cell phones."

Kelly cocked her head at him with a smile. "Like you don't believe in fairies, or like you don't believe in the need for mass mobile communication?"

Reis handed her the lighter of the two packs and said, "Oh, I believe in fairies."

She laughed and accepted the backpack. It was heavier than she'd imagined, and she set it on the ground as she threw the phone back in her purse and locked the whole thing in the trunk of the car.

They started slowly up the trail. For the first half hour the path was smooth with only the slightest incline. The forest grew dense and dark around them. The ground was wet from recent rain, and a heavy mossy odor filled the air. Max was in his glory as he zigzagged ahead. He'd run in one direction, only to stop short and follow his nose to something better. Every few minutes he'd run back to them, just to check in—dripping with mud and panting with happiness—before trotting off again.

"It's like we're in another world here," Kelly whispered to Reis. "I half expect to see a wood nymph or troll jump out ahead of us."

"I think Max has sent them all into hiding," Reis replied. They watched as Max started at the chirp of a chipmunk and took off toward the sound. "When I'm in a forest this dense, I always feel a sense of timelessness. These forests looked pretty much like this thousands of years ago, and with any luck, they'll look like this in another thousand."

The trail steadily grew steeper, and they had to navigate an increasing number of tangled tree roots. Large boulders began to appear, looking as if they had just erupted from the earth. The day became warm, and the cloud cover broke apart, sending beams of light through the trees. With the warmth, the mosquitoes descended upon them, buzzing around their heads in small dark clouds. "Just be glad black fly season is over," Reis told Kelly as she swatted at the air. She had begun to sweat—the uncomfortable feeling of hot moisture in her armpits, her head hot beneath the hat. She considered removing the baseball cap, but then the thought of her hair popping up in every direction put an end to that idea. A few people came up from behind and passed them with a smile. Kelly, who'd been chatting pleasantly about one of her coworkers and her most recent software ideas, grew quiet. After several minutes, Reis stopped and turned to her.

"What?" she asked.

"You've stopped talking," he said with great concern. "Something must be terribly wrong."

"You think you're funny, don't you?" She looked down at her feet. "I hate to admit this, but my feet are killing me. I should have at least worn socks."

They studied her soiled canvas shoes, her ankles splashed with mud. She narrowed her eyes as he returned to her face. She could feel the heat of her cheeks—the dampness on her face—and knew her bangs were slipping out from beneath her hat in wet, slimy strands, pressing against her damp forehead. "Don't laugh!" she warned.

He tilted his head—a kind little smile. "Let's just go a little further," he whispered. "I know just what you need."

They followed the trail for about ten more minutes before he turned left and led her along a narrow deer path that roughly followed a small stream into the woods. Even the most nimble of deer must have a difficult time ducking and leaping over the many small logs and branches Kelly was made to negotiate. As they strayed further and further from the main trail, the isolation began to nag at her. She was alone—very alone—with this man.

As if he sensed her unease, he smiled back at her in reassurance. "It'll be worth it. Trust me."

She repeated the words in her head. *Trust me.* She considered stopping and insisting they turn back, but after pushing through a heavy patch of sticky undergrowth, the path suddenly widened and flattened out. The stream was directly to their left, bubbling down, clear and sparkling in the filtered sunlight. The streambed was small descending steps of smooth, flat rock. Several hundred yards ahead the streambed dropped away. Kelly could hear the song of the falling water as she took in the greens of the trees that hovered softly over the water. She smelled the mossy wildness, and all thoughts of leaving were swept away. If he were a killer, there was no better place to die.

They carefully picked their way through the underbrush until they stood at the top of the falls. The water fell about ten feet, swirling momentarily in a small pool before gently cascading its way down the mountain. The banks of the pool were steep, with a soft green border of ferns on either side. They stood a long moment, looking down in silence.

"Here we are," Reis said softly. He reached his hand out to Kelly and nodded his head toward the pool below. Kelly took his hand and let him help her down the bank. The soft earth gave way beneath their feet, and they slid slowly along the carpet of ferns and moss, coming to an easy rest at the edge of the pool. "This is the perfect remedy for tired feet," he said when they'd reached the bottom. Reis sat down and began taking off his boots.

"How'd you know about this place?" she asked, looking around in wonder.

"There are not too many places I haven't explored up here," Reis said, kicking off his right boot and starting on his left.

Kelly sat down and undid her own laces. She groaned as she removed her shoes. Several large blisters stood out, bright red on her feet.

Reis gave her feet a good, sympathetic going-over before he said, "Come on."

He stood up and stepped into the water, the depth of it crawling up his ankles as he moved, stopping as it reached halfway up his calves. Kelly followed his lead, letting her feet slide into the pool. The water was surprisingly cold, and she sucked in a breath in shock. The bottom was soft and sandy beneath her toes, and she inched forward toward the center of the pool. Max went in also, lapping water as he walked along the edge. He stood there for a moment before leaving the pool, sending shimmering droplets in all directions as he shook.

"Better?" Reis asked.

"Ah, yes," Kelly answered and closed her eyes. She listened to the water as it fell into the pool. The cool current caressed her feet. She sighed with contentment and wiggled her toes in the sand.

"Watch out!"

Kelly opened her eyes with a start.

"There's a crayfish by your toe!"

Kelly jumped back out of reflex, then glared at Reis as he laughed. She reached down and shot a spray of water at him.

"Watch it!" he said.

"I'll have you know, I'm not the wimp you think I am! I bet I've caught more crayfish than you've ever dreamed of."

"That's quite possible, especially considering I've never dreamt of crayfish," he retorted. She splashed him again. "You better stop that," he warned.

"Oh yeah? What are you going to do if I don't?" she laughed, sending more water his way.

"Now you've done it!" Reis whipped off his hat, intending to scoop up a large volume of water to throw at her, but his feet slipped as he bent down, causing him to fall. Water flew in all directions as his backside hit the bottom of the pool.

When Kelly got her laughter under control, she said, "I certainly hope you haven't injured any poor, innocent crayfish."

Reis looked up at her with a grin. He took his hat, still filled with water, and flopped it on his head. Water trickled down his face and neck. "Okay, okay. I stand corrected. I now know you have a great passion for crayfish."

"That's right," Kelly said smugly. Reis sat on the bank as Kelly wandered down the stream. Stepping gingerly through the water, she'd stop every few feet and lift up a rock, peering carefully under it. She turned back his way. He was resting his head on his arms, which were crossed across his knees, and he was dripping and smiling and watching her.

"What are you smiling at?" Kelly asked.

"You," was his answer, and she tilted her head with a soft smile. She returned and sat next to him on the bank. He reached for his pack and pulled out the water bottle, a small Ziploc bag filled with plump purple grapes, and another full of crackers. "Are you hungry?" he asked, passing her the water bottle.

She took a drink, then passed it back. "A little," she answered. He brought the water bottle to his lips, then pushed the bag of crackers along the ground. Kelly took a cracker and chewed thoughtfully. "So, Reis," she said as she swallowed the last of the cracker. He popped a grape in his mouth and looked her way. She picked up a small pebble and threw it in the water. "You never told me where you used to teach."

He chewed for a moment, then swallowed. "Cornell," he said, leaning back and easing his body down amongst the ferns.

Kelly picked up another stone and sent it skipping across the water. "Cornell?" she said, glancing his way. "Should I call you Professor or Dr. Welling?"

Reis brought his arms up, rested his head into his hands, and closed his eyes. "I don't know. What did it say in my journal article you seemed so interested in?"

She flashed him a look. His face was calm, his eyes closed, his hair mingling with the leafy vegetation, his knees pointing up toward the sky. "It said," her voice tight, "Reis M. Welling, PhD."

"Oh. Well, that's way too long." Still, he did not open his eyes. "I think professor will do just fine."

Kelly gave him a hard look. He appeared asleep, except for the slightest suggestion of smugness on his face. "You're quite pleased with yourself, aren't you?" she accused. "Spying on me from your bedroom door."

Reis's eyes popped open. "Me?" he exclaimed as he sat up. "Spying on you?" He faced her. "Excuse me, but I believe it was my place and my papers you were pawing through!"

Kelly gave him a look of stubborn disbelief. "Well, how else am I going to find out anything about you? God knows you're not going to volunteer anything." She made her voice sound more wronged than she really felt. "I didn't even know you had your PhD! I thought you taught high school or something."

Reis folded his arms across his knees and put his chin on them, sighing with boredom. "What is it you'd like to know, Kelly?"

Kelly let out a little puff of air in exasperation. "Where you got your undergraduate degree? Your doctorate? How long were you at Cornell? Why you aren't still there?"

"Yale. Berkeley. Four and a half years. I'm no longer there

because it's always been my dream to work in a library."

"Fine!" Kelly said, kicking the water with her foot and sending a small wave across the pool. "I'm sorry I brought it up!" She crossed her arms over her knees and heavily rested her chin on her wrists.

They were silent for a time, both watching the waves slap gently against the opposite bank. Somewhere nearby a crow squawked loudly and was answered by a more distant call. The forest grew quiet again, except for the falling of the water. Reis put his foot in the pool and gently rotated it until a small eddy formed. "Kelly, look," he said quietly. "I had some problems after my dad died. I just couldn't teach effectively anymore, so I left. It's as simple as that." He paused. "Okay?"

Kelly looked at him—his hazel eyes pleading. "Okay." She offered him the slightest shrug—a little smile.

They didn't speak for a while. Kelly munched on some grapes and wiggled her toes in the mud of the bank. Max came over and panted happily in her face. She turned her head from the slightest odor of dead fish.

"How're your feet?" Reis asked.

"Much better." They both looked down at her mud-covered toes. She dipped them in the water, the mud slipping away. "But I think I'll have to go barefoot."

"I think I've got some things that will help," he said, reaching for his other pack.

"An extra pair of hiking boots?"

"No, but almost as good." He searched through the pack. "Let's see. Here are some Band-Aids. Oh, here's a cloth to dry your feet.... Ah, here we are." He pulled out a pair of thin wool hiking socks and showed them to her proudly.

"Socks! Wonderful! What else do you have in there?"

"A little of this, a little of that," he said, rifling through the contents. "You never know what you might need when you're out here."

"Do you have any dry clothes for yourself?" she asked with a smile.

He pulled his wet shirt away from his chest and shook it briefly. "No. It's the one thing I didn't think I'd need."

When Kelly had doctored up her feet, they continued up the trail. Kelly felt greatly refreshed—her feet cozy inside her shoes—and began to talk. She talked about her father, his love for fishing, and how she'd been hoodwinked into catching him crayfish in the stream behind their house. She'd believed him when he'd told her he was taking them to a better home, setting them free in larger waters. It was years before she'd figured out he was using them as bait.

The trail steepened, the trees began to thin, and small scrub trees took their place. As they picked their way through the suddenly rocky outcrops, Kelly continued to talk, telling Reis about the time her father accidentally hooked a baby duck, which was almost immediately snapped up by some large, unseen creature. Kelly could barely contain her laughter as she told Reis how her father had fought the battle to beat all battles, convinced he'd stumbled upon one mother of a catfish, only to almost lose his finger to the largest alligator snapper he'd ever seen.

"Where," Reis laughed, as the trail made one last large bend, "do you get this stuff? Do you just make it up?"

"No. Really! It's true. And then there was the time—" Kelly was forced into sudden silence. She opened her mouth with wonder at what surely must be the entire Adirondack Park. She turned to him in amazement. "My God," she whispered.

"Pretty incredible, isn't it?" Reis said as he scanned the view.

"We're up so high! I don't think I've ever seen a more lovely view. What lake is that?"

"That's Heart Lake. And over there," he pointed, "is Indian Pass Brook. If you follow it north, it flows into Henderson Lake, which connects to the Hudson River." They continued to walk around the mountain top—Reis naming various landmarks.

"Are you hungry now?" Reis asked when the panoramic tour was complete.

"Starved!"

"Come on." Reis sat on a large, flat rock that overlooked the view of Mount Marcy. He began to remove various foods from his pack. "My famous tuna and bean sprouts in a pita sandwich," he told her, handing her one of the sandwiches. "There's more fruit. And, for dessert, peanut butter cookies. Which, by the way, I made myself."

"Wow!" She removed the plastic covering from the pita pocket and admired the delicate green strands sprouting from its opening. "I expected trail mix and granola bars. This is great."

"That's the nice thing about a day hike: since you don't have to carry sleeping gear, you can bring better food." Reis undressed his own sandwich and took a large bite.

"So what's the longest you've ever been out here?" Kelly asked before taking her own delicate bite.

Reis negotiated the food in his mouth before attempting an answer. "Oh, about a month, I guess."

"A month?"

"Give or take a day."

"Man! You must feel awfully grimy by then."

Reis wiped at his mouth with the back of his hand and then brushed it across the side of his shorts. "You bathe in the streams." He shrugged. "Out here," he looked about with admiration, "no one cares how you smell, or how you look. What you say. Or what you don't say." He turned back her way and smiled. "But I will admit, that first hot shower feels pretty damn good."

When they finished with their food, they lay back upon the rock and took in the view. Kelly was uncharacteristically quiet, not feeling the need to fill up the silence. And she didn't feel awkward, leaning against the rock, the sun warming her body. This man, so close that all she had to do was stretch her foot out a couple more inches to have it rest against his thigh. And Brian? He'd hardly entered her mind. She peered down the mountainside and watched a red-tailed hawk float in lazy circles against the green of the surrounding forest.

"This is the first mountain I climbed as a child," Reis said. "My father and I. I must've been around four or five, but I remember it as if it happened yesterday."

Kelly watched the ever-widening circles of the hawk, afraid that if she looked Reis's way, he would stop.

"I felt as if I were on top of the world. I also remember suddenly realizing how small and really insignificant I was—just one very small member of this very large world."

She waited. He smiled gently, turning his eyes from the view, and she turned to face him. "We lay on this very same rock, and he said, 'I feel the power of God up here, son.' He asked me if I could feel Him too...." Reis turned back toward the hawk. "I told him, 'Yes.' But what I really felt was the power of the earth. The power of nature itself. The trees and animals. Their power. Their struggle for survival. And somehow, being a part of that—my insignificance, maybe, not so insignificant."

Kelly waited to see if he would say more. After a long moment, she said, "I think you and your father felt the same thing." She turned her eyes from the bird and tilted her head toward Reis.

"Your interpretations were just different."

He looked at her. "Yes, I suppose you're right. It's just my scientific nature to want to put more of a label on it than *God*."

Reis's gaze turned away, and he was lost in his own thoughts. This had been the longest he'd ever talked about himself, and she longed for more. "You must miss your father a great deal," she said.

Reis didn't respond, and that was okay. Kelly closed her eyes, drew in a long, slow breath, and felt not so insignificant.

"I'd like to think that he's out here," Reis's soft words flowed into her ears, "his soul having returned to the earth, and that he's part of everything we see and all that we feel."

The two of them stayed at the top of the mountain for another hour before they started their descent. "Going back down is always easier and quicker," he told her. It was a little before two o'clock when they started, and by three thirty they were back at Kelly's car. Max flopped in the back seat, exhausted.

"I'd like to join him," said Kelly, picking off various burrs and plant debris from her blouse and dropping them to the ground. "I know I'll sleep well tonight."

Reis threw the packs next to Max. "I'll drive back, if you'd like. Then you can rest."

Kelly looked at Reis, who looked bright-eyed and chipper— no worse for wear. "You could probably run right back up that mountain and back down and still not feel like I do."

"Probably." He grinned.

They both looked at what was left of her poor shoes. Kelly brushed at the dirt that was smeared into her white shorts and pulled her fingers through the tangle of her hair. She could only imagine what her makeup must look like. She slid into the passenger seat and pulled down the visor. "Oh my God! Look at my hair!" she exclaimed as she looked in the mirror. "I look terrible."

Reis leaned slightly against the door frame. "Are you kidding? You look great. The natural look suits you."

She shook her head at him with disgust and dug out a comb from the glove compartment. Reis shut the passenger side of the car and made his way around. Kelly fought with her hair as Reis pulled back the seat and adjusted the rearview mirror. He fiddled with the car keys, studied the console, leaned forward, and scrutinized the steering column, tapping his index finger gently on the ignition before sliding the key into place. He adjusted the mirror again. Kelly's attention strayed from her hair, allowing her eyes to shift slightly his way. He turned the key and jumped slightly when the car fired to life. He brought both hands firmly to the steering wheel, shifted his shoulders about, and rolled his head around. Finally, he brought his right hand down and shifted the car into reverse. He turned his head toward her to check his surroundings, his lower lip held gently between his teeth. As he eased his foot off the brake, allowing the car to roll tentatively back, Kelly turned her head his way and smiled softly. *It's okay*, she wanted to say. *It's okay.*

When he was safely on the road and relaxing into his driving, she leaned back with a tired sigh and said, "You realize, of course, that I work out three times a week at the gym. It's obviously done no good, whatsoever."

His lips went up in a smile, his eyes not leaving the road. "All you need are a few more mountains under your belt." He leaned forward slightly and pointed quickly with his right hand before returning it to the steering wheel. "See that one up ahead and to the right? That's Haystack Mountain. We'll do that next."

Kelly peered at the large green mountain capped with rock, which loomed in the distance. "In your dreams! I think we should tackle something a lot smaller. Like maybe...a large anthill. Or maybe one of those little mounds gofers leave behind."

He laughed. "It's not as bad as it looks. Then there's always Mount Marcy.... Algonquin.... White Face...."

Kelly slid further down in the car seat and brushed ineffectively at the dirt on her shorts. "And there're leather couches, feather beds, hot tubs...."

At five o'clock, when they were about forty-five minutes from home, Reis turned his eyes from the road and said, "I know a great place not far from here where we could have an early dinner...."

"I can't go into a restaurant! Look at me!"

He looked at her and smiled with approval. "It's a very dark place. Very cozy," he coaxed.

"It would have to be pitch black for me to go in!"

"Come on, Kelly. You look great. I already told you that. Besides, it's me who would be seen with you. If you really looked that bad, do you think I'd embarrass myself like that?"

She rolled her eyes and considered the invitation.

"Come on," he continued. "I'll buy. Will you *please* have dinner with me?"

"Okay. Geeze. If you're going to beg," she laughed.

A short while later they parked in the shade of the restaurant parking lot, rolled the windows down for Max, and brought him some water. The day was cooling quickly, and as Kelly watched him lay his face back down on his paws and close his eyes with a sigh, she decided that he would be fine. And Reis was right: the restaurant was dark and cozy, and the food came quickly, the steam rising from the plates, making Kelly's mouth water with anticipation. She eyed Reis's chicken parmesan and suppressed the urge to dig her fork into his plate.

Instead, she dug into her fish, eating quickly, chewing and

swallowing, closing her eyes, chasing the mouthfuls with tiny sips of chardonnay. She took a large bite of fish, then caught the look on Reis's face. "What?" she said, her mouth full.

He grinned. "I don't think I've ever seen anyone so thin eat with quite so much enthusiasm."

"Hey!" She chewed for a moment and swallowed. "I'm starved. I burned off a month's worth of calories today."

"You don't need to put them all back on in one sitting," he teased.

"Oh, yes I do! And I want dessert too! You did say you were buying, didn't you?"

"Yes, ma'am."

Kelly took another bite and closed her eyes to its pleasure. The fish was tender and sweet, its flavor enhanced by a delicate cream sauce. When it was all but swallowed, she topped it off with a gentle sip of wine and reached for her hot buttered roll.

"So, tell me about the boyfriend."

Kelly's hand stopped somewhere before the roll—hovered there momentarily—then secured the warm, soft bread, her fingers curving in until the crust gave way under the pressure. Her eyes lifted up to Reis, who was waiting for a response—the look on his face not quite readable. "Oh." She waved her other hand in dismissal and laughed. "The boyfriend." She picked up the roll and smiled. "The one that doesn't think I'm repulsive?"

"Is there any other kind?" he asked.

Brian. Her eyes went back to the roll. What about Brian... who was cocky with self-confidence, warm, and playful...who was teeming with the joy of life. And then there was Reis: not quite joyous, but there was no denying the physical attraction, and then there was the pleasure of his apparent vulnerability. The contrast between the two men was striking, causing her to evaluate her own needs—her own motivations. She tore the bread apart and felt the steam rise from its guts. Her eyes went back to his. "He's a lawyer," she said quickly, almost flippantly. She smiled. "A very busy lawyer. Kinda casual.... I hardly see him."

Reis nodded his head slowly. Kelly ripped off a large piece of the bread and popped it into her mouth, making it quite impossible to say anything more.

Reis waited, using his fork to put his own reasonably sized unit of food into his mouth, then chewed and swallowed. "That's it?"

She shrugged, then swallowed the last of what was in her mouth. "Pretty much." She popped another large chunk into her mouth.

"Wow." He took a sip from his own wine glass. "I can sure see why you like the guy."

Reis stopped Kelly's car by the curb in front of his apartment building and put it in park. He turned to her and said, "Home, safe and sound."

Kelly looked at him and smiled at the chaos of his hair, the tempting tinge of stubble on his face, and the soft suggestion of anticipation in his eyes. She wanted him to flee from the car, so that this wouldn't be—wouldn't become—their moment.

Max popped up with alertness and poked his head between them. She placed her hand on the dog's head. "Reis," Kelly said softly, looking away from his face and running her fingers through the rough hair on top of Max's head. "Thanks so much for inviting me. I can't remember when I've had a more wonderful day."

"Thank you, Kelly—" His hand was suddenly close to hers in a defensive move, the sound of his voice sending Max into action. He gently restricted the dog's access to his face. "For coming with me," he continued. Max was suddenly in his lap, and Reis's hands encased the dog. Reis gave the dog's body a good going over. Max grunted with pleasure, rolling on his back in Reis's lap and threatening Reis's wellbeing with his paws. Max froze in anticipation at the sudden stillness, his legs stuck straight up in the air as Reis's hands came to rest. Reis turned back to Kelly with a soft smile. "Well." He extracted Max from his lap, gently depositing him on the backseat. "I'll just get my things."

As he stepped out of the car and opened the backdoor for his packs, Kelly got out and walked around to the driver's side. Reis grinned like a boy, a backpack on each shoulder, and backed toward his apartment. "I'll probably see you Wednesday."

"Okay. Bye, Reis," Kelly called as he reached his apartment building's door. He shot her a wide flash of a smile before he pivoted and disappeared into his building.

Kelly saw Brian's car parked in front of her building when she was still a block away.

"Shit!" She ran her hand through her hair and cussed again. Max turned his head to her, a look of concern on his face. She frowned at the dog and eased her car behind Brian's. They both sighed. "Come on, Max. Let's get this over with."

Brian stirred on the couch and looked up from the game he was watching as she came through the door. "My God, Kelly! What happened to you?" Max rushed toward him in greeting and Brian put his hand out to impede the dog. "And look at poor Max! He looks almost as bad as you." Max sat down in muddy dejection.

"I told you I was going hiking today," she said, not hiding her irritation.

"Hiking, yes. But you said absolutely nothing about mud

wrestling!" As he laughed he became more delighted with his joke and laughed even louder.

She narrowed her eyes at him and did nothing to restrain her inner bitch as she said, "I'm taking a shower! I've already eaten, so why don't you order yourself a pizza or something. I'm way too tired to go out."

Brian's laughter stopped; he cocked his head to the side. "Okay…." He stood up and kissed her gently, picked a burr from her shirt, and looked down on her with wounded eyes. "Would you like me just to go home?"

Kelly was derailed, her anger deflated. He loved her. He did. She placed her filthy hair against the soft cloth of his Ralph Lauren polo, and he didn't pull away. "No," she whispered. "Of course not. Let me just clean up. We'll watch a movie or something."

Kelly disappeared into her bedroom and began removing her soiled clothing.

"So who all went?" he called.

"Just Reis and me." She picked out some fresh clothes and stepped back into the hallway, naked, tilting her head his way. "Remember? I told you that." She headed quickly toward the bathroom.

"Yes…" his words came out slowly as he watched her walk away, "I know…." Kelly smiled. Over three years and the sight of her naked body could still make him take pause.

"I thought maybe one of his other friends might have joined you."

Kelly disappeared into the bathroom, tempted to shut the door. "No," she called, reaching for the shower faucet. "It was just us." The water burst from the showerhead.

"So when am I going to meet this guy?" she heard Brian call over the drone of the shower.

Kelly had to smile once again. "Brian! I can't hear you! Wait until I'm done!" Jealousy: not an emotion Kelly would've believed Brian capable of entertaining. And her heart did indeed soar with giddy satisfaction. To be the one who rules. Who drives a thing forward. Or back. Or stops it altogether. There was, without a doubt, a certain joy in the power to cause pain.

But, as the hot water poured over her body, her thoughts turned from Brian to Reis, then back again to Brian, then once again to Reis, and then to the memory of what it was like on the receiving end: the snooty sneers of pretty girls, the cruel indifference of boys, being used and played, teased and picked on, and ignored. The power to cause pain was quickly no longer something worthy of her embrace, and she braced herself against the walls of the shower. "Oh God," she whispered.

n ine teen

Reis took the stairs to his apartment—three at a time—marveling at how well he felt. His mind hadn't felt this focused in ages. He let himself in, threw the backpacks to the floor, kicked off his boots, and paced about in his enthusiasm. He went to the phone and picked up the business card, flicking it with the tips of his fingers. Should he call? Let the doctor know how good he felt? Share the joy? But it was a Saturday night. Dr. Benson would surely be home with his family. He put the card down, carefully aligning it back with the edge of the phone. Who else could he call? He looked at the phone for a long moment. There was no one—no one he'd choose to talk to—so he walked away from the phone and surveyed his little domain, stepping among his abandoned journals and sliding them along with his feet. He picked up the latest issue of the *American Journal of Botany* and sat down at his little desk. He read the entire issue and reached for another, going back now to the oldest issue and working his way forward. He read them long into the night, amazed at all he'd missed in the last year and a half.

tw enty

Reis's tenure was officially announced one week before the start of the fall semester. Ellen threw him a small party at the house, inviting their hiking group, her family, his parents, and a few people from Reis's department. The day was warm, and people spilled out of the house onto the front porch and also the garden out back. Reis sat in the garden, sipping a beer and thoroughly enjoying himself. All his stress and his sleeping problems had disappeared once he'd gotten home from his field research, and he could hardly wait for the semester to start—to see the stunned young faces of the freshman class, to watch them wander around the campus lost and confused, and then to see that confusion replaced with the cockiness of independence and knowledge…and, yes, pride at being a part of Cornell. And he was looking forward to strolling among the ivy-covered buildings with the full weight of importance—the secure weight of the title of associate professor. How many years, he wondered as he tipped his head back and drew in some beer, before he reached the final frontier? Could he make it to full professor before he reached thirty?

"Congratulations, Reis." Reis turned from his happy musings and took Bob's hand into his with a grin. Bob gave him a rough slap on the back. "Now that you finally have a real job," he said with the enthusiasm of a few beers, "you need to buy a real house and have a couple real kids."

Reis saw his mother turn from the face of one of his fellow faculty members and look his way. He smiled softly toward her. He saw Ellen turn her face, knit her brow.

"What's wrong with this house?" Ellen demanded from across the garden.

Sandy walked by and handed Bob a Stella. "Here, Bob. I think you need another."

Reis looked up at Bob and said with a smile, "I've got to talk Ellen into marrying me first."

"What the hell's wrong with her?" asked Bob. "I'd marry you in a minute."

"I appreciate that, Bob. I'll let you know if it comes to that."

His mother smiled; Ellen looked away.

"Hey, Mike!" Reis called, standing as he saw Mike Green come around the house.

"Congratulations, Reis." Mike shook his hand. "I know how good it feels."

"Yes, it does. I don't think I realized the stress I was under until it was finally made official."

"That's right," said Jim, who was standing nearby. "Now you can sit back and do whatever the hell you want, and they can't just up and fire your ass."

Over people's laughter, Mike said, "God knows, that's what I'd do." Jim laughed louder, and Ellen was suddenly by Reis's side.

He kissed the side of her face, and his beer spilled just a tiny bit from the top of the bottle, dripping on his thigh and rolling down and onto his knee. Then his father was there, and Reis introduced him to Mike, and Mike was shaking his father's hand, and the two of them—the two men in Reis's life—were talking about him in a proud, fatherly sort of way. Ellen smiled toward his mother, who was smiling from a few feet away, and the two women in his life shared a moment. Reis smiled—the wetness of the beer forgotten.

The party went well into the night, with five or six of their best friends lounging around on the couches, with the apparent intent of permanence. Ellen finally threw them out, and as they closed the door behind the last of them, Reis captured her in his arms. "Thank you, Ellen. It was a wonderful party."

"I thought so too." She smiled and kissed his lips.

"So, when *are* you going to marry me?" he slurred in her ear. She laughed.

They stood near the front door; a puff of fall breeze teased the drapes of the front window, the material reaching out and caressing the back of his leg. "Really, Ellen. I'm serious."

Her hands were on his chest, pushing slightly away from him. "Reis, we've been through this before."

"But that was before my tenure." He leaned her way. "When things were still up in the air."

"Nothing's changed for me." Her hands pushed harder as she continued. She took a step back. "There's no guarantee I'll have a job here next fall."

"Your job's secure." He tightened his grip on her arms. An unsavory sensation wriggled through the room. "They love you there."

"Even if that's true, don't you think I'd like the opportunity for tenure?" She eased further from his grasp. "There's no reason to believe a tenure track position will open up in my department."

"What are you saying, Ellen? Are you saying you'd leave Cornell?"

She managed to extract herself fully, stepping back and looking him square in the eye. "If I felt there was a better opportunity, offering tenure, I would certainly consider it." She turned away and picked up an empty beer can off the nearby table.

"Jesus, Ellen!" Reis's hands fell helplessly to his sides. "You've never talked like this before! I just accepted tenure. Here, at Cornell! And now you're thinking of leaving?"

She picked up four more cans, balancing them carefully as she headed toward the kitchen. Reis remained suspended by the door. "No, I'm not saying that at all. I'm just saying that I'm not ready to get married yet." She was in the kitchen now. He heard her open the bin where the recyclables were and throw the cans in. The clanging sound as the cans settled in crawled up Reis's spine. He brought his hands to his ears. There was the dizzy sweep of alcohol. How much beer had he consumed? She returned for another load of cans, avoiding his gaze. "I have no plans to leave," she said, smiling at him, her lips curled in an unnatural sort of way. "Who knows, someone may die tomorrow and open up a position. I just want the opportunity to develop my own career, without the house and kids and everything else that goes along with being married." She disappeared again into the kitchen. He cringed at the sound of metal on metal, the bang of the lid of the bin. He covered his ears fully, pressing his fingers deep into the canals of his ear. He pulled them quickly away as Ellen reentered the room.

She faced him, her hands on her hips, her head cocked, that odd smile on her face. He closed his eyes to the sight of her. *Fucking bitch!* A fucking, fucking bitch.

"Being married doesn't have to mean a house and kids," he said, opening his eyes and concentrating on a small fray on the pocket of her jeans. "Nothing would change. I love this place too." His voice whined, "We could just stay here," and brought up the bile of self-hatred.

The room sighed. Her resolve softened.

"Then why get married at all?" Her words were gentle now, closing the distance between them. "Why not just leave things the way they are, for now." She stepped his way and reached for his hand, the anger gone. "You've got to admit they're awfully good."

The foreign feel of her fingers mixed with his. "You're right," he conceded. He fought the urge to pull away. "They are." He was suddenly exhausted. She brought his hand to her lips, slowly kissing each of his fingers—each kiss a deep and crushing sadness.

tw enty - one

Monday morning, Kelly sat at her desk in front of her computer, and instead of cleaning up the bugs on her latest software, she reviewed what she believed, and what she knew, about this man's life—this life in which she'd allowed her life to be tangled. She really knew so little about Reis; he was so vague about his past. His reason for leaving Cornell seemed too simple. Why hadn't he just taken a leave of absence and returned by now? Hadn't he told her his father died a year and a half ago? He'd only been at the library a few months. What had he been doing in the meantime? There had to be much more going on than he'd told her. As her screensaver turned off and the screen of her computer turned black, she made up her mind to find out what it was.

She did a quick search on her computer, and within minutes, the phone line was ringing in her ear.

"Cornell personnel. Paula Burns speaking. How may I help you?"

Kelly smiled at the sound of her old college roommate's voice. There was a reason why her old roommate worked at the personnel department. Paula not only had access to all the personnel files, she also had a marvelous way of knowing everything about everyone and loved to share it. If anyone could give Kelly information about Professor Reis Welling, Paula could.

"Paula, it's Kelly. How've you been?"

"Kelly! I'm doing great," Paula's bubbly voice came through the line. "I haven't heard from you in a while. How are you?"

"I'm doing fine, but I need a little favor. I was hoping you could help me."

"Sure. What do you need?"

"I was wondering if you could pull up a personnel file for me. I have this friend who used to work at Cornell, and I'd just like to know a little bit more about him," Kelly said casually.

"Is this a friend of the romance nature?" Paula asked, already interested. "You want to check out if he's married or something?"

Kelly laughed. "Yeah, something like that."

"What's his name? I'll look."

Kelly waited while Paula punched information into the computer, and it was only a short moment later when she said, "Okay. Here he is: Reis Welling, born September 8, 1979. Not married!" she proudly announced.

"That's good. What else do you have?"

"Let's see.... He started here in the fall of 2002. In the botany department." There was a long pause. "Wow! Pretty impressive CV! Bachelor's, Yale. Doctorate, Berkeley. Tons of publications. A couple of books. Sounds like you've got yourself a bright one."

"Anything else?"

"He received his tenure in the fall of 2006. Then it just says he took an extended leave of absence shortly thereafter."

"That's it? It doesn't say why he left, or why he hasn't returned?"

"No. Unfortunately they don't usually put the good stuff in the computer. Why? Do you think there's something deep and dark in his past?" When Kelly didn't answer right away, she quickly added, "I could find out! I've got a friend in the botany department."

"Do you think you could?" Kelly asked.

"No problem. It just might take a day or two; I'm a little swamped right now."

"That would be wonderful. Just call me at work. My number is 518-429-0034 extension 9."

"Will do."

"Thanks, Paula. I really appreciate this." Kelly hung up the phone. If nothing else, at least Paula had substantiated all that he had told her.

tw enty - two

In December of 2006, record amounts of snow fell across the Ithaca area. On Monday, December fifth, fourteen inches fell in two hours, closing Cornell and turning the steep streets of Ithaca into wonderful sledding hills. By evening the temperature had dropped twenty degrees. The wind picked up, forming drifts up to ten feet high, paralyzing the city for yet another day.

That night, as the wind whipped around the house, Reis lay awake in bed, not realizing as he listened to the wind and the soft sound of Ellen's gentle sleep that his sleeping problems had returned. He simply lay there marveling at the power of the storm as it rattled the windows of the old house, also impressed by the fact that Ellen was somehow able to sleep, untroubled, through all the chaos.

By Wednesday the university had reopened, and Reis trudged across campus feeling the fatigue of two nights with little sleep. Dark clouds hung ominously overhead as the cold wind smacked across his face. Only about half his graduate students showed up for class, and by the time Reis strolled up to the podium, it had begun to snow earnestly again.

He stood shuffling through his class notes and congratulated the smattering of his students who'd braved the storm. "You know," he said, leaving the lecture podium and turning the closest chair around, "perhaps we should reconsider the class syllabus." He smiled as he sat facing the lecture hall, the back of the chair to his chest. "At least for the day. What shall we discuss?"

"Sex," one young man offered.

"Drugs," suggested a lovely, dark-eyed thing that sat in the front row—within reaching distance.

"And then there's rock and roll," added Reis. The sound of the hard, icy pellets of snow hitting the high windows of the auditorium beat rhythmically throughout the room. "But I was thinking of something that at least hinted at botany." There was a small groan from the students, and Reis stood up from his chair and smiled. "A compromise then. *Cannabis sativa.* Division: Magnoliophyta. Class: Magnoliopsida. Order: Urticales." He looked around the room. "Family?" Someone called, "Cannabaceae," and Reis nodded his approval. He paced gently in front of the class. "Can anyone tell me the differences between *Cannabis sativa* Linnaeus subspecies *indica* and subspecies *sativa*?"

And thus began a lively discussion on the uses and history of *Cannabis*, which might have been a fun way to spend an hour if it weren't for the fact that Reis sensed the negativity of several of the students. Well, more than sensed it—he could hear their harsh words as if he were sitting by their very side. He felt an almost overwhelming blanket of disappointment and sadness. It wasn't like he was passing around a bong. If he were forced to defend himself in a court of law—to court the powers that be, to dazzle them with his powers—exactly where would he stand? At the podium? Baring it all in front of these hostile students? Bare and vulnerable. A fear quivered next to the sadness, and he sat and rested his chin heavily against the back of the chair and did not mediate the mild argument that had erupted concerning *Cannabis ruderalis*—because, really, it just didn't matter.

Mike walked past Reis's open office door and caught him deep in thought. He leaned against the door frame and said with a grin, "Are you plotting your next move on your plan to take over the department?"

Reis looked at him, taking a moment to register Mike's words. "Absolutely," he said with a smile. "I'm working on a three-year plan."

"Well then," his smile broadened, "I'll let you get back to it." He took a step away from the door frame.

"Actually, Mike, there is something I'd like to talk to you about." Reis rubbed his forehead. "That is, if you have the time."

"Sure," said Mike, stepping into the room. He sat in the small chair across from Reis's desk. Reis shifted uncomfortably. Mike settled into the chair as if he had all the time in the world.

Reis stood up, crossed the room, and closed the door quietly. He walked slowly back to his seat and took his own time settling into his chair. "It's something that happened this summer during my field research," he finally began. He hesitated, looking at Mike. "I don't know why, but I can't seem to shake it." Reis got up and began to pace behind his desk. He walked around it and checked the office door, making sure it was fully shut. Mike waited patiently as Reis made his way back across the room and resumed his pacing. "Mike," Reis stopped and looked at him, "you're a good looking guy. You must have the women students come on to you at times."

"Yes.... It's been known to happen."

Reis continued to pace. "Well, I have that problem too. I'm not a whole lot older than most of them. I guess they idolize me or something." He paused, laughed awkwardly, and appealed to Mike. Mike smiled back with understanding. "Anyway, I've always dealt with it professionally. Even with the most aggressive women, I was always able to gracefully bring them back to the subject of botany, without hurting too many feelings." Reis stopped again and looked at Mike. Was he making any sense?

Mike nodded. "Yes, I know what you mean. I've been there too. These young women can be pretty scary; one wrong word from them, whether it's true or not, can bring your career crashing down around you."

Reis nodded in agreement and took a few steps toward the door. "You know me pretty well, Mike. Wouldn't you say I'm a pretty laid back guy? Always under control?"

"Yes, Reis. You're a prince." He grinned. "Now are you going to tell me what happened this summer or not?"

Reis made his way back to his desk, sat back down, and looked at his friend. "It was Holly Maxwell. She came to me the last night in the field, wearing nothing but a white T-shirt. She just flat out kissed me, right out there in the middle of the woods." Reis paused, pushing his hand through his hair. "I know you think I'm going to tell you I slept with her, but I didn't. It was more bizarre than that." He stopped, pressing his fingers hard against his scalp. "Mike, I got angry. Really angry. I threw her to the ground and screamed in her face. Of course, she began to cry. It was a very bad scene." He rubbed his hands across his face. "I think I'd feel better if I had just slept with her."

Mike sat back and thought a moment. "How are things between you two now?"

"They're surprisingly good. She's actually a very nice girl."

"Well, her timing sure stunk. Wasn't that only weeks before the committee made their final decision on your tenure?"

"Yes. I was worried sick she'd make trouble for me, but she didn't."

"Then why is it still bothering you? I have to admit," he said a bit dreamily, "Holly Maxwell in nothing but a T-shirt...my reaction might have been different. But getting angry at a totally unwelcome advance is not that bizarre. You'd been out in the field for weeks. You had to be exhausted. You were under stress over the tenure thing. I think you just need to put it behind you and stop beating yourself up."

"Thank you." Reis sighed and smiled sadly. "I think I just needed someone to tell me that, Mike. It hasn't been something I wanted to talk to Ellen about. Thank you."

"No problem. Any other confessions? Moral dilemmas?"

Reis shook his head with a smile.

"Are we still on for lunch?" Mike asked as he got up.

"Sure. I'll drop by your office at one." Before Mike was out the door, Reis added, "And Mike...thanks. Thanks again."

Reis watched Holly as she ran analysis testing on some of the soil samples they'd collected over the summer. Was she the reason for the hostility? He'd seen the department heads snooping around, peering in from the halls—seen their shadows stopping to listen at his closed office door. He narrowed his eyes. She may need to be dealt with—removed. He must talk to someone...but who? Conversations with his colleagues had become senseless and irritating; they failed to see his importance and didn't understand his relationship to their survival. But he must not let that con-

cern him. What was important now was Holly. He watched as she
flicked her hair away from her face. She caught his presence, and
her almond eyes turned his way with a smile. "Oh, hi, Professor
Welling. I'm almost done with the last of the samples from area
twenty-five. I should have the results to you by the end of the
week."

"Fine. That's fine." And he turned and left the lab, retreating
to the safety of his office.

"Reis," Ellen said as she passed him the salad bowl, "you've been
acting a bit off lately. I know you're not sleeping well." He took
the bowl from her outstretched hand and placed it gently on the
table. He did not move to put any salad on his plate. "I assumed
you had a lot of work-related stress. God knows I get like that. But
it's gotten to the point…" she put her fork down and implored
him with her eyes, "I can't help wondering if it's me you're having the problem with. You barely talk. We haven't slept together
in over a week." She looked so sad; Reis had to look away. "Reis,
have I done something?"

Reis turned back to her blue eyes, looking more blue, more
intense, more soft with concern than he thought possible, and he
felt a rush of love that pushed into his throat and made him gasp.
"It's not you!" He urgently grasped her hand. "It's them! They're
always watching me."

"Who, Reis? Who's watching you?"

"The heads of my department. I'm not sure why."

She shook her head, and he immediately saw the error—his
miscalculation of trust. "Reis, that doesn't make any sense. Why
would they do that?"

His hand came down hard, shaking the salad to attention.
"Don't you think I wish I knew?"

Ellen jumped, and Reis looked away. "Reis," his name coming out with caution, "I think you're under a lot of stress right now. Maybe it's from not sleeping. I don't know. But think about this rationally." She continued, slow and patronizing. "You just received your tenure. There's no reason for anyone to be watching you." She paused. He waited. "I think you're being a little paranoid."

"Damn it, Ellen!" he yelled, his hand assaulting the table once more, the salad jumping out of the bowl. "What the fuck's wrong with you? Don't you think I know that? That's what makes it so bizarre!" He stood up and began taking angry steps around the room. "Maybe they think they've made a mistake! Maybe they think they have something on me! Why don't you believe me?"

He stopped his movement and took in her tears—saw them roll out of her eyes and trickle down her cheeks—turned his eyes to the quivering salad, and felt the shame.

"Well, even if they are watching you," her words slipped over the salad, "it's not as if you have something to hide."

Then it smiled his way, its green lips curling up around the tomato. "Oh, Ellen," he said, turning his face away from the salad and into his hands, reaching for his chair and sinking into its seat. "I'm so sorry. Of course, you're right. Of course, I am being paranoid. They can watch all they want. I have nothing to hide. I just wish they wouldn't be so obvious about it." He looked at her and could tell, even with his apology, she was still hurt and confused. He regretted bringing the whole thing up. He'd be sure not do so in the future. "Everything's fine, Ellen." He picked up the mischievous leaves of lettuce and popped them into his mouth. "Really, it is."

The phone rang on New Year's Day. It was Ellen who reached for it. "Hello?" Reis watched as her face changed, and as her eyes met his, the sudden rush of fear. She handed him the phone.

"Hello?"

"Reis." His mother's voice came through in tears. "It's your father. He's had a stroke. I'm at City Hospital. I think you better come."

tw enty - three

Late Tuesday afternoon, Kelly's head was beginning to ache, her gut queasy. She was considering leaving work early, going home, crawling into bed, and possibly watching a movie she'd recorded. She wanted to get to sleep early and get lots of rest—then Wednesday morning everything would feel better. The sound of her phone made her jump. "Hello?"

It was Paula getting back to her. "I found out more about your friend," she offered once the pleasantries were over. "You did say he was a friend, right?"

"Yes." Kelly rubbed her aching head and closed her eyes to the wave of dizziness. "What did you find out?"

"Well...I'm not sure I should tell you this—"

"Sure you should," said Kelly, trying to sound upbeat. "You're dying to tell me!"

There was a nervous laugh and a long pause on the other end. Kelly's head throbbed harder. "Well," Paula began and then stopped. "Is he, like a, good friend?"

"Paula, come on. Just give me the dirt."

There was an uncharacteristic laugh. "Well…" she began again, "apparently, his father died suddenly, and…and he had sort of a nervous breakdown." She paused again. "He was more or less forced into taking a leave of absence." Paula hesitated for another long moment. Kelly sighed. Paula wasn't really telling her anything she didn't already know.

"Yes, he told me that. But why hasn't he gone back by now? His father died almost two years ago. Taking your dad's death badly and needing a break from work, I can understand, but two years seems a bit excessive."

"Kelly, he didn't just take his dad's death badly. I said he had a nervous breakdown." She stopped. "I really don't know if I should tell you this."

Kelly stopped rubbing her head. "What, Paula? Tell me what?" She listened hard into the phone, a tight, little knot of fear grasping at her stomach. "Tell me," she whispered.

There was a slight sigh of resignation before Paula continued. "Apparently, after he left here, he totally flipped out. Kelly, he…I guess, he tried to kill himself—with a knife. Slashed open his gut. He all but died. No one's heard anything about him since. Or, at least if they have, they're not talking." She stopped.

His gut—slashed open.

"I'm sorry, Kelly. I knew, I shouldn't have told you."

"No. You should have," Kelly said weakly. "Thank you, but I really have to go." She slowly hung up the phone. "Oh my God." Her head spun, and she had to lean back against her chair. She had known there was more to Reis's story—something he was hiding. But this…this she could not fathom. Why couldn't it have been a sordid affair with a student or some such thing? Sexual misconduct she might be able to handle, but suicide.... How could she face him tomorrow, knowing what she knew? What could have possibly gone so wrong in his life that he'd wanted to die?

twenty-four

Wednesday afternoon as the clock crawled toward five, Kelly had still not entered the library, which wasn't a big deal since she never came in when she had Max in tow. And when she and Max failed to be on the library steps, it was also no big deal, for she was often running late and would meet him at the pond. When Reis got to the pond, he fed the ducks as he walked slowly around the edge of the water and laughed as they swam after him, pushing their fat feathered bodies into one another, snapping at the food and each other's rumps with mild quacks of complaint. When he got tired of this, he sat on the bench and watched the ducks swim around and around. *Is there really no more food?* they asked. The sun set and the temperature dropped. He was shivering slightly as the ducks gave up, nestling together on the shore, quacking softly, gently pushing their beaks through their feathers and tucking their heads under their wings. His stomach growled. A light rain fell. Another hour and the rain fell in earnest. He got up and slowly walked through the empty park and along the dark street. He opened the door to his poorly lit apartment house and made his way up the three flights of stairs and into his apartment, where he was greeted by no one.

tw enty - five

Ellen went back to Ithaca after Walter Welling's funeral. Reis stayed behind, as any good son would, under the assumption that he could somehow help his mother with the process of learning how to live without her husband of twenty-eight years. When he was unable to help her, he fell into wandering the house aimlessly or sitting despondently in his room for hours. Martha began to find her gloomy son's presence more depressing than the prospect of being alone. After a week, she suggested that perhaps it was time for him to return to Ithaca.

"I'll be fine, Reis," she told him in response to his look of despair. "It's time you get back to work, back to Ellen. Your father would not want us to suffer his death so. He would have us celebrate his life. You know I'm right, Reis."

"I'm sure you are," he said, closing his eyes to stop the tears from flowing again. "But I feel so betrayed. Cheated out of even saying goodbye. Defeated by the impossibility.... I'll never see him again…never have the chance to tell him how much I loved him."

"Reis, honey, he knew." She placed her hand gently against his cheek. "He knows now. Please go home, back to Ellen, your work, to the business of living."

The Sunday before the spring semester began, Ellen pulled into the parking lot of the bus terminal a couple of minutes late. She glanced around for Reis but didn't see him waiting for her. She parked the car in irritation. It was bitter cold; she was in no mood to leave the warmth of the car to search the terminal. Once inside, she spotted him immediately, standing alone in the middle of the bus station, his hands to his sides, his eyes to the ground. All irritation disappeared, her own sorrow rising in her throat.

Grief, bereavement—things Ellen had only known through the loss of a beloved family dog and the sudden death of her grandfather when she was six; it was not enough to prepare her for the rawness of Reis's pain. It shook her soul, and even though she feared that there was nothing she could say or do—no way to reach into that grief to retrieve him—she took a few quick steps his way, her arms wrapping around the sadness. "How're you doing?" she cautiously asked. He hugged her back, leaning his body into hers so that she could feel the full weight of his despair, could feel his tears drip onto her neck. She closed her eyes to the people who glanced at them with curiosity while walking past. "You'll feel better," she whispered, "once you're home for a few days." She pulled away and brushed his hair from his eyes. "I've made arrangements for Mike to take over your classes this week. So you can kick back and regroup. Okay?" He nodded, not putting up an argument about his classes as she'd expected. She gently pulled his hand, and they began to walk to her car.

Reis returned to work on Monday of the following week, not because he felt ready, but because he knew it was expected of him. He arrived at his office before eight and slowly tried to sift through his mail before his nine o'clock lecture. Shortly before nine there was a soft knock on his door.

"Come in," Reis called.

"Hi, Reis," Mike said as he entered his office. "I haven't had the chance to tell you in person how sorry I am about your dad." He stepped into the room and gave Reis a critical going-over. "How're you holding up?"

"I'm fine." Reis looked at him blankly.

"Are you sure you want to take over your classes today?" He tilted his head slightly. "You look pretty stressed. I'd be happy to continue with them a bit longer."

"I said I'm fine, Mike."

Mike stood there a moment, a slight frown to his face. "Well, if you're sure." He put out his hand, which contained Reis's class notes. "I've marked where I left off in both classes." Reis took a moment before taking the notes and setting them on his desk. He rubbed his temples slightly.

"Are you sure you're okay?" Mike asked.

Reis jumped at his voice, looking up suddenly. "What? Oh, yes," he managed a slight smile. "Thanks, Mike. I'm fine."

"Well, okay. I guess I better let you get to your class," he said as he looked at his watch. "I'll talk to you later." He left, leaving the door open.

Reis looked at his hand; he still held the same letter he'd been trying to read for the last half hour. He put it down and gathered up his notes for his introductory botany class. He took the elevator to the first floor of the building where the main lecture hall was located, pushing sadness aside and enjoying the sweet song of the elevator and the sensation of falling.

The introductory botany class, which consisted mainly of freshmen students trying to fulfill their science requirements, was large, almost filling the two hundred and fifty seats of the lecture hall. Reis entered the room just as the class bell rang, knowing that his well-deserved reputation among the students was the reason that many of them had picked this particular class. As always, he smiled as he stepped up to the podium. He felt a surge of pleasant anticipation.

The students, who were not already seated, quickly sat down, and all eyes turned to the man who would determine their final grade. He flipped through his papers. A silence fell over the room. Reis looked up from his notes and began to scan the class, already trying to learn the faces that he would be seeing three times a week for the next four months. An eye, a nose, a soft wet mouth. A puff of blonde hair. A flash of white teeth. A foot bouncing on the end of a leg. The unpleasant glare of the lights. The squeak of a chair. His notes slicing into his finger. He looked down and studied with great interest the red that pooled on his fingertip. A soft murmur broke his concentration, causing him to turn away from the fingertip and turn to the projector, where he wrote his name in large, sweeping letters on the transparency—a curious red smearing with the blue of the marker.

"I am, of course, Dr. Reis Welling," he began. "My office hours are on the top of your class syllabus, which I'm sure Dr. Green gave you last week. I apologize for not being here, but it was unavoidable."

He turned back toward the class with a slight smile, trying once again to scan the room. His smile dropped, and he began to scan his notes. "It's my understanding that last Friday you began a discussion on photosynthesis. Photosynthesis, of course, being not just a chemical reaction whereby the sun's energy is converted ultimately to water and glucose," he wrote out photosynthesis on the transparency, "but the very basis on which life depends." The students bent their heads and began taking notes.

"Can you imagine a world without light? A world without photosynthesis? A world in which there was no sun? No. It cannot be imagined, because there would be no life. No light reaction. No dark reaction. No reason for chloroplasts or carotenoids. You would have no reason for taking this class." The students laughed a bit nervously. Reis stopped and briefly checked his notes again before continuing.

"There are two basic steps in photosynthesis: number one being the light reaction," he wrote this on the page, "whereby the sun's photons are absorbed, and number two being the dark reaction, where the energy that has been absorbed and stored as ATP and NADPH2 is used to reduce carbon dioxide to organic carbon. We'll look at each of these steps in some detail over the next few days."

The students' pens scraped against their paper. A small cough, a slight sneeze, the rustling of paper, the soft murmur of discord. He turned away from the distractions and glanced up to the high windows of the auditorium. The sun was shining. Tiny particles floated haphazardly. "You might wonder, 'What is a photon?' Is it energy stolen from the sun? Without its energy, the sun would no longer be in power. The sun has, after all, ultimate power over whether we live or die." He turned from the window and queried the room. "Is it any wonder many societies worship the sun as their god? We might be wise to consider this." He paused a moment and paced gently, allowing each student the opportunity to ponder his words.

"Does all this come down to depending on the absorption of one small photon by a tiny fern struggling to survive next to an acid-filled stream?" he continued, turning back to the window. "The power of the solar system—this solar system—does it come down to depending on one little photon?" He turned back to the class and pointed at the sea of faces. "You may think the answer is *no*. After all, the sun is only a very small speck in the universe—a mere photon in the universe, so to speak."

Reis stopped and smiled a bit. He had always known the importance of photosynthesis, but he had never fully understood its impact on the entire universe. It all seemed so clear. He didn't know why he hadn't seen it all before. It was very important that he make the students understand. "Be it not for that photon," he went on, his voice rising in his enthusiasm, "wouldn't the earth just spin out of control? A sun without power! And what, you wonder, would happen to Jupiter and Mars?" One by one, students stopped taking notes; the room grew deathly silent. It was only right that they give him their full attention. He smiled at their confused faces. He could—he must—make them understand. "The death of the sun," he said, quietly, dramatically. "Surely the whole solar system would be lost…floating around, banging into other solar systems. And yet," he smiled ironically, "we take the sun for granted by not recognizing the importance of one tiny photon."

"Dr. Welling? Dr. Welling!"

Reis stopped his movement and saw the young man, midway back in the center of the sea, his arm held high above his head. "Yes?"

"That bit about Jupiter and Mars. Is that going to be on the test?" Several students laughed, while others sat up straight to listen for his answer.

Reis stared at him. "The test?" he finally said. "It is, I suppose, only natural for you to wonder about the test. But you know what they say about curiosity. You think right away of dead cats, and no matter how you picture a dead cat in your mind, it's not the lovely yellow kitten you had as a child."

Reis turned and checked his notes. "Now where was I? Oh, yes. Chloroplast, I believe."

Reis went back to his office and locked the door behind him. Wet with the descent of dread, he tasted the stench on the back of his tongue. He no longer felt exhilaration from his new understanding of photosynthesis but instead saw clearly how it led to the end of the world—the death of all plants—leaving all other forms of life choking for oxygen. He had years of data to prove it. The subtle changes in plant growth and distribution were directly related to the extent of human toxic waste. How much more could the earth take? If only he could make the people understand. He began to cry; he knew it was hopeless. Even if he had the energy to warn them, he knew they could never comprehend what was necessary to change the course of inevitable doom.

He stayed quietly in his office until his afternoon class. He did not respond to the few timid knocks at his door but stayed perfectly still, not breathing until they had gone.

Reis paced up and down in front of the small lecture hall. The twenty or so graduate students followed his progression—followed his movement, his words. Rapt. He had their total attention. This is how it would start: a small but rapt following, and then more would come, more would join, and it wouldn't be long before he would lead them all. He in the front of a long, pulsating throng of devotion, into the forest. He in the front, raising his hiking stick toward the heavens. "This way! This way to the an-swers! Into the earth's embrace. Clarification of the human soul!"

And they would join the earth, crawl to her on their bellies. "Forgive us! Forgive us our sins." And she would take them in and cleanse their wretched souls.

And he turned and smiled at his students—his students of the earth.

Then his smile slipped away. He stopped in his tracks and stared at the intrusion. Infiltrated. "I believe that we've pretty much covered all we need to today," he told his students. He watched them as they turned around and followed his gaze. His students took in the intruders, then turned their heads back to him.

"What do we do now?" they asked with their eyes.

"You may leave now," he told them firmly.

Then when the last of his dear students had left, Reis nar-rowed his eyes and said in such a way that there would be no ambiguity, "It's about time you finally showed up here in person. I'm so very sick and tired of this surreptitious monitoring." The two men looked at each other in confusion. "Don't act surprised," Reis said as he left the podium and started toward them. "Did you think I did not know? Could not see that which was so easily seen? You really thought you could advance without the vision of my knowledge?"

Reis watched as Mike turned to the chair of the department and said, "Ted, why don't I talk to Reis alone." Ted nodded his head and left the auditorium.

"Yes," called Reis as he drew closer. "Let's do that. Just you and me, my dear friend." He came close to this supposed friend and looked him in the eye. "And this is just one of the many things that hurts the most. I am not, in any way, surprised about

Ted. But, in all my many, many thoughts, the thought that you'd be involved in this failed to occur."

"Involved in what, Reis?" Mike asked gently.

The kindness of his words—the concern—crushed Reis's anger, confused his purpose. Deflated, he pressed his hands into his face.

"Reis," Mike's words were soft as he squeezed Reis's shoulder, "we've had complaints from your students—about your lecture this morning. And frankly, after listening to you here, I'd have to agree. I don't think you're ready to resume teaching. I know how close you were to your dad. I think you need more time to accept his death."

"Mike, I'm fine." His words were arduous, sinking heavily toward the ground.

"Reis, take a temporary leave of absence. Take the rest of the semester off. Continue with your research, if you want, but let me take over your classes."

Sinking deeper.

"Reis." Mike's other hand was now on Reis's shoulder—not an unpleasant sensation. Now Reis could lean in slightly, keep upright. "I'm speaking to you as a friend. You're not fit to teach right now. The department won't let you teach in your condition. Don't force Ted into taking this to the university. This can be all handled within the department, and you'll be back teaching just as soon as you're feeling better. All you need is a little more time. It hasn't even been three weeks since your dad died."

"You're a good friend."

"Yes, Reis. I am."

"I don't know what's wrong with me. It's like something's not right with my head." Reis brought his hands to his head; it felt like his brain was dangling from a thread.

"You're depressed. Depression does all kinds of weird things to people. You just need more time. Maybe you need a little help. You know, a quick course of antidepressants. They helped my brother when his wife died. A little time. Everything will fall back into place."

Reis studied his class notes he held in his hands. The papers rattled their complaint.

Mike grasped his shaking hands and stilled them momentarily before freeing the papers from his fingers. "Go home, Reis. Take care of yourself. I promise, I'll take good care of your students."

Reis sat on the edge of the bed, contemplating his shoes. After a considerable length of time, he reached down and put one on his foot. It did not feel right, so he took it off and tried it on his other foot. This felt worse, so he removed it and placed it back on the original foot. He sighed deeply as his eyes confronted the tangle of laces. He wished Ellen had not already left for work. Perhaps she might have tied it for him. He held the laces gently in his hands. The curves of the cloth strings were fascinating, bringing to mind earthworms—warm summer days spent sitting on the banks of lazy rivers, fishing poles, dancing silver fish in blue.... The fatigue of holding up his foot finally brought him back to the task at hand. The laces refused to cooperate; they had no intention of allowing him to tie them. He struggled stubbornly for several more minutes before he angrily kicked his shoe off, sending it flying across the room.

"You fucking bastard," he said as he watched it lying smugly on the floor, its tongue wagging with satisfaction. Reis stood up, went to his closet, and put on a pair of loafers. His intention had been to take a short walk on campus, maybe stop at the coffee shop. But by the time he reached the living room, he was exhausted. He sat on the couch, thinking he'd just rest for a bit.

Ellen walked in the door, and Reis looked up in surprise. "Did you forget something?" he asked.

Ellen gave him a funny look. "What?"

Reis glanced at the clock. It read five thirty. "Nothing," he said, regrouping quickly. "How was your day?"

Reis did not have to wait long for Dr. Rabin. The nurse called him back and checked his weight, temperature, and blood pressure. "So what brings you in to see the doctor?" she asked pleasantly as she put on the blood pressure cuff.

"Just routine, really. I've been a bit tired lately, that's all."

She smiled. "Well, your blood pressure's great. Temperature's normal. Why don't you just sit tight, and Dr. Rabin will be in shortly."

She left him sitting on the edge of the examination table, and he began to really take in the room. It was a typical examination room with bright pictures on the walls and little plastic models of various assorted organs sitting on the counter. There were jars of alcohol, cotton swabs, and tongue depressors. A row of pamphlets sat in a little plastic holder. Reis read the titles: *Self Breast Exams, Facts About Diabetes, Living with Stress, Migraines, Prostate Cancer, Coping with Depression.* He reached for the pamphlet on depression. On the front it had a drawing of a woman who was obviously not having a good day. He opened it but found it impossible to follow, so he quickly put it back. A deep, long breath flowed from his lips, and Reis reminded himself just how crucial these next few minutes were.

It hadn't been his idea to come here. He'd really had no choice. An ultimatum of sorts—Ellen and Bob ganging up on him. "If you love me…. Your father wouldn't approve…"—that sort of thing. And the idea—the audacity—of Bob suggesting he see a psychiatrist! Well, they'd like that, wouldn't they? Have him locked up somewhere so that they could be together. He'd always suspected something was up with the two of them. But he'd finally relented and agreed to see this family doctor. It was true: he wasn't sleeping well. It would be nice to sleep a little better… maybe get some sleeping pills.…

There was a small knock on the door, and Dr. Rabin walked in. He was about forty-five, with shocking red hair that came out of his scalp in curious little tuffs. He wore thick glasses over his bright blue eyes, which were, in Reis's opinion, not only too large, but hovering disturbingly just off the plane of his face.

"Professor Welling," he said warmly as he shook Reis's hand. "I'm Dr. Rabin." He sat down on the small round stool and studied Reis before saying, "Tell me why you're here."

Reis hesitated before answering. "It is my understanding that you've talked to Bob Morris. I know how you medical types like to stick together." He smiled. "Therefore, it's my guess that you know that I did not want to come here. Ellen, Bob—they're unnecessarily concerned."

"So you don't feel you've been acting strangely?"

"Well, certainly, I've been a bit depressed since my father's death. I've also had some trouble sleeping."

"How long have you been having trouble sleeping?"

"Just a few months."

"And you're feeling depressed?"

"Well don't you think that's normal? My father and I were very close. He was not an old man. His death was totally unexpected," Reis stated.

"Certainly it's normal," he said kindly. "Your father died, what, three months ago, in January?" Reis nodded. "Are you working now?"

"I've taken a temporary leave. I plan to return to teaching in the fall. Meanwhile, as soon as the weather breaks, I'll get back to my field research."

"What kind of research do you do?" he asked as he got up and began checking Reis's ears and eyes. "Open your mouth, please," Dr. Rabin said before Reis could respond. He peered down Reis's throat. "Say *Ahh*. Good."

"My specialty is phytogeography. I study the impact of environmental pollutants on our national forests," Reis answered as the doctor felt his glands and checked his heart.

"Do you spend the summer out in the woods? Lie back, please."

Reis eased himself down on the table. "Pretty much," he answered as Dr. Rabin prodded around in his gut.

"You can sit up now. Besides feeling depressed, have you had any other problems? Pain? Headache? Nausea?"

Reis sat up and shook his head. "No, not really. Just a bit tired. Maybe a bit achy."

"So what do you do all day? Are you getting out? Socializing?" He sat back down and faced Reis again.

"Look, I'm sure Bob told you, all I do is sit around all day. And that's more or less true. But I'm not sleeping at night. I'm tired. I sleep on and off during the day. As far as socializing...I've never been particularly social."

Dr. Rabin nodded his head. "How's your appetite?"

"No problem. I eat when I'm hungry."

"You live with Bob's friend. Ellen, right?" Reis nodded. "Sex? Any issues there?"

Reis sighed heavily. What the fuck had Ellen been telling Bob? He forced a smile. "If you're asking me on a personal level, you're really not my type."

Dr. Rabin laughed politely and skipped to his next question. "Do you think your feelings of depression are getting worse?"

"No. Not really."

"But you are not getting much better either?"

"I guess not." Reis was trying hard to hide his impatience.

"Have you had any bizarre thoughts? Strange things happening?"

"No," Reis said flatly and met his gaze.

"Thoughts of suicide?"

Reis managed another smile. "No."

Dr. Rabin sat back and studied Reis for a moment. "Tell me, Professor, what do you think is wrong with you?"

Reis thought about this question before answering. "I guess I'm having more trouble getting over my dad's death than I should be."

"Well, I think you're probably right. You seem to be suffering from a moderate case of clinical depression. It's very common, especially after a death in the family. It's very easily treated…and I do think you need treatment. I'm going to have Patty draw some blood, and we'll run a few tests to make sure nothing else is going on. In the meantime, I want to start you on a course of tricylic antidepressants." As the doctor talked, he wrote out the prescription and handed it to Reis. "These will help you sleep and help you feel less depressed, but it can take weeks before there's a significant improvement. It's extremely important that you continue to take the medication even if you don't feel better right away. Meanwhile, many people benefit from some group therapy or one-on-one discussions with a counselor."

"I'm not interested in anything like that," Reis told him firmly.

"Well, that's up to you. If you change your mind, let me know. Sometimes the medication has some minor side effects, like dry mouth, drowsiness, or constipation. These usually go away fairly quickly. I want to see you again in two weeks. Patty will make that appointment for you. If you have any questions or problems, don't hesitate to call me."

Dr. Rabin stood up and prepared to leave. "Do you have any questions now?"

"No," said Reis.

"Good," he smiled. "We'll have you feeling better in no time. I'll see you in two weeks."

Reis sat in his car outside the doctor's office. He could not quite remember where to put the key. After fifteen minutes his confusion became unbearable, and he left his car and walked the five miles home. Once home, he felt greatly relieved. He sat in his usual spot on the couch and stayed very still, gathering strength for when Ellen came home.

A little after five, Ellen came through the door. "Reis," she sighed with relief. "Where's your car?"

"I couldn't get it started. I walked home."

"You left your car there?" He nodded. "Did you call Triple A?" she asked.

"No. I think it was probably flooded or something. I'm sure it's fine now." He looked at her sadly.

Ellen sat down next to him and placed her hand on his leg. "How did your doctor's visit go?"

"Fine. He gave me a prescription. It's supposed to make me happy." He flashed his teeth at her, as if to show how it might work.

"Did you get the prescription filled?" she asked.

"No."

She gave him an exasperated look.

"I'm sorry, Ellen. I guess with the car thing it never occurred to me."

She put her arms around him. "It's okay. As hard as these last weeks have been for me, I know they've been harder on you." He did not hug her back but rested softly against her shoulder. "Tell you what," she said. "I'll jump on the bus and see if I can't get your car started. I'll get your prescription filled and pick up a pizza or something for dinner. How does that sound?"

"Sounds fine."

"Would you like to come?"

"I'm really tired, Ellen."

"Okay." She forced a smile. "I'll be back as soon as I can."

After she left, Reis sat as still as the soft rise and fall of his chest and the beating of his heart would allow. And maybe, just maybe, if he could sit still long enough, the shattered chunks of his brain would tumble back together.

twenty-six

Thursday afternoon, Reis walked into Dr. Benson's waiting room and sat down in the chair closest to the door. Sue looked at him a moment before saying, "Good afternoon, Dr. Welling." He did not acknowledge her. She watched him thoughtfully for a few minutes. "Dr. Welling, are you all right?" she asked.

Reis looked straight ahead and did not turn to her as he said, "A lot of people ask me that. It's really not a question I'm fond of."

"I'm sorry," she said kindly. "Is there anything I can get for you? Coffee? A glass of water?" Reis shook his head as an older woman walked out from Dr. Benson's office. "The doctor is ready for you now," Sue told him.

"You seem a little down today," Dr. Benson observed as Reis sat down and melted into the folds of the chair cushions.

"Good days. Bad days. Days that are sad. They all go around and around. A big soft bagel. The world's funny like that. When you step on it, it gives just a bit beneath your feet. If you are not careful, it can suck you in," Reis said without taking his eyes off his right hand, which lay limp on the arm rest.

Dr. Benson sat back and looked carefully at Reis. Reis did not meet his gaze. "How was your trip to the mountains with Kelly?" he asked.

"That was a good day. The best so far, or so it had seemed. You can never be sure. You think things are going well, that everyone is happy, but later you wonder. Was it all just in my head? How much of it was actually real?" He lifted up his hand and brought it to his face for closer inspection.

"Why would you think it hadn't been real?"

"Perhaps things went very badly, and I'm too insane to see it. That would explain what happened yesterday. Wouldn't it?" Reis continued, bringing one finger to his mouth and biting at the side of a nail.

"Yesterday? What happened yesterday?"

Reis brought his other arm up and rested his chin carefully in his hands, focusing somewhere beyond the doctor. "Kelly never came. I waited much longer than any sane person would have. Of course, time's a funny thing too. What seemed like hours could have easily been minutes. Life seems very long today." He briefly turned his sad eyes to Dr. Benson before looking away.

"There could be many reasons why Kelly did not come. She could've been called out of town. Maybe she was ill. I wouldn't assume that you offended her in some way," Dr. Benson told him.

"Insane people can be very offensive," Reis stated.

"Why do you keep referring to yourself as insane?"

Reis sat up and looked at Dr. Benson. "Well, isn't that the official diagnosis?"

"No. No, it's not. You have a brain disease. A disease that, especially in your case, is well controlled by medication. You should not think of yourself as insane."

"Medication! Now that's interesting. You almost had me convinced that all that was standing between me and a trip to the hospital were those damn pills. You really have no idea what they do to me. One illness replaced by another. The cancer's gone, but the chemo killed the patient. Radiation! Slow poison for the masses."

"Reis," Dr. Benson said, alarmed, "have you stopped taking your medication?"

"It's all a matter of control, isn't it?" Reis's eyes narrowed a bit. "The captain of the big ship of sanity, doling out the saltpeter. Is there really any evidence that the captain maintained control? It should be an individual thing, an individual decision."

"Reis, you and I had an agreement. We made that decision together. Your side effects are minor with these medications. And you know, as well as I do, the statistics."

"Fuck statistics," Reis muttered.

Dr. Benson sighed but continued. "The relapse rate in an unmedicated schizophrenic is unquestionably higher than those who are medicated. The first year is most critical. Each time we've tried to decrease your meds, your symptoms have increased. Different drugs have been either ineffective or caused worse side effects."

Reis was no longer looking at the doctor but staring stubbornly ahead.

"How long has it been? When did you stop your meds?" Dr. Benson asked quietly.

"I don't remember."

Dr. Benson stood up and walked to other side of the room, where he poured a glass of water. He set it next to Reis and returned to his desk. He looked briefly through his top drawer before removing a small bottle of pills. He shook out three of the yellow pills and placed them by the water. "Take them, please."

Reis made no move. He sat rigidly upright, staring out the window. "Reis, I will not hesitate to call your caseworker and start the ball rolling to get you back into a more supervised environment. You have a history of self-violence. I would have no problem convincing a judge of that," Dr. Benson said firmly.

Reis turned to him angrily. "You know, I don't have to come here every week! You can threaten all the legal bullshit you want, but when it comes right down to it, I can do whatever the hell I want, short of breaking the law! Even if what you said were true, I could be in Taiwan before your fucking ball made its first rotation!"

Dr. Benson leaned forward and put his hands on the table. "Reis, please. You know I'm right. I promise, in a few weeks, when you're more stable, we'll try decreasing the dosage again. Right now it's extremely important that you continue with the present dosage. Now is not a good time to change that. You have too much going on. You probably do not even realize it, but you're already slipping back into more schizophrenic thinking. Do I need to remind you what it was like before? When you were very ill?"

The two men locked eyes. They struggled briefly before Reis finally looked away. As Reis reached for the pills, he said, "You know, I wasn't always like this."

Dr. Benson looked at Reis. "I know, Reis. I know."

tw enty - seven

Reis never took the medication that Ellen brought home. He simply flushed it down the toilet each day. There was no telling what kind of poison Ellen and Bob were trying to pass off as medicine. He no longer trusted the food Ellen brought home or prepared, so he started making dinner each night before she got home. She took his renewed interest in cooking as a sign of improvement. The fact that she encouraged his culinary feats did not in any way dissuade Reis. He knew, without a doubt, that she was trying to poison him.

"You know, Ellen," he told her one morning. "It might be best if I do the grocery shopping from now on."

"That would be wonderful." She tried to look cheery. "I'm so glad that you feel better and want to get out."

He bit back his words, wanting to scream and tell her he had no choice, but he instead narrowed his eyes and stared her way. Then he saw the hurt. He was forced to turn away, to bear the guilt and accept without remonstration his worthlessness.

Reis saw Dr. Rabin in two weeks as instructed and succeeded in convincing him that he was taking the medication and that things were improving. Oh, yes, he could play the game as well as anybody else; he'd always been able to. He knew the only way to fight them was to appear to be going stupidly along with the conspiracy. And at night, while Ellen lay sleeping in the next room, he could pace about the room, cower in the corner, fight the dark cloud, and battle the enemy—because someone had to fight them. He had been chosen, and it made sense that he had been chosen, because he had always been up for the task. And even though they were trying to drive him insane, he would not fall prey to their trickery.

By the second week of May, he was scarred and battle-weary. It was possible, just possible, that the enemy had taken a strong hold. The cloud of terror, loud with its flapping wings, was within inches from descending upon him, and he was just so tired. The flapping, near deafening, no longer beat randomly but had an unmistakable rhythm—a message from the enemy. A code. He concentrated on the rhythm, trying to interpret its meaning. And then the meaning became as clear as words. *He's right about her.* Loathsome words.... *Oh, absolutely! She pretends to care, but all along she's busy fucking anything that moves.*

Where were they? Behind the drapes. *God, he's an idiot!* A laugh—worse than the words. *He thinks he's going to find us.* Nothing! *Look how scared he is. He's too dumb to know we're here to help him.* The closet! *It's that Ellen. She's doing this to him.* Only coats. Coats and laughter. Hands over his ears. *He'd be best off to get rid of her.* To push this out of his head! Press hard...until the brain seeps out and trickles down the neck. *What do you think would be the best way? I personally would enjoy slitting her throat.* Laughter—worse than the words. *He would never have the balls for that.* Retreat onto the couch. *Yes. Yes, you're right about that. He can't even screw her.* The laughter filled the room.

Sink into the folds of the couch and be very still. Let the brain tumble back into place.... Push the chunks back where they belong and breathe…just breathe.

Ellen woke up the next morning to find Reis sleeping in a ball on the couch. He looked more filthy and disheveled than she'd ever seen him look. She shook her head and said into the air, "I don't know how much more of this I can take." She tiptoed around the house as she got ready for work, trying her best not to wake him. He was still asleep when she left for campus. She shut the front door behind her, relieved that she'd escaped. A warm spring breeze blew gently. Tiny, new green leaves fluttered in the trees. Ellen took a deep breath as she stepped off the front porch and relished the sweet aroma of spring flowers. The further she walked from home, the better she felt. This was her favorite time of year, and she'd be damned if she was going to let Reis ruin it for her.

That evening, Ellen did not go home but went to Stewart Park and played volleyball with some friends. Afterward, they went out for pizza and beer. Ellen headed home well after eleven. It had been months since she'd gone out with her friends, and the feeling of freedom was exhilarating. She hadn't realized how lonely and isolated she'd become. She stood outside her front door dreading a confrontation with Reis. As she slipped quietly in the door, Reis's eyes turned to her from his spot on the couch. He still had not showered or changed his clothes. Had he moved all day? Any compassion she'd once felt was now replaced by disgust.

"So, Ellen," he said. "Where have you been?"

"I played volleyball at Stewart Park, and then we got pizza

at The Chariot," she said lightly as she put her coat in the closet.

"We?"

"Just a few people from the game." She looked through the mail.

"Was Bob there?" He stood up and came toward her.

"Bob?" She looked up. "You know Bob doesn't play volley-ball."

"So, you would have me believe that you've just been inno-cently eating pizza with some of your friends?"

Ellen suddenly wished that she'd had a few more beers. "You know, Reis, I don't need this shit! I really don't."

"Sometimes," he continued, "I just wish that if you want to get rid of me, that you'd just do it and not try to accomplish it surreptitiously."

"Oh Christ!" Ellen slapped down the mail. A few letters slipped to the floor. "Believe me, Reis, when I'm ready to call it quits, there'll be nothing surreptitious about it!"

"Really?" he yelled. "And I don't need to be sitting around here, dealing with all the shit you're throwing at me, while you're out fucking Bob someplace!"

She closed her eyes and took a breath. "Are you kidding me?" Her hands flew apart in frustration. "How dare you accuse me of such a thing? Bob? Christ! At least you could have me sleep-ing with someone who's heterosexual! I have no patience for this anymore. You're making my life as miserable as your own." She turned away. "I don't even want to come home to my own house!" Her words caught in her throat. "You need to get yourself togeth-er. It's obvious you being here isn't doing either of us any good."

She paused a moment, catching her breath. Angry tears fell from her eyes. Reis opened his mouth to speak, but she raised her hand to silence him, then continued. "You're dragging me down with you. I can't live like this anymore! I want my house back, my life back! I want you to leave. I want you out!"

Reis looked at her dumbly. "You're kicking me out?" He turned away, defeated. "And so they've won…." he mumbled.

"I think it's best if you leave…at least for a while." She sucked in her breath. "It'll give you a chance to get your head together. I can't help you. I really can't. God knows, I've tried, but we're only growing further apart. I need my life back, Reis."

Reis sank back down on the couch and ran his fingers through his hair. "Where will I go?" he asked, more to himself than to her.

"I don't know. Why don't you visit your mom for a while? You haven't seen her since your dad died," Ellen said, with only a hint of impatience. She, too, was suddenly defeated. She sat down next to him and allowed his body to sink into hers, trying her best not to be appalled by his foul odor. "I guess you'll need a day or two to get your things together," she whispered into his hair. "I'll stay with Sally. Can you manage to pack your things by Wednesday?"

"Wednesday?" he said as if he hadn't the faintest idea what she was talking about.

"Yes. Can you manage to move out by Wednesday?" She emphasized each word as if she were talking to a small child.

"I believe that I can." His eyes met hers, and although she could not read his emotions, she found that she had to look away.

twenty-eight

Kelly sat on the couch, nursing her unhappiness like a fine wine. She pushed her fork through the mess on her plate and finally had to say, just one more time, "I can't believe you'd bring me Chinese food when you know I've been throwing up for a week."

"Kelly," he said patiently, "you went back to work on Monday. You must be feeling better."

"Work, yes. Hunan chicken, no!" She dropped her fork with an unpleasant ting against the plate and sat back on the couch with an equally unpleasant pout.

"Would you like me to go get you something else?" He was trying to be kind.

"No. Never mind. I'll eat the rice," she said sullenly. Everything about Brian seemed to irritate her tonight. It didn't make a bit of difference that he'd taken time out of his busy week to come here on a Tuesday night. It was the least he could do after conveniently going out of town the day she got ill, leaving her alone to struggle with the worst flu she'd ever had. Now he was trying to poison her fragile system with spicy Chinese food. She placed a small amount of rice in her mouth and rolled the dry, tasteless morsels around with her tongue. A slight flicker of guilt crept through her, and she searched for something pleasant to say. "I talked to my sister today." She looked at him and forced a smile. "Out of the one hundred people invited to my parents' anniversary party, eighty-five have accepted so far. It should be quite a party."

Brian shifted a bit in his chair. "Ahh.... Kelly, about the party—"

Kelly rapidly turned to him. "Don't even say it, Brian! We've had this planned for months!"

Brian sighed, but his confidence and determination did not falter. "Tom McMann asked me to his fishing cabin. Several big clients are going. My clients! It would look really bad if I didn't go."

Kelly glared at him in disbelief.

"He's my boss, Kelly. He's never asked me to his cabin before. It's not something I really have a choice about."

"You're a partner now. It's not like you need to keep kissing their asses."

"A junior partner. And I wouldn't call all the work I do there 'ass kissing.'"

Brian tried to sound hurt, but Kelly wasn't biting. She was too angry—too angry to speak. She closed her eyes and fought for control.

"I'll make it up to you somehow," Brian offered meekly.

"No! No, you won't!" she exploded. "You're not going to get the chance. You're absolutely unbelievable! You can't even give me one weekend of your time. What am I supposed to tell my family?

'Brian couldn't come. He just had to go fishing! Oh, yes, he sends his love, but fishing is ever so much more important than fifty years of marriage!'" Kelly glared at him.

He all but shrugged. "Kelly, I already told Tom I could come."

"I can't believe you would do this! God forbid if you had to spend any real time with me, not to mention my family! This is all getting a little old. You are totally incapable of any sort of commitment!"

"Oh, Jesus! Here comes the marriage thing again." He rolled his eyes.

Kelly stood up, unable to sit next to him any longer. "Oh, I'm sorry you find marrying me so offensive!" Max jumped from the couch and gave her a worried look. She walked a few feet away, then turned. "You claim to love me, Brian!" Her voice cracked with self pity. "People in love tend to want to be together. Marriage is a natural progression."

Brian's mouth was fixed; he didn't say a word. Kelly returned the look. Max slunk down onto the floor and placed his head on his paws.

A long moment ticked by. "What do you want me to say?" he finally offered.

Kelly looked at him, her anger pulsating, her voice dropping. "I can't go on like this. I refuse. This relationship needs to progress or stop altogether."

He stood and faced her. "Are you giving me an ultimatum?" His anger almost matched her own. "Either I marry you or we're through?"

"Yes! Why not? My life is a fucking cliché. Who cares? Biological time is ticking away! Tick! Tick! Tick!"

"I will not tolerate being pressured!"

"And I will no longer tolerate the way things are!" she yelled.

"Decide what you want. Just don't do it here! Take your damn Chinese food and get out!"

"Okay! Fine!" he said, roughly snapping on the lids of the food containers. "I am so fucking out of here!" He shoved the containers back in the bag and grabbed his coat.

"Don't forget these!" Kelly flung packets of soy sauce at his back as he headed toward the door. He turned and caught one. He started to throw it back at her but thought better of it. He tossed it up in the air and caught it gracefully as it fell. He gave her the look he reserved for a witness during cross examination—when he knew his point had hit home with the jury. Kelly flung one more packet his way as he shut the door. It hit the wall and landed with a plop on the floor. Max trotted over and sniffed it hopefully.

"Bastard!"

twenty-nine

When Ellen returned to her home early Wednesday morning, Reis's car was gone, just as he said it would be, but she wasn't sure if he'd actually left until she entered the house. She sat on the couch and looked around the room, taking in each small possession of her house. She rested her head against the back cushions and stared at the ceiling. Drawing in a deep breath, she felt momentarily relieved before she was struck and then overcome by grief.

th irty

Reis had no itinerary as he drove through the streets of Cornell Wednesday morning. He'd simply started the car and pulled away from Ellen and her house and Cornell. He found he needed most of his energy to remember how to shift the car through the hills of Ithaca. The car was packed with only things he really cared about: his books, journals, publications, and hiking gear. He'd brought clothes only out of necessity, leaving most of his wardrobe behind. He hadn't taken the DVD player Ellen had given him for his birthday the year prior, and he'd left behind the blender and coffeepot his mother had given him. He had not even considered taking the few pieces of furniture he'd contributed to the household. As he'd carried the last of his things from the house, he'd slipped his house key under Ellen's welcome mat, stopped, and studied the word *welcome*, considering its implications before making the final trip to his car.

The voices, which had up until now left him alone during

the day, began a running commentary on his inability to drive. It seemed to take hours before he finally reached the city limits. He followed Route 89, north along the west side of Cayuga Lake. The voices eased up a bit as he shifted into fifth gear and cruised along the fifty-mile shoreline, through the heart of wine country. At the foot of the lake he turned east onto Route 20. The Saab took on a life of its own as it sped up and down the hills, slowing down only for Auburn, Skaneateles, LaFayette, and Cazenovia. Reis did not take note of the lovely white and pink blossoms that covered the trees as the car flew down through the apple orchards. He was oblivious to the pretty green haze of the new spring leaves on the gently rolling hills or the spattering of cows and horses grazing contently in the fresh new grass. The handsome red barns that dotted the hillsides also went undetected. Thirty miles later, he turned off the curvy, hilly beauty of Route 20 and made his way onto Route 28, heading north to the Adirondack Mountains.

It won't be long until we can rest. Yes, he's finally taking us home, where we can all rest. "Yes, rest," answered Reis. "That's all I need is a little rest." *Sure, Reis. We'll all be fine. We're going to help you make everything good again.*

Reis pulled into a gas station a short while later. The nozzle tap, tap, tapped against the car as he tried to fit it into the gas tank. He mumbled to himself as he filled the tank. "Pollutants. Everywhere. Gas goes in…poison itself…carbon monoxide comes out…even worse. Choking plants. It's my fault as much as the next person. Everyone likes to think they're innocent, when we all should burn in hell—the hell we're making right here on earth." He was distinctly aware that people were staring at him. The more they stared, the louder and faster he talked. He felt as if he might explode—light a match and explode into a fiery blast of man and Saab.

The roads began to wind around the foothills of the Adirondack Mountains. He drove through tiny towns clustered around the small lakes. He drove until the towns disappeared, through the High Peaks area, until he was surrounded by only mountains and forests. One hour out of Canada, Reis parked the car at a pull-off. He checked his pack and hoisted it onto his shoulders. Patting his car goodbye, he locked it and headed for the trail.

For three hours he moved at a fast pace up the steep mountain. The forest sang its sweet song. The trees swayed; the fragile leaves of spring shuddered. His mind slowed and calmed. As he warmed with exertion, the evil toxins drained from his body until his clothes were wet with evil, but an evil that was at least gone and out of his body. The sun was low in the sky when he turned off the trail and headed west along the top of a deep ravine. The going was considerably slower now, the fading light making the tricky footing even harder to negotiate. Far below he could hear the noisy chatter as the creek rushed by, swollen by the spring thaw. Then he made his descent before the walls of the ravine became too steep. When he reached the bottom, he walked against the flow of the bitter cold water of the creek, the rising roar of the waterfall assaulting his ears until all other senses were consumed. Turning a small bend in the narrow ravine, his hands against his ears, it stood out before him. One hundred feet up, the water gushed from a hole in the mountain. Shattering apart on sharp rocks as it fell, the water formed large orange jewels in the rays of the setting sun. Reis left the stream, threw off his pack, and stripped off his clothes. He dove into the shallow pool and swam directly under the falls. Standing on a small rocky ledge, he closed his eyes to the cold water of a faded winter that pounded against his body.

His father laughed next to him. "Did you ever feel anything

so good, my boy?"

"No, Dad. I haven't," Reis laughed back.

"I bet we're the first ones to ever find this place. This can be our secret."

"Yes, our secret place in this world."

Reis stood under the falls until his body was blue with cold, until his father had drifted away, until the sun was a memory and the moon was a frown. He swam back across the water and lay his nakedness down on the mossy soil. He rested his head on his pack and closed his eyes to the spray of the water, to the cool breath of the spring night. He was almost at peace. Yes...he might be okay, his soul having returned to him in these woods. He no longer felt chilled but was warmed and comforted by the earth below—his breath slow and steady, his eyes closed, his ears opened to the music of the night.

And it was then that things started to go wrong. He opened his eyes and looked at the trees high above. The moonlight struck each new leaf, creating tiny silver lanterns in the sky. One by one, the large black birds appeared in the glow of the lanterns. Within a moment they filled the trees, wings flapping, beaks snapping their angry complaint. And with that anger, the descent of cold, creeping fear. He eased into the earth, covered his head with his hands, and tucked his knees to his chest, feeling the soft suck of the mossy soil while breathing in its decay. The branches of the trees swayed and bent; the weight of their burden pulled toward him. The crows were close now, only inches from his face, their quick red beaks reaching for his eyes.

"No!" The angry growl of the wind. The condemnation of the forest. The betrayal—by the very thing he loved the most. The intense pain snaked through him, reminding him of his culpability—an evil he housed and nurtured. Death pecked impatiently at life, and it was almost welcome: the peacefulness of death. But still he closed his eyes, his arms wrapped about his head.

Reis—a kind voice. Moments passed. A sweet wisp of air. *Reis, look at us.* Reis slowly turned toward the voice and opened his eyes. Two shiny black crows stood inches from his face, their eyes a golden glow. *You're having a really rough time, aren't you?* Their heads cocked to one side. *We're here to help you. We know how to make everything all right.* Sweet seduction. *It hurts so much. Doesn't it, Reis?* Their heads tilted the other way in unison. *Do you feel the pain?* He nodded. *We can help you. We can help you make it stop.* The sweet sigh of the trees. *You'd like that, wouldn't you?* He nodded. *Get your knife, Reis.* "My knife?" *We can stop the pain. Wouldn't that be nice? To be free of pain forever? We must free the evil. That's right, Reis. Get your knife.* The blade glowed in the moonlight. *Feel the sharpness of the blade, Reis.* He ran his finger along it, cutting deeply into his flesh. The blood flowed from the wound, but he felt no pain. He ran the knife gently along his arm and watched, with interest, the trail of blood it left behind. *No pain, Reis. Only peace. Finally, you'll be able to rest. You can remove the pain.* Their eyes glowed to red, their voices sweet, sweet seduction. *It's so easy to free yourself.* The knife quivered in his hand. *Remove the pain.* He closed his eyes. Peace, if only it could be.... Reis plunged the knife deep into his abdomen, sweeping the blade downward. The pain was hard—biting. He threw his head back and screamed. His eyes wide, he watched as the large black birds flapped up and away and disappeared into the moon.

thirty-one

Wednesday morning, Reis felt too tired to go to work. He hadn't slept well for over a week now, and it was beginning to catch up to him. He stood before the mirror, trying to shave, but it seemed to be taking a very long time. Perhaps he should call in sick, although he had yet to miss a day at the library. He mulled it over in his mind. Dr. Benson was already suspicious. Any peculiar action may send up red flags. The last thing Reis wanted to do was draw attention to himself. Dr. Benson would like nothing better than to get him back into the hospital and have ultimate control. Then there was Kelly. If he went to work and she did not come, it would be obvious their relationship was over. Reis wasn't sure he was prepared to deal with that. If he stayed home, he'd never know if she'd shown up or not. Perhaps that was preferable. Then again, maybe Dr. Benson was right: there may be a very good explanation for Kelly's no show. It was possible—because it had been known to happen—that he was just being paranoid. He turned it over and over in his mind. When he finally decided to go to work, he was an hour late.

"Reis! We were beginning to worry about you," said Lanie, right as Reis walked in.

"Sorry," Reis mumbled. "I overslept."

"It's not a problem. I was just a little worried. Are you sure you're okay?"

"I'm fine," he said flatly. "I'm going to get to work," he said, indicating the stacks.

Reis tried to keep himself calm, but as the day wore on, his anxiety became volatile and leaked through his shaky hands, dripped from his brow, and threatened to erupt from his gut. By three, he gave up all pretense of work and paced up and down the stacks, stopping every few minutes to stare through the books toward the door. He mumbled to himself as he walked. "Even if she does not come here, she may meet me in the park…."

At three thirty, Kelly walked through the door. She briefly looked around before sitting down at her usual table. Reis saw her as he peered through the stacks and burst into tears. He pressed his fists to his eyes and slipped into the back room, where he attempted to compose himself. He frantically dug through his rumpled paper bag and struggled to open the bottle of Ativan. The tiny white pills rained to the floor. He picked up two and placed them on his tongue while he gathered up the remainder, putting them back in the bottle and shoving it deep into his bag. He splashed cold water on his face from the bathroom sink and used the rough paper towels to rub his face dry. He looked at the redness the towels left and studied the familiar lines of his face. How exactly had he gotten to this point? He ran his hands slowly along his cheeks, ending at the blunt point of his jaw. And what exactly was the point? He carefully contemplated the pattern of the engorged blood vessels that coursed through the sclera of his eyes—a tortuous, torturous plot. And he waited—time the only deterrent to the magic of the drug.

Reis approached Kelly's table a short while later. Her research material was scattered across it. She did not look up with her usual warmth but appeared strained and hesitant in her acknowledgment of him. He waited.

"I've been sick," she finally said.

"I'm sorry." Reis sat down across from her. "Were you very ill?"

"As sick as I've ever been." She smiled at him then.

He reached across the table, touched her hand, then pulled his away. "You should have called me. I would have brought you some soup or something. I would have at least walked Max for you."

Her smile deepened. She cocked her head. "I don't even have your number. You don't believe in cell phones."

And that was true.... He looked at his hand lying limply on the table. He had no cell phone...no car...no real source of employment...hadn't had sex in—"Are you okay, Reis? I hope you're not getting sick."

He looked up from his hand and took a moment before he answered. "I'm fine." He smiled at her then, trying to make his face normal. He saw her uncertainty, her discomfort, and something else.... Distrust. And judgment. She was judging him...and the verdict wasn't good. He looked away, the punch of sadness prevailing. Of course. Of course. He nodded his head in acceptance. Of course.

"Well," he told her. "I better get some work done too."

He slipped, unseen, among the bookshelves—a sloth, an agile spy. She was always visible, through a tiny slit of space above the books, around the edge of a bookshelf, down the long, straight row of books. She flipped through her books and twisted the locks of her hair, penned quick notes, chewed the tip of her pen, knitted her brow, and played her part well. And when her cell phone beeped, she looked at it and slapped it back down on the desk, pushing it away and putting her pen in her mouth. But it would not be ignored, and the phone fired back to life with a low but insistent jangle of notes. Reis watched Kelly close her eyes and reach for it with resolve. He slipped closer, holding his breath and keeping his cover.

"Brian, I'm working."

A silence. A pain across her face. A swipe through her hair. A sigh. She closed her eyes and rested her head against her hand, rubbing her forehead, the gentle rise of her chest, then the slow exhale of air.

"I know.... Yes." Another long pause. "Tonight?"

Edging closer, he watched her face change into a gentle longing, then the tiniest of smiles.

"Yes.... I know. I know you do."

Her tongue came out and swept over her amazing lips.

"Of course."

Her lips parted—a soft sigh of peace.

"Yes, I've always loved you..." a gentle laugh, "ever since I looked up from that nasty old urinal and into your crotch."

Her face turned—his way. He was unable to move. Her green eyes lifted, seeing him, and then, across her face, the subtle panic of being caught.

thirty-two

Kelly sat across the table from Brian, picking through her food. He was chatting about his business trip, but she wasn't listening. She was thinking about Reis and the look on his face—his awkward but graceful acceptance when she'd told him how sorry she was that she couldn't go to the park that evening. She'd asked if they could pick things up the following week. She'd convinced herself that it was best this way…wasn't it? He'd heard enough; he knew now that perhaps there was more to her relationship with Brian than she'd initially revealed. It wasn't like he'd ever given any real indication of wanting more; he'd never even tried to kiss her. They'd barely touched. And yet…. Why then did she feel like she'd betrayed him? Why was she consumed by guilt? She suddenly realized Brian had stopped talking and was staring at her.

"You're still angry, aren't you?" he said softly.

She looked at him. Her eyes filled halfway with tears. She shook her head.

"Kelly, I already told you how sorry I am. I know how important your parents' anniversary party is to you. I was wrong to even consider backing out. I told Tom McMann, before I left the office, that I can't go to his cabin." Kelly opened her mouth to speak, but Brian quickly continued. "Kelly, I love you. I know I don't always act like it. It may seem that I have no room in my life for you, but that's simply not the case. In fact, I cannot imagine my life without you."

Kelly looked at him in bewilderment. "Brian, I—"

"No." His hand came up. "Let me finish." He caught the look on her face and frowned in apology. "I'm sorry. Please, please let me finish. I've done nothing but think about this since our fight last night. I think we should get married. I know that's what you want." There was a slight pause, then the quick addendum, "What I want!"

"Oh, Brian—" Then it was impossible to stop her tears, so she put her face into her hands and just gave in to them.

thirty-three

Thursday afternoon, Kelly left her office and drove across town. She found a parking space near the park and walked the few blocks to the library. The afternoon was hot and muggy, and there was no doubt as she looked up at the queer color of the sky that a storm was coming. The air conditioning of the library wafted over her as she opened the door, and she shivered slightly, wrapping her arms around herself and rubbing at the eruption of goose bumps. She didn't see Reis as she made a quick search of the stacks. Perhaps he was in the back. She waited for a while, browsing through the books, pulling one out every now and then, flipping through its pages…. She checked the time on her cell phone: four forty-five. Kelly glanced at the woman behind the desk, who was busy typing away at the computer. After a couple of more minutes, Kelly made her way to the desk.

"Is Reis here?" she asked.

"Oh, I'm sorry. You're his friend, aren't you?" Kelly nodded.

"I was so wrapped up in this thing," she laughed, indicating her monitor, "that I didn't even recognize you. He's not here. Didn't show up today." She leaned toward Kelly and whispered, "I'm a little worried, you know…. I tried his number. No answer. I'm not sure who to call. Maybe you know?"

Kelly checked by the pond, in the woods, by the pavilion, and up in the trees. By the time she left the park and made it back to her car, the sky was ominous with storm clouds, and daylight was slipping away. She drove the short distance to his apartment and parked in front of his building.

The stairway and hall were longer and darker than she remembered—the dull yellow bulb casting eerie amber shadows on the gray walls. Lightning flashed in the window at the end of the hallway, turning the scene into the makings of any good, scary chop-'em-up. "Whoa." Kelly jumped at the crack of thunder. The rain began to pound against the roof of the building. She reached his door and knocked. Nothing. Lightning flashed again, and she laughed at the absurdity.

"Reis," she said, knocking harder, the thunder rolling overhead. "Reis, please. Open the door. It's Kelly."

What did she really know about this man? What had happened to his life? She pictured the knife in his hand and shivered slightly at the thought. Maybe it wasn't even true. She knew how stories could grow over time—to the point where they barely resembled the actual facts.

She knocked again.

And if he were dead, whose fault would it be? And if he was very much alive and dangerous—if his actions fit the scene—whose fault would it be?

She tried the door. It opened. Lit by only a tiny desk lamp,

Reis's apartment was even darker than the hall.

And if he was there, somewhere in the gloom, then he could see her silhouetted against the light from the hall.

"Reis?"

She stepped carefully into the shadows of the room, leaving the door open behind her. Listening hard, she thought she could just make out the sound of his breathing. As her eyes adjusted to the new lighting, he slowly came into view. Surrounded by the clutter of his papers, he sat in the far corner of the apartment, rocking ever so gently, his hands wrapped tightly around his legs.

"Reis," she tried again. He did not look at her. She walked slowly toward him until she stood only a couple of feet away. Squatting, she tried to make out his face, which was half buried in his knees. "Reis," she said gently. She touched his arm. "It's Kelly."

At first he did not respond, but as she rested her hand more firmly, feeling the sticky coolness of his flesh, he slowly turned his vacant, red-rimmed eyes her way. "Oh, Reis," she said softly. "Tell me what I can do."

He did not speak but brought his hands to his head and pressed. A curious, dark liquid mixed with his fingers and stained his legs and forearms. "Reis, are you bleeding?" Fresh blood dripped down his cheek and below his left hand, in which a small silver object was nestled. "Give me your hand." Kelly gently pulled his hand from his head. The tiny clang of a small paring knife as it hit the floor made her jump. Fresh sprays of blood pulsated from his hand.

"Dear God," Kelly whispered as she made his hand into a fist and pushed it back against his face. She picked up the knife and held it away from her body between her index finger and thumb. Walking quickly into the kitchen, she wiped at her eyes with the back of her free hand, then passed it along the wall until she located the light switch. Blinking through her tears and the sudden insult of light, she dropped the bloodied knife into the sink. There was a gentle moan from Reis as she searched for a cloth. Her hands trembled, new tears filling her eyes as she pulled open one drawer, then another. Finally, near the stove, a neat stack of dish cloths.

Reaching Reis's side, she took his hand into hers and wiped away the blood. How could there be so much blood? She located the deep gash between his thumb and his hand before new blood obstructed her view. She pressed the cloth against the wound. "Hold this," she said, folding his fingers around the cloth. "Hold it tight." His fingers tightened around it slightly, and she was satisfied.

Kelly went to the phone on the desk. Her wet, sticky fingers slid across the receiver, leaving a red smudge against the white. As she put her index finger on the nine, she saw the business card lying neatly lined up with the front of the phone. "Dr. Jerome T. Benson, Psychiatrist," she read aloud. Reis moaned again. "Oh please, God." Her hands shook as she punched in the number.

Rain fell hard against the windshield, the lights from the hospital smearing across the glass as Kelly tried to locate the emergency room entrance. Dr. Benson had told her he'd meet her outside the ER; he had warned her not to try to bring Reis in herself. Maybe she should have called the ambulance—called an ambulance and then gotten the hell out of there.... But the doctor had been so kind on the phone, expressing how it would be easier on Reis without the police or an ambulance. And he had been right; Reis had come without any resistance. She'd carefully bound his wound shut with strips of the cloth as she told him she was going to take him to see his doctor. And Reis had stood without complaint, and they'd made it down the stairs and into her car. He had been quiet—hadn't said a word as she drove, his hand tucked into his chest, his head tucked toward his hand, the hood of his sweatshirt pulled down low.

But where was the ER? She searched through the rainy gloom. Then it was there but seen too late. She had to circle around the block again. On the next pass, she made the turn and pulled right up to the door. The rain had slowed, but still the three men who stood behind the double glass doors were smeared, unfocused, looming figures. She shut the engine off, and Reis looked up, examining his surroundings. The door of the hospital slipped open. Reis turned Kelly's way, stunned, shaking his head. "How? How could you do this?" he said. Then the car door was open, the splatter of rain hitting the seats as he left the car. He paused just a fraction of a moment, but as he turned to run, it was already too late. The three men were there and ready, their arms out, their hands spread, ready to stay his flight.

Kelly stepped from the car.

"Reis. It's me. Dr. Benson. Please, just let me help you."

"No, no, no, no, no!"

He turned to her—the panic of his impending death in his eyes—before he spun, shoved past Dr. Benson, and began to run. He made it only a few yards before the two other men were on him—large, oversized orderlies, grasping him by his arms. Reis exploded into action, screaming in his efforts, knocking off the bandages, reopening the wound, and sending blood squirting across one orderly's face.

"Shit! You crazy motherfucker!"

There was an angry warning look from Dr. Benson. "Would you please just help me get him inside!" The two men tightened their hold, and Reis was dragged, kicking and screaming, into the hospital. Kelly followed in horror.

Once inside, all heads in the waiting room turned to watch this screaming, bleeding man as he was pulled across the room, past the desk, through the doors that said *No Admittance*, and down the hall. The doors shut automatically with a sharp hiss. Then all eyes turned from the door and onto Kelly, who stood wet and dripping. She looked down at her hands. Covered with diluted blood, the wet mixture coursed through her fingers and dripped gently to the floor. She sat in the chair nearest to where Reis had disappeared and absently rubbed her hands into her jeans. After a moment, people stopped staring at her, but Reis's distant yells of complaint could still be heard. People shifted uncomfortably in their chairs and exchanged glances, some shaking their heads slightly. It wasn't terribly long before the screaming stopped. A collective sigh seemed to run through the waiting room. An orderly came out and carefully mopped up the trail of blood Reis had left. Kelly's cell phone rang. She turned it off. She waited.

Dr. Benson came out nearly two hours later, looking exhausted as he reached to shake Kelly's hand. As she extended her hand to him, they both saw the blood. "Sorry!" She pulled her hand back. He looked at her.

"How are you holding up?"

She shook her head in bewilderment. "I don't know.... How's Reis?"

Dr. Benson sighed slightly. "Only a bit calmer. I was hoping I could bring him around tonight. I'll have to admit him. We're going to transfer him across the street shortly."

"What's wrong with him? I mean, I know he's...well...not right. But what exactly is wrong with him?"

He considered the question before saying, "I really think it would be best if you discussed that with Reis—when he's better. Patient confidentiality aside, I don't think it's my place to give you an exact diagnosis."

"I think it's my fault he ended up here," she said quietly.

"Why would you think that?" He sat down next to her in the hard plastic chairs of the waiting room.

Kelly looked down for a moment, fighting tears. "Reis's told you we're friends?"

"Yes. He's told me a good deal about you."

Kelly nodded her head and wiped her eyes on her sleeve. "I knew. I knew how Reis felt...about me.... And then Brian—" Dr. Benson gave her a questioning look. "My boyfriend. I never really told Reis I was, you know...seriously involved." She looked at Dr. Benson. "I may have given him the wrong idea. I don't know...I care a great deal about him. I shouldn't have led him on. I never wanted to hurt him."

Dr. Benson nodded his head and thought for a moment. "One of the worst things about mental illness," he said kindly, "is the guilt it inflicts on those closest to the patient. Don't let yourself get lost in guilt. And don't assume you had anything to do with this relapse. If you really care about Reis, the best thing you can do is show him compassion and understanding. The last thing he needs is your guilt." He paused, letting her digest his words. "Why don't you go home? There's nothing more you can do for Reis tonight." Dr. Benson stood up. "I'm going home myself, as soon as he's settled in next door." He gave her a tired smile.

Kelly also stood up. "Can I see him tomorrow?" she asked.

"That's hard to say. It depends on how he's doing. He may not be up for visitors."

"Okay. I'll wait and see."

When Kelly got home there was a message on her machine. She hit the play button as she gently scratched Max on the head. "Kelly," Brian's voice came through the machine, "I'm back at the office. Call me." She hit the erase button. Brian could wait for a change.

She stayed in the shower for a long time. She stood there long after the last of Reis's blood had flowed down the drain. The dull numbness that had kept her going for the last few hours began to fade. She sat in the shower with her face in her hands and shook as the reality of what had happened overtook her. Reis was—had become—so much more than some kind of mild entertainment. All those weeks, all those hours she'd spent in the company of his quiet gentleness. The rare times she'd made him laugh—each note an award, a gift—making her feel better about herself, able to bring such simple joy into someone's troubled life. And he eased away her own undeniable loneliness, filling up some deep void with undeniable joy.

The sudden thought that it would end was crushing, causing her to drop her face between her upturned knees and wrap her arms above her head. She loved this man. There was no denying this, yet there was something terribly wrong with him—something that may not be fixable. And to feel this way now—when everything she'd ever wanted was within her grasp…. But everything she'd ever wanted was now tainted and wrong; she couldn't possibly love Brian while desiring someone other than him. As confused as she was, one thing was very clear: everything was lost—to her, to Reis, to Brian. And she was, quite decidedly, alone.

thirty-four

"How is he this morning?" Dr. Benson asked the orderly, who sat watching the monitors of the twenty-four-hour observation rooms.

"He's a bit calmer."

Dr. Benson peered at the little screen. Reis sat on the floor, naked, shaking his head as he rocked back and forth. "Has he taken his bandages off?"

"Only once," the orderly answered. "I told him if he did it again, I'd put the jacket back on. He's been better since then."

"I see you've taken away his hospital scrubs."

"Yeah, we had to. He tried to strangle himself with the pants," said the orderly, shaking his head. "It sure ain't a pretty sight, watching a grown man try to kill himself with a pair of pants." He chuckled a bit to himself. "You know, though," he continued, looking at Dr. Benson, his smile gone, "seeing some of these sorry bastards, you wonder if maybe it wouldn't be better just to let them do it."

The doctor's eyes left the screen and turned to the orderly. "How long have you been here, Lloyd?"

"About two years now."

"You'd do well to remind yourself that these are human beings you're dealing with. They have hopes and dreams and feelings, just like the rest of us. It's our job to get them well enough so that they have the chance to realize some of these dreams."

Lloyd looked squarely at him. "Well that may be true, but you're not the one who has to scrape their shit up off the floors," he said with a slight smile.

Dr. Benson did not return Lloyd's smile but looked again at Reis. "Do you think he's ready to talk to me?"

"No, sir. He can't talk to no one."

"All right." Dr. Benson nodded his head. "I'm going to order his meds increased. Then, in a couple hours, I want you to clean him up and give him his clothes back."

"I'll do what you want, but if he chokes himself to death, don't blame me."

"You call my office if you have any problems." Dr. Benson put his hand on Lloyd's shoulder. "I'm sure you'll take good care of him for me. I'll be back early evening to check on him before I go home."

thirty-five

Kelly went home Friday evening and let Max out before heading to the hospital. Her answering machine was blinking, but she did not listen to any of the messages. Her cell phone had six missed calls—none from Dr. Benson, only Brian. She still did not feel ready to talk to him and was greatly relieved he'd not shown up at her apartment. When she got to the hospital she went up to the reception desk and asked the nurse if she could see Reis.

"I don't believe Dr. Benson has approved visitation," the nurse replied kindly. "Dr. Benson is in the hospital now, though. I can let him know you're here and that you'd like to see Professor Welling."

"Thank you," Kelly said. She went to the waiting area the nurse had indicated. The room was empty except for an older, well-dressed woman. The woman acknowledged Kelly with a slight smile and nod, before continuing to stare blankly ahead. Kelly glanced at her stoic expression and wondered if it was this woman's family member or a friend who was locked up somewhere behind those doors. If this had been the waiting room in the cancer ward, they would only feel compassion for one another, but as it was, a heavy cloud of shame and embarrassment filled the room. Kelly picked up a magazine and pretended to read.

A short while later a young man approached the waiting area. "Mrs. Welling," he said, "Dr. Benson will see you now." Kelly watched with surprise as the older woman stood up and followed him down the hall.

Kelly went back to the nurse's station. "Excuse me," she said. "Could you please tell me? Was that Reis Welling's mother that he just took back?"

"I'm sorry," she said pleasantly. "I can't answer that. You know, HIPAA and all…."

Kelly looked in the direction that Mrs. Welling had gone and thought for a moment. "Oh, by the way," the nurse continued, "I just talked to Dr. Benson on the phone. He wanted me to tell you that Professor Welling is better but is not up for visitors yet."

"Thank you," Kelly said. She sat back down in the waiting room. She'd wanted to ask the nurse how long Reis was going to be there and what they were doing to him. She especially wanted to know what was wrong with him. But if this woman would not even answer the most basic of questions, she certainly wasn't going to answer something that was perhaps none of her business. Kelly sat patiently and waited.

It wasn't long before Mrs. Welling came back down the hall. Her face appeared calm, but Kelly could tell that she'd been crying.

"Mrs. Welling?" she said as she stepped from the waiting area.

Martha stopped and gave Kelly a questioning look.

"My name's Kelly Adams. I'm a friend of your son's."

"Of Reis's?" she asked, surprised.

Kelly nodded her head. "Yes. I met him a couple of months ago." Mrs. Welling seemed to be thinking about this and considering its implications. Kelly decided to plunge ahead. "I was hoping that you could help me. No one's really told me anything. I don't know how Reis is doing. They won't let me see him."

"Kelly. It is Kelly, isn't it?" she asked kindly.

"Yes."

"I don't think I know a whole lot more than you. I've not seen Reis myself. In fact, I haven't seen my son in almost a year." Her voice caught in her throat. "I believe you could probably tell me more about how Reis is now than I could tell you."

Kelly felt a sudden rush of compassion for this woman. She could only imagine what she must be going through. "Would you like to get some coffee someplace?" Kelly asked. "Maybe we could help each other."

thirty-six

They sat down in a small café close to the hospital and ordered coffee. Martha studied Kelly with great curiosity. "How did you meet my son?"

"I met him in the park," Kelly said with a smile. "He was up in a tree. Scared me half to death." Her smile grew wider. She brushed nervously at her bangs.

Martha smiled. "Reis has always loved his trees." The waitress brought the coffee and they spent a moment with the sugar and the cream. Martha stirred her coffee and asked, "Then you two just became friends?"

"Well, it wasn't that simple. I'm not sure Reis was all that interested." Kelly took a sip of coffee. "But there was something about him that made me want to get to know him." She hesitated and peered into her coffee. Martha waited. "He seemed so gentle and, I don't know...lonely. Lost maybe." Martha took in a quick breath. Kelly looked up at her. "I'm sorry," she said. "I'm upsetting you."

"No. Please go on. I want to know how he's doing." Martha waited.

"Mrs. Welling, what exactly is wrong with Reis?"

Martha sat back away from the question and considered how to respond. "He hasn't told you?" she finally asked.

"No. He's told me very little. I felt he was struggling with something. There were times when he seemed so sad or confused. He told me that he took his father's death badly. I know he had to leave Cornell." She paused a moment, then quietly said, "I know he tried to kill himself." Martha looked away. "Mrs. Welling, I care about Reis. I'd like to help him. I'm the one who brought him here. I saw how he was. But I have no idea what's wrong with him."

Martha sighed, looked back Kelly's way, and took in the pleading face of this young woman. How many times had she struggled with this question? It was so hard for people to understand. How could they, when even she found it so hard to fathom—so hard to accept? "Reis has schizophrenia. He was diagnosed about a year ago." The word slipped easily from her tongue but then hung ominously in the air between them.

"What is that, exactly?" Kelly finally asked. "Some kind of multiple personality?"

Martha shook her head. It was always the same. She commenced with her well-rehearsed response. "A lot of people think that, but it's nothing like that. It's a brain disease—a disease that makes it very difficult for those affected to process and respond to things the way normal people do. It's a thought disorder. Usually schizophrenia involves hallucinations, but there's a bombardment of other things going on." She paused, considering whether to take another sip from her coffee. "Reis wasn't always sick." She looked back to Kelly. "He was perfectly normal most of his life. Schizophrenia doesn't usually strike until the teen years or early adulthood. In Reis's case, it came on rather late." She sighed. "He was such a smart little boy. Kind and gentle." Martha paused to dab her eyes. As well rehearsed as these lines were, the *smart little boy* part always made her cry. Reis had been a perfect child. No one could have seen this coming. They'd been good parents. He was not abused or mistreated. He'd been truly loved. She wanted to tell Kelly this—make sure she understood this was not due to poor mothering—but she knew this was her own need and perhaps irrelevant to the conversation.

"He still is," Kelly told her. Martha looked at her. "Kind and gentle," Kelly added.

Martha gave her a grateful smile, tears welling up again. "I'm sorry," she said. Kelly gave her a compassionate, encouraging look. Martha blew her nose gently in a paper napkin from the dispenser on the table and continued, "I don't know when things began to go wrong for Reis. As far as I knew, everything was going great in his life. He had his tenure. He was living with a girl he obviously loved. They came up for Christmas, right before Walter died. I guess we noticed Reis seemed a bit on edge, but we didn't think much of it. When Walter died, that's when things really fell apart. If only I'd seen it coming, maybe it wouldn't have been so bad."

"I'm sure you had your own pain and grief to deal with," Kelly told her.

"Yes, that's true. But I did know that Reis was taking it harder than I. I should have somehow realized he needed my help." Martha narrowed her eyes. "I also blame Ellen." She paused. "That was his girlfriend. She never told me how bad things were. Not one word. If I'd known, I would've made sure he got the help he needed, before—" She paused, trying to collect herself.

"Before he tried to kill himself?" Kelly offered.

"That's right," she said quietly. "To be fair, I know Ellen did not realize how bad things were. She would never have kicked him out the way she did if she'd known how very ill he was."

"That's when he tried to kill himself?"

"Yes. Way up in those mountains. If those other hikers hadn't stumbled upon him, he'd be dead. As it was, by the time they got him to the hospital, he was near death. The doctors did not expect him to live. He was in the hospital for months. Even when they knew he would live, they could not make him well. They confused his psychosis with delirium. When his fever broke, they kept treating him for depression. It wasn't until I found Dr. Benson that Reis was properly diagnosed and treated."

"It must have been a terrible time for you, so close to your husband's death," Kelly said sympathetically.

Martha nodded. Martha's whole world had fallen apart. The death of her husband, her son's sudden illness, his desertion of her…her perfect, idyllic life—gone. She knew bad things happened to people, but somehow she'd always believed that she was safe. She was a good person. Had done everything right—or at least she'd thought she had. How much wasted energy and tears had been spent going over the past, trying to see what could have caused this terrible thing that happened to her son? Blame had made the full rounds and eventually landed on Ellen. It was easier that way, and yet she knew in her heart that it was wrong. Blame and guilt had no home with mental illness. "Oh, yes. It was very hard. Then, when Reis finally started getting better, he refused to see me or his family anymore. He just cut us out of his life. Even his grandmother…."

"Why would he do that?"

"I've asked myself that a thousand times. I've worked through a lot of guilt. Maybe he blamed me for his illness…that kind of thing. But I think it comes down to pride." She stopped talking and pulled out another napkin from the dispenser. Reis was so much like his father: so very proud, cavalier in his approach to life. He'd never failed at anything he'd ever done. And then to have failed in the most basic way—in his ability to maintain his own sanity. Then, she believed, when he got well enough to realize how very sick he was, he just couldn't face her. She sighed sadly and mopped at her face. "This relapse is going to be so very hard for him to deal with," she continued. "I just wish he'd let me help him," she gasped back a sob and had to stop again to collect herself.

Kelly reached forward and grasped Martha's hands in hers. Martha looked up and felt the comfort of this girl's hands and saw the tears that were rolling down her face. She managed to compose herself enough to ask, "How close are you and my son?" Her voice mingled with both kindness and concern.

"We're friends." Her hands squeezed Martha's and then Kelly reached for her own napkin to wipe at her eyes. "I care what happens to him. I want to help him, if I can. If he'll let me. But he's… he keeps a distance from me, also. I only hope he still wants to be friends when he gets better." She paused. "He will get better, won't he?"

"Dr. Benson seems to think so." Martha's voice trailed off sadly. "I do hope you and he remain friends. One of the hardest things about schizophrenia is that no one understands. I haven't been able to talk to anyone, other than my family and a few close friends. It's been good for me to talk to you like this. It also helps me to know that Reis has been well enough to maintain a friendship with someone such as yourself."

Kelly's cheeks grew red. "I've never met anyone like Reis," she managed to say.

"Let me give you my number. If there is anything you need or something Reis needs, will you call me?" Martha asked.

"Of course."

thirty-seven

Kelly booted up her laptop and hooked into the coffee shop's wireless. She Googled schizophrenia and was amazed—28,200,000 results. She spent a few hours reading until her eyes could take no more, until her mind was swimming with facts, and until her head ached.

Brian was waiting for her when she got home. He looked tired and stressed. Max was lying next to him on the couch, the dog's head resting on Brian's thigh. Neither one of them bothered to get up and greet her as she walked in the door; they simply turned from the TV. "I was beginning to think you weren't coming home tonight," Brian said. Kelly sat next to him on the couch and sighed. "You never answered my calls," he told her.

"I'm sorry."

He leaned over and kissed her lightly on the lips. "What's going on, Kelly?" he asked.

"My friend's in the hospital."

"Who?" He sat up a bit with concern.

She looked away. "Reis," she whispered.

"Who?"

"My friend Reis."

"That guy you went hiking with?"

She nodded and began to cry. He, of course, did not move to comfort her. Her head went down in her hands. "God, everything is so messed up." Max came over and licked her face. She reached for him, pulled him onto her lap, and buried her head in the brown fur of his back.

"Why's he in the hospital?" Brian asked, not quite hiding the pleasure he was feeling at this man's misfortune.

Kelly looked up at him blankly. "He's sick." She dabbed her eyes with her shirt sleeve.

Brian narrowed his eyes. "Okay…so you've been sitting, holding his hand all this time?"

"Why do I feel like I'm being cross-examined?"

"I don't know. Do you have reason to feel guilty about something?" Max cocked his head at Brian's tone.

"We're not having an affair, if that's what you mean," Kelly shot back defensively.

"I'm not sure that's what I mean, Kelly," Brian said, dropping his cross-examination voice in defeat. "I have a feeling there's more going on here. If you were simply having sex with this guy…. Well, maybe I'd have a fighting chance. But something tells me I'm losing you to something else."

"I'm not so sure you're losing me," Kelly responded quietly.

"But you're not so sure I'm not," he countered.

Kelly put her head back in her hands. "Brian, I'm so confused." He put his arm around her, and she turned to him and leaned into his chest.

"I know I haven't always been there for you," he whispered. They were both quiet for a moment. "Can you just give me another chance to make you happy?"

An unpleasant-sounding sob escaped from Kelly's mouth. "Brian, you've always made me happy." She wiped at her nose with her shirt while trying not to ruin his. "It's just that…I'm not sure we want the same things."

"And this man: he wants what you want?" Brian asked, his own voice straining.

"I have absolutely no idea what he wants. It's not what you think," she said, pulling away from him. "I don't even know…. I just need a little time—to sort things out."

He dropped his hands from her shoulders. "Is that my cue to go home?"

He was so wounded and hurt, and she'd done this. Strutting about, leaving the broken remains of men everywhere she went— knocking them down, *Pop! Pop!* one at a time.

thirty-eight

Dr. Benson came into the room and sat in one of the fake leather chairs. Even though the hospital consultation room had been designed to give the feeling of warmth and home, Dr. Benson would have preferred the plastic chairs in the waiting room. To him, the decor reeked of disingenuousness. He opened Reis's file and began to write a few notes in his short, wispy handwriting. A few minutes later there was a light knock on the door.

"Come in," he called. Lloyd opened the door and gently led Reis into the room. "Thanks, Lloyd," Dr. Benson said, indicating that he could leave. "Have a seat, Reis," he said softly.

Reis moved slowly to one of the chairs. He looked uncertain on his feet and seemed to collapse once he hit the chair. It had been six days, and he was greatly improved.

"The nurses tell me you're better," Dr. Benson said. "You had a good night?"

"I slept," Reis stated, his voice almost inaudible. "When do I get out of here?"

"I think very soon. I do have a few things I'd like to talk to you about."

"I suppose I could suffer through one of your lectures if it will get me out of here." Reis's eyes held no humor as he looked at the doctor—only a mixture of boredom and depression.

"I know that you're not happy with me for admitting you, but I felt it was necessary."

Reis pressed his lips tighter together and closed his eyes. "Kelly brought me here, didn't she?"

"Yes."

Reis rubbed his hand into his face and almost smiled. It was the kind of smile Dr. Benson did not like to see.

"She was here last night wanting to see you. She's been here or called every day. I imagine she'll be back today," Dr. Benson told him.

"I don't want to see her," Reis replied, his voice suddenly strong.

"I thought you might feel that way." Dr. Benson sat back in his chair. "Are you angry with her about her boyfriend?"

Reis looked at him, surprised.

"Kelly told me a little about her boyfriend," Dr. Benson added.

"Why would I be angry? She's only spent the last two months telling me her whole life story. She acted like this boyfriend was nothing serious. Apparently, the fact that she was deeply in love slipped her mind."

Dr. Benson looked at him and cocked his head in gentle reprimand.

"You don't think I should have expected her to tell me something of that significance?" Reis asked.

"I believe there are some very significant things about your life that you failed to tell her."

Reis sat back further in his chair. "Touché," he said quietly.

"Kelly blames herself for your relapse."

Reis laughed slightly. "The pathetic thing is, she's probably right."

Dr. Benson tilted his head and narrowed his eyes. "Let's talk a moment about your medication." Reis shifted in his chair and looked at Dr. Benson with bored expectancy. "Why did you stop taking your antipsychotic, Reis?"

Reis looked toward the window as he said, "The meds make Reis a very dull boy. Now a dull man, I might be able to handle. But a boy…." He shook his head. Dr. Benson waited for him to say more, but he didn't.

"You know that's not totally true. The Seroquel has proven to have very few side effects for you. If you were feeling off, you most likely needed an increase in dosage, certainly not a complete withdrawal from it. Why didn't you talk to me?"

Reis shrugged. "Just a little experiment gone wrong…. I wanted to impress her with my charm, my wit." He smiled ironically. "Well, I ended up impressing the hell out of her, didn't I?" Reis began to absently pick at his bandage.

Dr. Benson watched him for a long moment before he asked, "How are you handling this relapse?"

Reis did not answer right away. He appeared to have found something very interesting as he poked around his wounds. "How am I handling it?" he finally said. "I'm not sure I ever really believed that I was that ill. Maybe that sounds absurd. I'm still not convinced that it's not some kind of mistake. A weak mind. A fragile soul. I always believed I could do anything I set my mind to. If there was something I could not do, well, I just did not want it badly enough. The human spirit, if strong enough, can overcome all adversity. You know—that kind of bullshit." Reis laughed a bit. "It would appear that I failed," he continued. "That failure could mean several different things, none of which I care to accept. You have no idea what it's like, to lose everything. Look at me now. I'm a walking mass of drugs and fucked-up neurons. Is this how I'm supposed to spend the rest of my life? Hell, I can't even brush my teeth without it becoming a major mental production. Do you have any idea all the steps involved in brushing your damn teeth?" He paused and looked at the doctor. "I don't think I can live like this." Reis stated the last sentence very simply, not looking away from Dr. Benson—challenging him to disagree.

Dr. Benson sat forward and folded his hands on the desk in front of him. "You're right. I don't know what it's like, and I can't tell you everything will be fine. I can't say whether you'll ever be able to go back to the way your life was. Even with the best case scenario, that you reach full recovery, your life has been altered. No one can go through what you have and emerge unchanged. You have one of the cruelest illnesses known to man—one in which you cannot trust your own mind. You understand, better than anyone, the fine line between sanity and insanity. It's up to you what you do with this knowledge."

Dr. Benson paused and waited until Reis looked at him before he continued. "You must first accept your illness for what it is: An illness. A brain disease. It's not something you can control simply by wishing it to go away. You must continue your medication, just as a diabetic must continue their insulin. You must learn the warning signs of relapse. Don't allow your cavalier attitude to prevent you from asking for help. You've pretty much insisted on going through this alone. There are many people willing to support you. I know you've thought of yourself as independent and self-sufficient, but accepting friendship and emotional support is not a sign of weakness. You've always succeeded in all you set out to do. Use that ability to succeed in learning to live with schizophrenia. It may be the hardest thing you've ever done, but use the strength you have in building the best possible life for yourself. There is no strength in allowing yourself to wallow in self-pity and depression."

Dr. Benson stopped and sat back a moment. Reis had returned to his hand, and having successfully removed the tape and gauze, was pulling gently at the stitches. "It would probably be best to have someone here remove those. I'll have it done today," he told Reis.

Reis looked up, a bit startled, then smiled slightly. "Is the lecture over?" he asked.

"Yes. I believe I'm done for now," Dr. Benson said, also smiling lightly.

"So when do I get out of here?" Reis said, leaning forward.

"I think we can get you out of here in a few days."

"Why not today?" he asked with little confidence.

"I don't think you're ready. Today is Tuesday; let's plan on Friday, if all is well." Reis sighed with relief. "But I want to see you in my office, Monday at four."

"Not a problem," said Reis, who suddenly seemed to have a lot of energy.

"Okay. We'll talk again on Thursday. Oh, by the way," he continued, "your mother was back again yesterday. She wanted to see you." Reis looked at Dr. Benson. "I told her I didn't think now was a good time."

"Thank you."

"She left these," Dr. Benson said as he looked through his briefcase. He pulled out a set of car keys and set them on his desk.

"My car?" Reis asked, dumbfounded.

"It's in the parking garage. Third floor. You'll need to eat well and rest for the next couple days if you want to have the energy to drive out of here."

"You're kidding!" Reis smiled. It was the kind of smile Dr. Benson liked to see. "You said Friday, right?"

th irty - nine

Reis did not have any trouble finding his car. He walked around it once, running his fingers gently along the metal. He wondered how he could feel such warmth toward a toxic, spewing hunk of modern technology. He sat in the driver's seat and smiled as he gripped the steering wheel, enjoying the odor of the soft leather seats. No matter how he felt about global warming, world hunger, racism, and organic gardening, he was not granola when it came to his car. He drove carefully out of the parking garage and took the shortest route out of the city. For two hours he drove, savoring the freedom he hadn't known in months.

forty

Kelly went directly to the hospital after work on Friday, determined to see Reis. This was absurd. Even prisoners get visitation rights. Today she was going to pitch a fit. "Dr. Welling has been released," was the answer to Kelly's request to see him. Kelly was dumbfounded.

"He's not here?" she asked, confused.

"No." The nurse shook her head. "He left hours ago."

"Did he go home?"

"I don't know," the nurse answered with a shrug and a smile.

Kelly drove to Reis's and parked. She sat there for several minutes. Seeing him in the hospital setting had somehow seemed safer. Now she felt a lot less confident in what she might say and how he might respond. It would be so easy just to drive away and allow her life to return to the way it had been. She rubbed her hand across her forehead, then looked at herself in the rearview mirror. Who was this woman? Kelly wasn't sure she knew any-more; maybe she never had. She'd always believed her capacity for loyalty and honesty was more or less tangible, but now it seemed fleeting and questionable as it blew with the prevailing wind. She looked away, closing her eyes for a moment before stepping out of the car.

When she reached Reis's door, she hesitated. She could hear someone moving around inside, and she was both relieved that he was there and filled with dread at the prospect of facing him. She knocked quietly. The noise inside stopped, and after a moment, she realized he was not moving toward the door.

"Reis. It's Kelly," she said as she knocked again, louder.

When he ignored her the second time, she tried the door. It opened. As she stepped inside, she heard Reis say, "Do you always just walk into people's homes?"

His voice held no humor. He was squatting on the floor, packing a box. He glanced up at her before returning to his box. Kelly had forgotten how compelling his eyes were and was taken aback by a sudden rush of emotions. She took a moment before answering. "Yes, I do," she said stubbornly. "Especially when I know they're at home and they choose not to answer their door."

Reis sat on the floor and looked at her. She sensed he was fighting off a smile, and she relaxed. He was himself again, or at least someone she recognized. Kelly looked around the room. It was pretty much cleared out. Only a few boxes lay scattered about.

"Are you moving?" she asked. A small surge of panic rushed through her.

"Kelly, why are you here?" he asked, impatient now.

Kelly walked over to him and sat down by his side. "How's your hand?" she asked softly.

"It's fine." He allowed her to take it. She turned it over and examined the wound.

"Wow. It looks like it's healing nicely," she whispered. "I tried to see you in the hospital," she said, not looking up from his hand. "They wouldn't let me."

"Well, they're funny that way." He pulled his hand away.

Kelly looked at him. "I'm so sorry." He met her gaze with his face set. "I'm sorry I never really told you about Brian."

"There was no reason why you should have told me about your love life," Reis said, returning to his packing.

She watched him as he eased a scattered pile of magazines together. She touched his arm lightly, then brought her hand to her lips in uncertainty. "I can't help but think that it's my fault that you ended up in the hospital."

An unkind laugh came from his throat as he lifted the stack of magazines and dropped them with a plop inside the box. "It's nice you have such a high opinion of yourself—that you can drive a man insane."

Kelly closed her eyes with a sigh. "Reis, I never told you much about Brian because, I guess, I didn't want you to know I was seriously involved with anyone. I guess I wanted our relationship to evolve naturally. That wasn't fair to you, or Brian. I don't think I even realized how exactly I felt about you."

Reis reached for the packing tape. There was the loud, harsh scream of the tape as he ripped a piece away. "I don't give a fuck about Brian." He slapped the tape across the top of the box, sealing its edges. He turned to her, impatient. "You and I were just friends. That's all."

"Reis." She looked away. "You know as well as I do that's not true."

Reis abruptly pushed the box away and shook his head in disbelief. "And who's the crazy one here?" He shook his head again and laughed. "Kelly, has it registered with you, at all," he spoke slowly so she'd be sure to understand, "where I've been the last eight days?"

"I know where you've been! I took you there." She was getting a little angry.

"I've got a little bit more going on than you and some Brian guy," he said, ignoring her comments. "I was in the nut house! Rolling around in my own shit. I'm a schizophrenic, Kelly! I'm sure you've heard the word. It means crazy, mad, insane, psycho, deranged, nuts, a fucking lunatic, a—"

"Reis, I know what schizophrenia is. I know all about it." She hesitated before adding, "I've talked to your mother."

He closed his mouth to the words he was about to say. He shook his head in confusion, his face collapsing.

"I know everything," she said softly. She put her hand lightly against his cheek. "It doesn't change the way I feel about you."

"Then, there is no doubt that your insanity runs far deeper than mine." He pulled away from her hand and rubbed at his temples.

"We can fight this thing together," she said eagerly. She scooted a little closer. "I've done a lot of reading about schizophrenia, and there is a pretty good chance you'll fully recover. The fact that it came on so fast and so late.... That's to your favor. You know, twenty-five percent of schiz—"

Reis laughed, sending shivers down Kelly's back. "So you've done a little reading, have you?" he said, his voice laced with mean sarcasm. "Read a few fucked-up statistics. And now you think that you and I can just waltz off into the sunset, our love strong enough to cure me! I'm sorry, but you have no fucking idea what you're talking about!" He sucked in a quick gasp of air before continuing. "You have no idea what my life is like. My brain doesn't work like yours. I'm right in the middle of a civil war of the brain. And here," he said, as he jerked up his shirt and pulled his pants down a bit, "is my badge of dishonor to prove it! Do you see it, Kelly?"

She looked at the large, angry scar that ran the full length of his abdomen.

"Take a closer look." He took her head and pulled it closer. "It's my daily reminder of just how fucked up I am." He let her go. Her eyes filled with tears.

"Good old Heckle and Jeckle, my constant companions, were kind enough to give me that! Their evil minds, the hideous things they say, keep me constantly entertained. But you know, their putrid, macabre witticisms are not transmitted to my brain by some devil or morbid god!" He shook his head. "No. No. It's all me! Me! It's my putrid, macabre mind. I am this hideous, evil thing. I am this thing that I have become."

He stopped and closed his eyes. He breathed deeply and exhaled. Kelly sat in stunned silence. Reis's eyes opened. "I never should have let you into my life," he said quietly. "I'm sorry about that. Maybe I thought for a moment that I could have a normal relationship, but I was wrong." He hesitated. "Marry Brian, Kelly. He loves you. Forget you ever met me."

Kelly sucked in a sob. "I don't think I can," she cried. She put her arms around him and cried against his shoulder. Reis let her stay there, unmoved, until her crying slowed.

"Kelly," he said, gently pushing her away. He looked at her, making sure he had her full attention. "Trust me on this. There is nothing for you here."

"Can't we at least go back to the way it was and see what happens?" Her voice was still choked with tears.

Reis shook his head. "I'm leaving."

"Where are you going?"

He shrugged his shoulders. "I'll know when I get there."

"You're coming back."

"No." He looked away. "Kelly, go on with your life. It's going to be a great one." He stood up, put his hand out to her, and helped her off the floor. "You're a great girl. And I'm glad for the time we had. But now I really need to get out of here. Will you let me finish packing?"

forty-one

Kelly spent Saturday looking out the window at nothing in particular. She was attempting to figure out exactly how her life had become so messed up. She had not been unhappy before she met Reis; she'd been content. But he'd somehow come into her life, affected all aspects of it, then simply left, leaving her miserable. And she certainly hadn't helped his life. Now she could see no way to go back.

The sun set behind the clouds, and the sky grew red, purple, and orange. She stared out the window while the last of the color faded and was slowly replaced by the soft black haze of night. There was a knock on her door, but she made no move to answer it. Brian used his key to come in. "Kelly," he said as he entered the room. He turned on the light, and she covered her eyes in pain. "I saw your car. I knew you must be here." He stepped across the room and sat down next to her. She turned her moist eyes to him. "Aw, Kelly. Please don't be so sad."

She buried her face in his chest. "Reis's gone. He's left. He's not coming back. I don't even know where he's gone."

Brian was quiet for a long time. He placed his arms loosely around her. "Where does that leave us?" he finally asked.

She shook her head in confusion.

"Let's go get some dinner," he said. "You look like you need to get out of here."

Kelly pulled away and looked at him. His blue eyes were intense and full of love. "How can you just keep on loving me?" she asked.

"It's not something I can change. Not something I want to change." He took her hands and kissed them slowly. "Come on, let's get out of here."

"Where would we go?" she asked, her eyes wide like a child's.

"To the moon, gorgeous. I'll take you to the moon!"

fo rty - two

Reis drove a few miles out of town and spent the weekend at a small motel. He spent much of his time organizing his hiking equipment and running to various stores for supplies. Sunday evening he sat in the small room of the motel and began to write slowly and methodically:

Dear Mom,

I am sorry I have been unable to see you. I cannot explain why the idea is so terrifying to me. The pressure of what you might expect, or even not expect, is overpowering. Never question how much I love you, or doubt my knowledge of your love for me. No child could ever want for better parents than you and Dad.

Not a day goes by that I do not miss him. I'm sure you feel the same way. As hopelessly sad as his death was, I prefer him dead, rather than him knowing me the way I am now. I guess that's the silver lining of this dark cloud.

This last year has been very difficult for me. It is not, of course, the life I envisioned for myself. I'm not sure that I am strong enough to adjust to its new boundaries and limitations. I know that I have hurt you deeply. Please forgive me for any pain that I have caused and any future sorrow I may inflict.

Please remember, I love you. Kiss Grandma for me.

Reis

On Monday morning, Reis checked out of the motel and ate a large breakfast at a local diner. The waitress, young and pretty, smiled at him as she filled his coffee cup. "Are you from around here?"

"No, not really." He smiled back.

She stood there for a moment, waiting for more. When he said nothing, she said, "Well, let me know if you need anything else." Her smile flashed again.

"There is something I can't seem to find," he told her. She smiled expectantly at him. "I can't find a mailbox—anywhere." He pulled out his letter to his mother and gave her his boyish grin. "It's to my mother."

"I'll mail it for you." She gave him a warm, soft look. "The mailman stops by in about an hour."

"Thanks." He handed her the letter. As she walked away, she turned and gave him one more smile.

Reis drove to a gas station and filled up his tank before placing a call from the payphone. "Dr. Benson's office," said Sue when she answered the phone. "How may I help you?"

"Hi, Sue. This is Reis Welling. Would it be possible to talk to Dr. Benson a moment?"

"Oh, good morning, Dr. Welling. Sure, hold on. Let me buzz him."

Reis waited patiently for a minute or two. In all the months he'd known Dr. Benson, he'd never called him. He was only a little surprised how easy it was to get through to him.

"Reis, is everything all right?" Dr. Benson asked when he picked up the line.

"Well, that's an interesting question. I suppose its answer depends on what you're really asking," Reis said casually into the phone. "If you are asking me if I am psychotic, the answer is *no*. If you are asking me if I'm happy, healthy, and fully sane, well then, I guess the answer is also *no*."

"Reis, where are you? The social worker went by your apartment. She said you'd moved out."

"That's really why I'm calling. I felt I owed you at least that. I'm leaving. I've thought a lot about what we talked about last week. I need to make a decision. I can't make it there, with all those external complications."

"What decision do you need to make?" Dr. Benson asked.

"Come on, Doc. You're a smart man."

"Reis, suicide is not the answer."

"That, Dr. Benson, depends on the question."

"Reis, listen to me. Come on in to my office. Let's talk about this."

"I appreciate your offer, but this is something I need to work out myself."

"You called me. You must want my input," Dr. Benson insisted.

"That's where you are wrong, Doc. I merely called to thank you. You've made the worst moments of my life slightly less unbearable. I just wanted you to know that no matter what happens, you've done a superb job. I wouldn't want to be a black spot on your record. I also wanted you to know that I am taking my medication as prescribed, and any decision I make will be mine and not that of a raving psychotic."

"Where are you? I'll meet you there. We can talk a little before you go."

"Thanks again, Doc."

"Reis, wait! Will you at least call me in a few days?"

"Tell you what: if I run across a phone where I'm going, you'll be the first one I'll call." Reis hung up the phone, purchased a soda from the vending machine, and walked slowly to his car.

forty-three

The transition between summer and fall was rapid in the Adirondacks. The large green leaves of the forest took on a dull appearance as if they knew their days were drawing to an end. The grasses turned amber, and the late summer flowers of aster and goldenrod stood brightly in the fading warmth. The bushes were the first to burst out in color. Berries and nuts were abundant. Small animals and birds relished this abundance in preparation for winter. The fall rains had not begun, and the streams flowed gently. Many waterfalls no longer existed. Cool nights and warm days decreased the bug population, making life more bearable for the warm-blooded creatures of the Adirondacks. The migratory birds stopped defending their territories and began to gather in increasingly larger groups as the days passed and their departure grew near. There was a sense of waiting and anticipation, but it was a gentle anticipation. The passage from fall to winter would not be so pleasant.

In many ways, this was Reis's favorite time of year. The hiking trails were dry and relatively empty. The low humidity made for bright, clear days that dazzled under blue skies. At no other time of year were the views more beautiful. He'd returned to his favorite area of the park: the far northern section. It was close to the small bluff he'd looked over the night Holly had kissed him. It was also close to the waterfall he and his father had discovered. He knew that if anyone searched for him, this is where they'd look; but he'd not been able to help himself. He'd parked his car well off the road and hidden it in bushes. Even if they were seriously looking, he would be very hard to find.

Reis spent his days walking slowly through the forest, absorbing the beauty and using the time to calm himself. He did not think of his past or future but only what he saw or did at that moment: where to place his foot, the best way to climb a ridge, what he would eat the next meal, the best place to sleep. He walked carefully on the earth, so as not to disturb its delicate balance. His every move was calculated, doing only what he thought would please the forest.

When he reached the summit of small mountains, he lay naked in the sun, sharing the power of its rays with the surrounding forests. At night, the power carried him through, and he slept peacefully under the stars. It was easy to avoid other hikers during the week, but on weekends, he stayed off the trails, spending his time sitting quietly among the branches of the great old trees.

One afternoon, a warm, gentle rain formed rainbows and created smoky mists in the valleys. Reis rejoiced in it and danced among the raindrops. That evening, the air was warm and felt like flannel. He painted his body with mud and crept up on a young doe as she nestled down for the night. She turned her brown eyes to him. He kept perfectly still, and after several minutes, she lay her head down and forgot about him. He slept also, only a few feet away.

There were days when he did nothing but study an ant colony as it went about its business of surviving; or he'd sit quietly by a small pond and observe its complex ecosystem. He did his best to clear his mind of human needs and concerns, only reacting to his basic instincts.

Weeks went by and the days grew cooler. The leaves lost their green as they shifted to red, yellow, and orange, and then, one by one, slowly floated toward the earth. Crows complained. Large flocks of Canada geese honked overhead. Squirrels rustled through the leaves. Stags shook their massive antlers. Does looked up with mild interest. Reis turned in his sleeping bag to the crunchy noise of morning frost and the start of cold rains, and he knew the first, early flakes of snow were soon to come. When his food supply grew low, he supplemented it with roots, dry berries, and small, wrinkled apples. As the nights grew colder and he was forced to expose himself with small fires for warmth, he began to consider his options.

He knew the earth was contemplating him, unsure if he could be trusted, unwilling, as of yet, to share its secrets with him as it had done so freely before he became ill. He could not seem to break through the barrier that kept him from his sense of wholeness. How long, he wondered, could he stay here, living off the earth somewhere between sanity and insanity? He counted his pills—they, too, were dwindling. He must prepare for winter if this was going to go on. How would he get more meds? He was so tired. Perhaps he was just delaying the inevitable with this quest for acceptance and wholeness. He did not believe that he was afraid to die, but he was afraid to die without his soul being fully intact. The thought of also failing at this was more than he could bear. He looked up into the red and yellow leaves. "What can I do?" he asked them. They did not answer but only swayed reticently in the night breeze.

It was mid-October when Reis hoisted his pack one morning and began to hike with a definite destination for the first time. He was finally going where he was afraid to go. The day was clear but cold, and the fallen leaves crunched beneath his feet as he walked. His breath blew around him in wispy clouds. He did not hurry, for he knew it was waiting patiently for him. The closer he got, the more clear his purpose became. As mid-day approached, he fully understood why he'd been chosen to suffer. He felt strengthened by this new understanding. The earth's power surged around him; he could almost grasp it in his hands.

He sensed it before he reached the gorge; its malevolence filled the air, even before the sound of the falls could be heard. Reis walked carefully to the edge of the gorge and peered down into the falling water. It no longer gushed from the mountain as it had the spring before last. Instead, it gently caressed the rocks as it fell. His gaze went from the falls to the pool and then rested on the soft, mossy bank. He pictured, in his mind, how it must have appeared to those hikers who'd found him. Had they seen him from above, as he was now? The image of him lying naked, bloodied, and dying must be something that still comes to them at night. There was no physical evidence that he'd ever been here. The blood had long been washed away, but the memory.... It lay like a filth across the ground. This was the center of the boil—the source. Had he left it here? Was this the reason the earth could not forgive him? Or had he merely stumbled upon an ancient evil, left by generations of human corruption and waste? Reis closed his eyes and sighed. In either case, he must face it and reclaim it as his own.

He walked along the top of the ravine, traveling about a half mile downstream to where the walls were less steep. Slowly picking his way down into the gorge, he reached the bottom and headed back upstream, slowing as he drew nearer. The air, which had been cool and light above, grew still and heavy. There was a foul odor of death and then the bloody horror: the carcass rotting, butchered and thrown casually over the ravine. The deer's tongue fat and grossly misshapen, its neck twisted, its eyes still shocked by its own death.

He stopped and stood in the stream, the cold water flowing around his boots, his arm covering his nose and mouth. He didn't believe that he could do this. As he stood there, hesitating, the deer staring up at him, a sudden rush of cool wind blew up from behind, hitting hard against his back and pushing his hair forward. Leaves flew all around him as he began to walk on against the flow of the water. He reached the last bend of the stream, and there, in the dim light of a late fall afternoon, the falls stood out in front of him.

His pack, his coat, his clothing—he dropped them onto the soft, mossy earth. The sudden coldness of the water and the force of the current were not a problem. And there, under the steady fall of water, the odor of death rinsing away, he felt the calmness of acceptance—he felt resolve.

The forest was holding its breath as he swam back across the pool and pulled himself upon the shore, carefully placing his body down on the soft moss. The ground, plush and mushy, gave way under his weight. A wave of dizzy movement ensued, and he lay down and peered up among the tree branches—skeletons against the grey. Only a few brightly colored leaves remained.

His mind cleared. A place of refuge. He offered himself up—a sacrifice, a martyr. He waited, relaxing, the water's music singing in his ears. The pain, the sins, the suffering of all mankind: dancing in the spray of water, splashing on his face. The earth's power flowed around him and whispered in his ears, but he was not quite able to grasp the message. Then there was confusion as the whispering became more distinct. What he thought had seemed so clear became fuzzy but then refocused. When it refocused, it had totally changed.

He began to laugh. He finally understood what the earth was telling him. He had nothing the earth wanted. He could not excrete or absorb evil. He could not take this evil with him. His laughter rang through the trees. Even in his death, he had thought he could be superior. But he was not the earth's savior. He was only a troubled, sick man who wanted to die. When his laughter stopped, he lay there for a long time. He felt slow tears roll down his cheeks, but he did not believe that he was crying. He felt he was ready. Now it was just a matter of logistics.

forty-four

Reis sat by the fire, slowly stirring the coals with a stick. It caught on fire, and after a while, he was forced to throw it in. He was considering his options. A gun, of course, was most efficient. Fast and foolproof. A man's way to die. Hemingway had used a gun, putting the barrel to the roof of his mouth and neatly blowing his head away. He'd never really cared for Hemingway's macho, manly characters, though. And then there was the other problem of obtaining a gun. He'd always supported strict gun control and didn't think his last living act should be hypocritical, even if it was efficient.

He had his doubts about knives. His pathetic, psychotic attempts with knives did not lend much confidence. Efficiency was definitely questionable. Was a vertical or horizontal cut to the wrist more effective? The popular method seemed to involve a bathtub of hot water. Was that done strictly for neatness's sake, or was the hot water necessary to prevent the blood from clotting?

He supposed he could warm water in a fire and place his wrists in his cooking pots. He laughed at this. The image of him lying on the ground, each hand in a pot, was just too absurd.

Freezing to death had a definite appeal, but he knew he would starve to death long before it grew cold enough to kill him. Starving to death had absolutely no appeal. There was an abundance of poison plants and mushrooms in the summer, but this time of year they were hard to find. There was also the question of proper dosage and delivery....

Then it hit him; he laughed at its simplicity. How could he have not seen it immediately? He was sitting among some of the highest peaks in that part of the country. The area was teaming with cliffs and deep gorges. How simply perfect—to soar to one's death. And he knew just the place.

The following day, Reis broke camp early. He was a day-and-a-half hike away from his destination. The air was cold and damp, and the heavy clouds that hung overhead threatened rain. A breeze blew around him, bringing the remainder of the leaves floating toward the earth. He did not hurry. He walked steadily but slowly. At noon he did not eat but continued to walk; he did not feel the need for food. Sunlight filtered through the clouds and warmed the air by late afternoon. As the sun set, a wet fog descended, and the visibility dropped quickly with the fading light.

Reis stopped for the night and camped near a slow-flowing stream. The darkness settled rapidly around him as he attempted to start a fire. The dampness made things difficult, but after considerable effort, he had a small blaze burning brightly in the darkness. For a long time he nursed the flames. An owl screeched from somewhere close by, but the only other noises were the crackling of the fire and the gentle murmur of the stream.

Reis poured some water into a small pot and placed it over the fire. When it was boiling gently, he took out his last package of stew and poured it into the water. The last supper. He laughed. He sat back and closed his eyes, waiting for it to thicken. The fire crackled, and a nut popped loudly as it burst from the heat. The owl flapped overhead. Reis opened his eyes, but it was already gone. He closed his eyes again and pulled his coat a bit tighter around him.

Moments ticked by, his mind calm and clear. He suddenly sat up, his eyes wide open. Something wasn't right. He stared out into the misty fog and did not breathe. He was not alone. There was nothing but blackness beyond the glow of the fire. He heard the noise again and turned toward it.

The fog seemed to part, and a man much older than Reis stepped into the firelight. Wild gray hair flew from his head, and a heavy white beard stuck out from his chin. He wore an easy smile and a face that was ageless. He could have been one hundred or he could have been sixty. Reis blinked, but the man did not go away.

"I saw your fire," he said in a slow, pleasant drawl. "It's been a while since I've seen anyone up here. Mind if I join you? A body gets a little lonely for someone to talk to after a while." He looked at Reis steadily, his smile never wavering.

"Sure. I guess so," Reis's voice was strained as he spoke. He hadn't used it in so long; the sound of it was startling.

The old man sat down a few feet from Reis, laid his pack down, and untied his boots. Reis watched him carefully. "Whatever you're cooking smells awfully good," he said.

"Well, you're welcome to some," said Reis. He did not believe the man was real. This was certainly a new twist to his hallucinations, and he was willing to play along with it.

"How long have you been out here?" the man asked as he

pulled out a cup from his pack and began spooning out some stew.

"I'm not sure. What's the date?" He watched as the man took another spoonful of stew.

"Let's see," he said, raising his eyes to the sky. "Must be about October twenty-eighth."

"Then I've been out here almost two months," Reis stated. He leaned forward and took the remainder of the stew.

"That's a pretty long time," the man said.

Reis did not respond.

"This isn't too bad. Is this reconstituted?" he asked as he chewed a large mouthful.

"That's right," answered Reis.

"Last week, I got myself a young rabbit. Now that was some good food." He wiped his mouth on his sleeve.

"How long have you been out here?" Reis asked. He made no attempt to hide the suspicion in his voice.

"Just a couple of weeks. I've got to go back soon," he sighed. "Unfortunately, sooner or later, the real world catches up to you—job, house, family responsibilities. You know what I mean."

Reis nodded his head.

"Of course, a young fellow such as yourself, you probably don't have too many ties. I remember when I was your age. I felt I had the world by the tail. When you get older," he smiled, "you realize that it's got you."

They ate in silence for several minutes. The old man finished his last bite of stew. "I've got some coffee," he offered. "I could brew it up real quick."

"No, thank you," answered Reis.

The old man looked at him. Reis met his steel blue eyes, then looked away. "I've got something I think you'll like," the old man said. He fished through his pack. "There you go, son." He pulled out a large navel orange and offered it to him. "I bet you haven't found any of these out here." Reis took it cautiously. The man took out another one for himself. "I've been carrying these around for weeks now, waiting for a special occasion. This seems as good a time as any." He split his open. Reis smelled its sweet, tangy aroma as the man pulled the fruit apart. He threw the peel into the fire.

Reis watched the edges of the peal curl in and enjoyed the whiff of burnt orange. He turned his attention to the hard round-ness he held gently in his hand. He carefully shifted it from one hand to the other, feeling its firmness and measuring its weight. He brought it up to his nose and smelled the bitter bite of the peel. He used his thumbnail to split the peel apart, sending a tiny spray of pungent pleasure to his nose. The peel came off in two neat pieces, and Reis threw them into the flames. He carefully broke apart the sections of the orange, feeling its wet stickiness on his fingers. He placed one section in his mouth and held it gently against his tongue. A moment passed before he brought his teeth down on it. He closed his eyes and moaned from the tangy sweet-ness that burst upon his tongue.

"God, this is good," he told the old man.

The old man's face broke out in a smile. His eyes gleamed in the firelight. The sweet, burnt smell of oranges mingled in the air. "I've been coming to the Adirondacks for fifty years," the old man said. "These mountains make you think. Everything seems closer to you out here. I guess there are a lot of reasons why people come out here."

He looked at Reis, who looked back in silence.

"Why are you out here?" the old man asked.

Reis shifted a bit. "For the beauty of nature," he said flatly.

"The way I see it," the old man said, "no one lives out here for weeks without some reason." He popped a second piece of orange into his mouth. "Either they're looking for something or trying to leave something behind."

Reis laughed a bit. "Is that so? Then why are you here?"

"Me? I'm looking for the meaning of life." His eyes crinkled.

"And, have you found it?"

"No. But I'm still looking." He looked steadily at Reis. "What are you looking for, boy?"

Reis met his gaze. "I'm looking for the meaning of death."

"And have you found it?" he asked, unblinking.

"Yes. Death is meaningless."

The man shook his head. "If death has no meaning, then life also must have no meaning."

"Well, there's your answer," Reis told him as he sat back against the tree, settling in with his orange. "You don't have to look any further."

"No. I just can't see it that way. Think about it. It doesn't make any sense. This is something I've thought a lot about." He sat forward and looked at Reis intensely. Reis smiled patiently back. "Let's start with the most basic forms of life…say a protozoan. It responds to light and dark. It responds to temperature. Each response is in order to survive. What is the purpose of its life? Its purpose is to survive and propagate. It doesn't seem like much, does it? But what would happen if there were no protozoa? Their existence is crucial. They are a primary component of the first link in the food chain, adding great meaning to their lives, and to their deaths.

"Now let's move up a bit in the food chain. Consider a frog. What is the meaning of its life? It certainly relates to other frogs. It maintains a territory. It searches out a mate, food. But again, everything it does is for one purpose, which is to survive so that it can propagate, allowing its species to continue and adding its own significant link to the food chain."

"I understand about each living thing's dependence on one another," Reis interrupted. "I fully agree with the importance of the food chain. But let's jump right to the top and consider human beings. Their importance to the food chain is nil. Not only would the earth survive without man, it would be better off."

"You have a point," the old man agreed. "But human beings do exist, and isn't that really the question? Why are *we* here? What is the purpose of *our* lives? Isn't everything we do driven by that same survival instinct? Survival in order to propagate. Propagation in order for the species to survive."

"Certainly not. If you claim our life has purpose, due to our ability to propagate, then people without children would have meaningless lives," Reis argued.

"That would be the logical conclusion, but is that really the case? Every human being, unless a total hermit from birth, affects other people's lives. With any luck at all, these effects are positive and are carried over to the next generation."

"So you're saying the meaning of our lives is to positively affect the next generation, so as to ultimately improve the human race?"

"Yes! That's it," said the old man, sitting back with confidence.

Reis laughed. "If that were true, don't you think we would see some evidence of that? Do you truly believe modern man is superior to the Neanderthal?"

"I believe there have been some considerable improvements, yes."

"Where? How have we improved?" Reis leaned forward to emphasize his words. "Have we improved because our lives are easier now? If we're lucky, we have warm houses and cars to drive around in. We can sit in our living rooms and be connected to the entire world, overwhelmed with technology. Is this improvement—the fact that our greed and thirst for technology have produced so much toxic waste that the earth's very survival is threatened?

There is an overpowering lack of respect for the other living things we share the earth with. There is even an overpowering lack of respect for the majority of human beings who live in poverty and despair. We are supposedly more civilized. Cultured. But if you look at the human race as a whole, it reeks of evil and hatred. The earth is full of wars, injustices, selfishness, and famine." He sat back, having made his point.

"I did not say the human race is fully evolved," the old man argued pleasantly. "I merely said it has improved. I believe that we have improved in our understanding of things. Neanderthal man did not understand his relationship to the rest of the world. He worked primarily on survival instincts. Modern man understands the consequence of their actions, and struggles to correct it."

Reis smiled again. "Well first of all, I don't agree with you. I think ancient man better understood his place in the world. He did not have any superior attitudes concerning how he fit in. But let's assume, for argument's sake, that what you said is true—that improved understanding has led to no improvement in our behavior."

"Evolution is a very slow process, my boy. Too slow to detect in one lifetime."

"Okay." Reis sat back a bit more and stretched out his legs. "By the time we evolve into these great and wonderful beings you imagine, how do you know that it won't be too late? How can you be sure the earth will still exist to support these enlightened, evolutionary marvels?"

"I can't be sure. That's why it's important for those of us who are already, shall we say, further evolved, to share our knowledge. Speed up the process a bit."

"I see," Reis said with a smile. "Even that could take a considerable length of time."

"Well," the old man smiled in response to Reis's look of amusement, "there could be other, faster methods, but they're more extreme."

"Such as?" Reis asked as he finished his last piece of orange.

"The Lord saw that the wickedness of man was great in the earth. And the Lord was sorry that he had made man on earth. But Noah found favor in the eyes of the Lord. Genesis Six."

Reis laughed. "That is a bit extreme, and if it worked, it was only temporary."

"Hitler also tried to speed up the evolutionary process," the old man said.

"Yes," Reis agreed, "using his version of what was superior. And therein lies the problem. Each individual has their own idea of what constitutes the perfect human being, the perfect society, the best way to interact with our world. Hitler began his crusade with the eradication of Jews. A different individual might have started with gays or blacks or right-wing Republicans. There is no way the peoples of this world could come together and agree on what is ideal. We could not agree on how to educate our children in order to improve the human race."

"And they don't need to," the old man argued. "You are missing my point. The evolutionary process will eventually make that decision. That's why it's extremely important that each individual not only strive for survival, but strive for the betterment of themselves and the betterment of those around them. If we truly be-

come the best person we can, and transfer that ability and knowledge to those around us, then the correct evolutionary path will
be followed."

Reis sat back and shivered slightly. He reached for his sleeping
bag and pulled it around him. He felt the old man's eyes on him
and suddenly wished he'd go away. "That's not such an easy thing
to do," Reis quietly told the old man. "Human beings are very
complex, selfish, and often inadequate. People have their own individual agendas—their own ideas on how they spend their lives.
It's often difficult to look beyond one's self and one's own needs."

"But it's not impossible. There must be some purpose to our
lives other than egoism. If we fulfill this higher purpose, then in
our deaths, our lives will continue through the knowledge we
have passed on, thus adding not only meaning to our lives, but
meaning to our deaths. We must strive for that greater purpose if
we are to survive as a species."

Reis was suddenly very tired and closed his eyes. The sound of
the fire crackled in his ears. There he was, a small boy standing by
the river. "Where does all the water come from, Daddy?"

"It comes from the North. Raindrops fall in the Adirondack
Mountains. What is not used by plants and animals or filtered
through the ground collects in small lakes and streams. This great
river starts in places like Lake Tear of the Clouds. Its waters flow
down, growing ever larger. Each individual tiny stream along the
way contributes to its greatness."

"Where's the water going?" Reis asked. His father took his
hand, and they soared over the river, flying below the clouds.

"Look, son. Can you see? It's going to the sea." Reis held his
father's hand tightly as they sailed past New York Bay and out
over the ocean. They were suddenly far above the clouds, the earth
far below. The sun's heat blazed upon their backs. "Look at our

world, Reis," his father said. It lay below them, beautiful in its blues and greens.

"It's so tiny," Reis said with amazement.

"Yes. And it's all we have."

Reis's eyes opened suddenly. He looked toward the fire. The old man was still there, sitting quietly as he pushed a stick through the flames. Reis's eyes fluttered closed again.

"Go ahead and sleep," he thought he heard the old man say. "Tomorrow comes all the sooner when you sleep."

Reis awoke to a cold, wet sensation on his face. He opened his eyes slowly, almost afraid of what he might see. White flakes floated gently around him. The tree branches were black against the gray sky. A faint sun glowed dimly above him. He sat up suddenly. It was very late in the morning, almost noon. He shook his head and rubbed his hands into his eyes. The smell of orange was still on his fingers. He looked around in confusion. He was alone. A thin layer of snow covered the ground, hiding all evidence of the night's activities. He shook his head, trying to clear the fog that pushed from within.

It was imperative that he move on. Much of the day had been wasted in his sleep. He crawled out of his sleeping bag and quickly threw his things into his pack. He staggered to his feet and splashed water from the stream on his face. Returning to his pack, he picked it up and hoisted it onto his shoulders. Reis glanced in the direction he'd been heading and then back toward where he'd been. He knew there was only one way he could go.

forty-five

Martha Welling snipped off the dead rose buds from her bushes. She cut back the canes and raked the mulch away from the base of each plant. Taking fresh, soft soil, she formed neat little hills around each bush to protect them from the harsh winter weather that would soon be upon them.

A cold wind blew in from the river, and she buttoned up her coat snugly around her neck. *November already*, she thought. *Soon Thanksgiving will be here, then Christmas.* She sighed deeply. Never would those holidays be the same. She sat down on the ground and looked toward the river. She'd tried hard not to feel sorry for herself, but it had not been easy.

Almost two months had passed since she'd received that awful letter. She knew that it was only a matter of time before her phone rang or someone pulled up to her house carrying the news that they'd found him—found him in God only knows what state. When he'd disappeared, the authorities had refused to embark on a long, massive search for someone who did not want to be found. She knew that he'd gone up to those damn mountains. She'd insisted they search, but the car was all that had been found, so far.... Was anyone still really looking?

If only Walter had been alive. He would've known where to look. He would've brought her son home. But now she was alone. It was incredible how one's life could change—its path greatly altered from that envisioned.

She'd been so angry with Reis when she received that letter. She was still angry. With whom was she angry now? Dr. Benson had been quite understanding when she'd called him crying and yelling on the phone. It was she, after all, who had given him back his car. Why? It had seemed like a good idea. A show of faith? Hope? And Reis had used it against her—a getaway car. To get away from life? Oh God! How she prayed he was not dead! She had, of course, since talked to Dr. Benson and apologized. No one had ever been able to change Reis's mind or stand in the way of what he wanted for himself. Car or no car, she knew he would've gone. She'd just made it easier.

"You must trust Reis," Dr. Benson had told her. "Only he knows how difficult his life is. Only he knows what he needs to do to deal with the changes in his life. Reis is very strong—stronger than he believes. Don't assume the worst. I must believe that he will work through this. You should also. He just needs to do it in his own way." At the time, his words made sense, but she'd lost faith. It had been too long.

A small flock of crows landed in the trees near the river and cawed back and forth to one other. Martha stood up and brushed the dirt from her hands, suddenly feeling very old as she walked a few feet closer to the river. It rushed by, fast and deep from the recent rains. "So much water," she said aloud.

"Hey! Lady!" She turned around quickly. "Mind if I take a shower in your house?"

She recognized him immediately; his wild woodsman's look was something she'd seen before. In a moment he was there, and she was hugging him, his rough beard scratching her forehead, the smell of the earth on his body.

He pulled away from her slightly. "Do you have anything good to eat? I'm starved!"

She began to cry.

"Aw, Mom," he said and held her close again. "I'm sorry. Don't cry. If you don't have anything good," he said, "scrambled eggs will be just fine."

forty-six

Reis sat on the stool in the kitchen, like he had as a boy, and watched his mother cook. He'd already showered. His beard was gone and his hair combed neatly back. It felt strange to be clean.

"I talked to your grandmother," his mother was saying as she rinsed lettuce under the faucet. "Her arthritis is really bothering her in this damp weather."

"That's too bad," said Reis.

"Are you sure this is all you want? Just pasta and a salad?"

"Yes, Mom." He smiled. "It's best to work your way back to real food."

"You look terribly thin."

"There's not a McDonald's to be found in the Adirondack forest."

"Well, thank goodness for that," Martha said as she reached for the carrots and peeled them with passion into the sink.

There was an awkward silence.

"Doris Miller from my bridge club called me yesterday. I don't think you know her. She told me her husband ran off with a friend of her daughter's!"

"A friend of her daughter's?"

"Yes! The poor woman's a mess."

"I'm sure the daughter is not too happy either."

Martha finished with the carrots and reached for the lettuce. She began to pick through it, removing the wilted or brown parts and ripping the rest into bite-size pieces. She seemed to be searching for something to say. "Oh," she said after a couple of minutes. "Did I tell you that my roses won first place in the fair this fall?"

"No, Mom. You didn't."

"Well they did. I'll show you the ribbon. Jane Ray was so jealous. You remember Jane? From down the river?"

"Of course. She's been there all my life."

"Yes, of course you remember. How silly of me." Martha became flustered as she washed the tomatoes. One slipped from her fingers, bounced off the edge of the sink, and landed on the floor with a thud. She looked as if she might start to cry again.

"Mom," he said kindly. "It's okay." He stood up, walked over to her, picked up the tomato, and placed it back on the countertop. "I'm okay." He put his hand on her shoulder.

She turned off the water and turned toward him.

Her eyes were moist as she said, "I don't know why it should feel so strange, talking to my own son."

"A lot has happened since we've seen each other. I'm not quite the same son you used to have."

"Oh, I don't think that's true."

Reis looked out the window and did not comment.

"I can't tell you what it means to me, that you're here. That you've come home," she said.

"It feels good," he told her, turning away from the window and facing her again. "It's where I want to be right now. I'm just sorry it took me so long to get here."

After dinner, Reis started a fire in the fireplace in the den. It wasn't long before the warmth from the flames had heated the room. He sat back in the chair in which his father had always sat.

"It's nice to have a fire again," his mother said as she came in with a tray of tea and slices of cake. "I never bother to start one for myself." She sat down in the other chair. "I brought you some herbal tea."

"Thanks, Mom." Reis reached for a cup and sipped it. "You must be very lonely in this big house. Maybe you should sell it."

"It's my home. I can't imagine being any less lonely somewhere else."

They stared at the flames, both drinking their tea in silence. "Mom?" Reis said after a while. "Do you ever hear anything from Ellen?"

Martha set her tea down. Her face was slightly tight, her mouth set firm when she turned to him. "She came to the hospital. Once." She hesitated, giving him time to contemplate her last word. "When you were very ill. When they said you would not live. I'm sure you don't remember."

Reis laughed a bit. "No." He stared back at the fire.

A few minutes went by. "She wrote to me," his mother said. "Some time later." Reis turned back to her expectantly. "I saved the letter. Would you like to see it?"

Reis met his mother's gaze and hesitated before answering. "Sure," he said casually, shrugging his shoulders slightly.

"It's in my room. I'll go get it."

Reis watched the flames while his mother was gone. He remembered how Ellen had looked that evening in her garden. He'd fallen in love with her then, as she'd looked up at him, the fiery sky reflecting in her eyes. And everything he'd ever wanted had fallen into place—too tight...too neat...too perfect.

He turned to the sound of his mother. She sat, flicked the letter gently with her index finger, then handed it over. He turned it over a few times. It was safely in the envelope and addressed to his mother. He pulled out the sheets and carefully unfolded them. The letter was dated the previous November. He began to read.

Dear Martha,

I know this letter is long overdue. My only excuse is that I did not know what to say. Mike Green told me that Reis was out of the hospital and doing pretty well. I am so glad that he's doing better. I cannot describe the sorrow I felt when they told us he would die.

I realize how angry you were with me when I saw you at the hospital. I hope you have found it in your heart to forgive me for my inability to help Reis. You were right: I should have told you how bad things were. I only wish I had understood how badly he needed help. I was too busy being angry with him for how he was affecting my life, to consider what was happening to his own.

Martha, I loved your son. I still ache for him. I wish I were selfless enough to love him still. It's easy to say that you were not there and that you did not know how his attitude toward me changed. It was a natural progression for my feelings to change for him. He became a man I did not know. He was, in no way, the man I fell in love with. I know now that he was very ill. I am ashamed to admit that even if I had fully understood the depth of his illness,

I do not believe I could have stood by him. I am not capable of the unconditional love needed for such a thing. I always felt that Reis and I were a lot alike. We both had similar interests, both strong and driven in our attempts to succeed. But there was one fundamental difference: his capacity for kindness and compassion greatly exceeded mine.

Please know that I only want the best for Reis. If I truly believed that I could help him, I would. But I cannot. I believe that any contact with me would only do him harm.

I will always hold the memory of him close to my heart. I can only hope he has a small place in his heart for me.

Love,
Ellen

Reis set the letter down in his lap and did not brush away the tears that fell from his eyes.

"I should not have shown it to you," his mother said.

"No," he said. "This is good. I'm glad I read it."

They were silent for a while. "Mike Green called not long ago," Martha said. "He calls every few months to see how you are doing."

"That's nice," Reis said flatly. "I'll have to call him."

"He told me this last call that Ellen had taken a tenure track position up near Boston. I don't remember the school."

Reis nodded his head. "I'm sure she'll do well."

"I'm sorry, honey. I know how much you loved her."

Reis shrugged his shoulders.

His mother was silent again. It was some time before she

spoke. "You know," she said hesitantly. "I met your friend Kelly."

"Yes, I know."

"She's also called several times, asking if I'd heard from you." She paused, waiting for him to respond. When he did not, she continued. "I promised her if I knew where you were, I'd let her know."

Reis turned to his mother. "Mom, that's a promise I'd like you to break."

She stared at him a moment before saying, "If that's what you want."

"That's what I want," he said with finality.

forty-seven

Reis walked into Dr. Benson's waiting room and smiled a bit sheepishly when Sue looked up. "Dr. Welling!" she exclaimed warmly. She glanced at her watch. "I see you're right on time, as always."

"Of course," said Reis. He scanned the room and shook his head when he eyed the crooked paintings on the wall. "Don't you ever straighten these things?" he teased. He walked over and carefully straightened each one.

"Dr. Welling, that was your job. It's not my fault you've been absent from your duties for so long."

Reis glanced at the magazines lying on the table. "What's this?" He picked up a magazine and held it out to her. "*People?*" he asked, his eyebrows raised.

"It's a great magazine," Sue said defensively. "A lot of our patients really love it."

Reis shook his head again. "I'll tell you, I'm gone for a few months, and this whole place goes to seed." Sue was about to respond when the door to Dr. Benson's office opened.

"I thought I heard your voice," said the doctor as he stepped into the hallway and extended his hand to Reis. The two men regarded one another; a long moment passed before Dr. Benson said, "Come on in."

A hint of a smile passed over Reis's face as he walked into the room. "You thought I was a goner. Didn't you?"

Dr. Benson shut the door and walked slowly to his chair. "No," he said as he sat down. "I really don't think I did."

Reis sat down also and smiled. "Is that so?"

Dr. Benson smiled back. "Reis, I've always had more confidence in your strength and ability to survive than you." He paused a moment and added, "You do, however, have schizophrenia—by definition, unpredictable. I am glad you're back. How are you?"

"Great. Just great." Dr. Benson studied him. Reis shifted his gaze to the window before reaching into his pocket and pulling out a prescription bottle. He placed it on the desk and said, "Two left, with no refills."

The doctor picked up the bottle and toyed with it in his hands. "I'll write you a new prescription."

"I don't know. I took them the first months I was in the forest. When they got low I rationed them along with my food. First, two a day. Then one. Then I cut them in half. I've been taking one hundred milligrams for weeks now, and I think I'm okay." Reis looked at Dr. Benson with uncertainty. "I know how much you love these damn pills. What do you think I should do?"

"I have never advocated unwarranted medication; if you're doing fine, let's continue with the hundred milligrams."

Reis was uncertain.

"Let's do this," Dr. Benson suggested. "Get the new prescription filled. I'll write it for ninety pills. If you feel things getting shaky, you can always increase the dosage. I'll refill the Ativan too. You'll have it, if you need it. How does that sound?"

"All right, I guess."

Dr. Benson sat back. "Talk to me, Reis. Tell me how you're really doing."

Reis hesitated before he sat forward and began to speak. "Oh, I'm sane. I'm so sane it's frightening. Scares me to death. I feel like I'm just waiting. Waiting and wondering how long it will last. Each day I wake up and do a reality check. Everything appears okay. But that's the problem with being crazy, especially in the beginning: it's impossible to see. I keep waiting for the look. You know, the *What the hell's he talking about?* look. I got it all the time when I first got sick. I'd be talking to someone and I'd get that look. Well, of course, what I said made perfect sense to me, so my only possible conclusion was that whomever I was talking to was an idiot. Before long everyone was an idiot." He smiled a bit when he said this. "So far everybody seems pretty bright, but I can't seem to stop waiting for it. And what's worse, the people who know that I've been ill, my mother included, step around me as if I'm the china shop and they're the bull. The pressure's enough to drive me insane."

"What you're going through is normal, Reis. I believe it's a good sign that you're afraid. With time, it will fade into the background as you grow more confident in your recovery. It's important that you keep in tune with what's happening to you. Any changes in sleeping patterns, radical mood swings, and certainly any hallucinations, you need to contact me, and we'll deal with them, but do not let it absorb you."

Dr. Benson stood up and walked across the room, where he poured himself a glass of water. "Would you like some, Reis?"

"No, thanks. I'm fine."

Dr. Benson returned to his chair and drank some before saying, "When you left here, you had every intention of killing yourself. Am I correct?"

"Yes," said Reis quietly. "I did not intend to come back."

"What changed your mind? What happened out there in the forest that made you want to live?"

Reis thought about his answer for a long time. He did not wish to share all that he had felt and experienced while he was away. "It wasn't so much that I was afraid to die," he finally answered, "or even that I did not want to. It was more that I was afraid not to live. As screwed up as my life is, who am I to say it's not an integral piece of the puzzle that keeps us all going? No matter what shape that piece is in, even if it's totally fucked up, it's not my place to decide when to discard it."

Dr. Benson nodded his head. "What are you going to do now, Reis?"

"Well, let's see. I have so many choices! I could continue to live with my mother for the rest of my life, or hers—whichever comes first. Maybe the local ladies would let me join their garden club! I do, after all, have a degree in botany. Or I could move back here to Albany and try to get my old job back at the library. God knows that was a position of bottomless fulfillment!"

Dr. Benson gave him an impatient look, but Reis was on a roll.

"I know! I could go back to the hospital! They were in desperate need of a good gardener. Or I could return to the woods. I could become the great madman of the Adirondacks. People would hike for miles and miles just with the hope of spotting me—"

"Reis, please," Dr. Benson interrupted. "I think we need to

look seriously at your options."

"Doc, I'm serious. Serious as death," he said with the slightest of smiles.

Dr. Benson sighed. "Reis, do what you do best. Go back to Cornell. Teach."

"You, of all people, should understand why I can't go back there."

"Okay. Forget Cornell. Obtain a position somewhere else."

"You make it sound so easy."

"I'm sure it would be no more difficult than anything else you've done or been through these last few years."

"Right. I'm sure there are just hundreds of universities that would jump at the opportunity to take on a schizophrenic professor."

"Reis, you're not a leper. You are also under no moral or legal obligation to discuss your medical history with anyone. You cannot spend the rest of your life waiting for your next relapse. It may never come. You've made the decision to live—now reclaim your life."

Reis looked at the doctor and nodded his head slightly. "Reclaim my life," he stated. "I'll give it some thought."

forty-eight

Reis stared at the phone a long time before he reached for the receiver. He cradled it in his hands for several more minutes. He closed his eyes and sighed deeply before finally forcing his fingers to dial the number. Nevertheless, he was unprepared when the phone was answered on the first ring.

"Hello?" the voice said into his ear.

"Um...hi.... This is Reis."

"Reis! I'm so glad you called. I was just thinking about you."

"Only good thoughts, I hope."

"Always. Where are you?"

"I'm at my mom's." The hesitation he'd felt about calling Mike quickly faded. He could sense nothing but friendship and warmth in Mike's voice.

"She must be so relieved to have you home."

"Yes." Reis hesitated. "I understand you've talked to my mother several times. Thanks, Mike. It's nice to know she's had someone to turn to. It's not been easy for her."

"Nor for you, I'm sure," Mike said.

"No. It hasn't."

"How are you, Reis?"

"I'm really doing quite well. Feeling better every day. That's one reason I'm calling. Mike, I'd like to start teaching again."

"Great! We'd love to have you back as soon as possible. When do you want to start?"

"I appreciate that. I really do. But I won't be coming back to Cornell. I just can't see myself there anymore. I hope you understand."

"That would depend on your reasoning. If you think the department doesn't want you back, you're wrong," Mike said firmly.

"It's not that. I just need a fresh start. Maybe something not so grandiose," he said with a laugh.

Mike laughed back. "Grandiose, huh?"

"You know what I mean. There's a lot of pressure to produce there. I'm not sure I'm quite as productive as I once was."

Mike was quiet for a moment. "I'd really like you to come back."

"Thanks, Mike. But it's really not what I need now."

"Okay," Mike said softly. "Then tell me, how can I help you?"

"I've been out of it for so long. I know the department gets inquiries now and then from universities looking for a botany grad. I'd really like to stay in this area. I was wondering if you knew of anything."

Mike thought for a moment. "I know of only one position in this area, but I don't think you'd be interested."

"Try me," Reis said.

"I understand SUNY at Plattsburgh is looking for someone."

"Plattsburgh. Really?"

"That's right. I guess the wife of an old professor died. He'd been dead for years. She had a great deal of family money and left a large endowment to the college with the stipulation it be used for greenhouses and gardens. They're looking for someone to come in to help organize its construction and teach a few botany courses. I thought it sounded more like they needed a gardener than a botanist," Mike said.

"Still, it might be worth looking into," Reis said.

"I'll give you the dean's name," Mike said. "Meanwhile, I'll ask around and let you know if there's anything else out there."

"Thanks, Mike. Maybe I'll head down to Ithaca in the next few weeks, and we could get together."

"Anytime, Reis. You just let me know when you're coming, and I'll clear my schedule."

forty-nine

Reis was thinking of the forest. His fingers hovered, almost touching the square black keys of his laptop, the words taking form, his index finger striking the letter *T*. He began to type slowly, but in less than a half hour, his fingers were moving easily across the keyboard—his mind focused on the task, the entire manuscript suddenly clear in his mind. Now it was strictly a technical issue. As his typing took on an urgent rhythm, there was a small knock at the door. "Come in," he said, not looking up. He finished the sentence he'd been writing as the door opened. He looked up reluctantly as his finger hit the period key.

"Dr. Welling," she said, a bit timidly, "I wondered if I could talk to you…um…about my midterm grade?"

She wore a tiny, tight floral dress that seemed so popular with the college women these days. *Barbie dresses*, he called them. Her high platform sandals were a bit ridiculous, her pink toes easing over the front. But it was undeniable: they made her already long, shapely legs all the better. Her long blonde hair was loose, its tips falling around the swell of her breasts, her eyes suppliant, her lower lip tucked between her teeth. Reis sucked in a breath as he smiled slightly, closed his laptop, and sat back. "Certainly, Ms. Reilly," he said. She smiled sweetly and shut the door. He indicated for her to sit down. She sat across from him and crossed her legs, her sandal bobbing gentle with the beat of her foot.

"I don't know if you know this or not," she started, "but I'm pre-med. My grade point average is 3.88."

"Congratulations," he said.

Her face constricted slightly, her lips turning into a pretty pout. "I wasn't very happy with my score on the midterm," she continued. "My grades are very important to me."

"As I recall, you did pretty well. The low eighties."

"Dr. Welling, *B*s just won't cut it." She sat up taller. "I need an *A* in this course. There must be some way I can improve my grade." She leaned closer to his desk, expanded her chest with an influx of air, and waited.

"Ms. Reilly, the material is not that hard." He concentrated on her face, returning to her mouth, which was now set in anticipation. "Certainly, if you intend to go to medical school, you should have no trouble learning the parts of a plant. The human body," his eyes involuntarily flicked down to the soft white curves above her dress and then back to her face, "is a bit more complex."

"I signed up for this class because I thought it would be fun to take in the summer. I never thought studying would be so hard. It's so hot out." She fanned herself to emphasize the point.

"True. It's hard when the weather's hot. When I was a student, I took classes every summer. But, I discovered the perfect way to get good grades, even when it was so hot all you wanted to do was hit the nearest lake." He hesitated, her look expectant. "This is what I'd do," he said, leaning toward her. "I'd get my books, and I would walk across campus." He paused and looked toward the door, leaned a little closer, and dropped his voice. "I'd walk across campus," he repeated, "to the library. The library was always air conditioned! I'd find a nice cool corner, and there I would study until I learned all I needed to know. Then, and only then, would I go swimming."

She smiled slightly. "There's no other way?"

He sat back. "I'm afraid not. If you start now and do a good job on your paper, the final should be a breeze. I see no reason why you can't pull your grade up to an *A*."

She frowned and sighed. "Well, then, I guess I'm on my way to the library." She stood up, pulling slightly on the hem of her skirt, letting her hands linger a moment at her inner thighs.

"I'll be looking forward to reading your paper," Reis told her.

After she'd left, he sat back and chuckled silently as he ran his fingers over his laptop. He allowed himself a moment of entertainment—a quick, alternate scenario running through his head. He shifted at the stirrings in his crotch, sighed, then reopened the laptop.

Reis had followed up on Mike's lead; he'd sent his credentials to SUNY Plattsburgh and had arranged for an interview after the holidays. "I was surprised when I received your CV," the dean had told him during his interview. "I found myself wondering why someone with your background would be interested in our little school." He looked at Reis for a moment. "I guess I'd like to know why you left Cornell."

Reis thought he was prepared for this question. He'd gone over a dozen different answers in his head, but when it came, he grew unsure. He nodded his head slightly, with resolve. "Dean Miller," he began, slipping his hands between his knees to hide any possible signs of anxiety. "I'm sure you've noticed from my CV that I have not worked in well over two years." He hesitated a moment and drew in a subtle but deep, calming breath. "I've spent part of that time in the hospital. The remainder has been spent attempting to reorganize my life." Another breath and then, "I was diagnosed with acute schizophrenia almost two years ago." He paused, letting his words sink in. "I know the word schizophrenia conjures up all sorts of images, ranging from the mumbling street people to the raving psychotic who strangles little children. And as popular as that perception is, it's far from accurate. I'm one of the lucky people dealing with schizophrenia—" He paused and smiled. "I'm not so sure the words *lucky* and *schizophrenia* have any business being in the same sentence, however.... But, in any case, I've had the family support and the financial ability to be properly diagnosed and treated. I have responded well to that treatment. As of today, I have not had any significant symptoms for almost five months. It's my belief and the opinion of my doctor that I will not relapse. I could go back to Cornell, if I wanted to, but that is not my wish. You have a wonderful college here. It has a good reputation. I believe that I could contribute greatly to its faculty. I only hope that the general prejudice against this misunderstood disease will not keep me from obtaining this position." Reis sat back, sighed gently, and waited for the review.

The dean leaned back and folded his hands under his chin. "I appreciate your honesty. And you're right: schizophrenia is probably the most misunderstood disease known to man."

Reis looked at him, surprised.

"My sister has schizophrenia," the dean continued. "She's had it for years. Unfortunately, in her case, it's chronic. She's been in and out of hospitals most of her life."

"I'm sorry," said Reis, simultaneously accepting the little bit of luck that life had suddenly thrown his way—of not having to find out, at this very moment, the cost of stigma.

"Dr. Welling, if this position is something you really want, we would be honored to have you. Your reputation in the field of botany is well known to me. You can make this position whatever you want. If you choose to continue your research, I will support you. The money and funding possibilities here are not what they are at Cornell, however. I have to wonder if you'll be content here."

"Dean Miller, let me be frank. If you had offered me this position prior to my illness, I may have laughed politely in your face. This illness has not so much changed my ability to obtain my goals but has caused me to reconsider what those goals should be. Even with all the research and publications, my true passion has always been teaching. That is what I want to do. If I do any writing or research, it will be secondary to what I love the most."

"Then am I to understand that we are in agreement that you will be joining us here at Plattsburgh?"

Reis smiled. "Yes, I believe we're in agreement."

It had been that easy, Reis thought as he turned away from the computer screen and toward his window. He hadn't even bothered looking into any of the other leads Mike had given him. It were as if this college, nestled near the Adirondacks, had been constructed just for him. Small and unpretentious, Plattsburgh was one of the thirteen colleges of arts and sciences in the State University of New York system. Situated in the small town of Plattsburgh, New York, in the Champlain Valley, the college was immediately west of Lake Champlain and east of the far northern sections of the Adirondack Park. It was just a short drive to the foothills.

Reis scanned the tops of the rather unpicturesque buildings of the campus, letting his mind drift to the distant Adirondack

Mountains. On a clear day, from just the right perspective, they could be seen—large and powerful in their beauty. He turned his attention back to his computer, thought a moment before tapping out a few unsuccessful words, frowned, and glanced at his watch. His office hours were officially over. He needed to eat lunch before his class. When the weather allowed, Reis ate by the tiny pond that sat just off the main section of the campus. He grabbed the small paper bag off his desk, locked his office behind him, and walked the short distance to the pond.

The pond, a popular spot on very hot days like today, shimmered in the summer heat. Several students sat with their feet in the water. A golden retriever made an impressive splash into the pond when it jumped after the Frisbee its owner had thrown. Reis quickly made his way along the edge toward a couple of large oak trees. He was relieved to find his normal spot beneath the first of the two trees free of students or dogs or other intruders. The branches of the old tree swayed low, almost touching the water's edge, and he ducked under the foliage and sat on the ground, easing between the roots and leaning against the trunk. He sighed and watched as the dog made its way back to shore, the orange, plastic disk securely between its jaws. Reis took his sandwich out of his bag and unfolded the first crease of waxed paper. "Good afternoon, Professor Welling," said two young women as they walked past the tree.

"Good afternoon, ladies."

He appreciated them as they walked away along the pond's edge. One turned to the other, leaned in with a giggle, and said, just loud enough for Reis to interpret, "He's so cute!" He shook his head and smiled. The Frisbee sailed; the dog leapt back into the pond. Reis sighed again, looked at the sandwich he held in his hand, and pulled the waxed paper open further. He really needed to get out more—force himself to meet some people closer to his own age. There must be hiking groups.... Something for people pushing thirty....

He picked up half of the sandwich and took a bite, the peanut butter slipping out onto his finger. The air was hot, and his shirt clung to his chest, beads of sweat forming at his neck. The golden retriever reemerged from the water, dropped the Frisbee, and shook, sending tiny drops of refreshment toward Reis. He put the sandwich down, licked the peanut butter free from his finger, and unfastened a couple of buttons of his shirt. He pulled the material away from his chest and used its tails to fan up some air. The young man called his dog. Reis took another bite just as a sweat bee landed on the bread. He swept the sandwich away from his face, causing a small piece of crust to fly free. The bee buzzed obstinately around his head and danced on his sandwich. One more good swat—making contact this time—and it was gone. A sudden, sharp snarl ensued, and Reis jumped. He looked up just in time to see a small, fuzzy brown dog, only a few short feet away, leap at the golden retriever's throat.

"Max! Stop that! I'm so sorry," a woman apologized to the dog's owner. Reis's eyes went quickly to Kelly as Max returned to her sheepishly. "He really thinks he's much bigger than he is. You see, it's the terrier in him." Reis frowned and cocked his head ever so slightly. She smiled at the young man and pushed her damp bangs away from her eyes. Reis felt his stomach twist. "He's really totally harmless." Her hair was a bit longer than it had been a year ago. Her skin was tan and contrasted nicely against the light green of her T-shirt. Her shorts were white, her legs curving down toward her feet, which were housed in light canvas shoes. No socks. He smiled.

"No problem." The dog's owner smiled. "Shane can handle

it." He ruffled the large dog's fur.

"Maybe you could help me," Kelly said. Max continued to eye the other dog suspiciously, growling. "Max! No!" Kelly laughed. "Sorry!" She paused and smiled another apology. "I'm looking for Dr. Reis Welling...from the botany department...."

"Dr. Welling? He's right there," the young man pointed. "Eating his lunch."

Her eyes met his. She tilted her head for a better view, her smile becoming deep and private. "Thanks," she said to the young man, her eyes not leaving Reis.

"I should have known to look under a tree," she said as she drew near, dropping under the branches as she laughed. Max was already at his side, sending Reis wet-tongue hellos.

Reis fended off the dog and picked up the sandwich from his lap. "And I should not be as surprised as I am to see you here."

Max sat, his tail wagging, his lips turned upward, his tongue lolling Reis's way. Kelly sat next to Reis, crossed her legs—her left knee brushing against his leg—and peered up at the tree branches. "So, what is this? Some sort of maple?"

"Oak."

"I knew that, of course." Her smile widened. "I was just testing you." Max suddenly jumped forward and snapped up Reis's wayward piece of crust before flopping down, grunting happily, and rubbing his back against the ground. "So this is where you hang out now?" Kelly glanced around the campus.

"This is it." He paused and admired the soft summer freckles on her face. "Would you like some sandwich?" he asked.

"I don't want to take your food." She eyed the half he was holding toward her.

"Go ahead," he coaxed. "I remember how much you like to eat."

"Well...I am hungry." She took it gently from his hand. "You look great, Reis." She bit into the sandwich, pulling the fingers of her other hand through her hair.

"Thanks. I feel great too." They ate in silence for a few minutes, watching the retriever swim across the pond.

Kelly turned to him as she swallowed a bite of the sandwich. "So everything's fallen into place for you." Her words came out thick as she struggled with the sticky peanut butter, her green eyes searching his face.

Reis offered her his water bottle, which she took and drank. "It would appear that it has."

Kelly set the remainder of the sandwich down on her thigh and looked at the ground. She nervously plucked a small weed from the dirt. "I've missed you. I never felt right about the way we said goodbye." She looked up. "There was something terribly wrong with it."

"I was having a pretty rough time then, Kelly."

"I know. I know you were. But I haven't been able to stop thinking about you. I haven't stopped thinking about you since I saw you that very first day, up in that tree."

"I'm sorry."

She gave him an exasperated look. "Reis, I like thinking about you. I just don't like thinking about you when you're nowhere to be found."

"And how did you find me?"

"Don't worry. Your mother was very loyal to you. But you know," she said with a smile, "it's amazing what you can do with a Social Security number and a computer."

Reis laughed. "I don't think I even want to know how you got hold of my Social Security number."

"Oh, that was the easy part." Kelly paused for a moment and

looked out at the pond. "So, Reis," she said quietly. "Do you ever think about me?" She looked back his way.

He looked at her, his smile gone. "Yes, Kelly. I do."

She dropped her chin slightly and cocked her head, her words tumbling out. "It seems to me that if I'm thinking about you and you're thinking about me, and I'm assuming that you're thinking good things about me, because I'm thinking good things about you, that maybe we could think together. I bet if we put our heads together, we could think some really, really good thoughts." She stopped and brought her hand to her mouth, bit the nail of her thumb, and waited.

Reis nodded, narrowing his eyes. "Sounds reasonable. But where does Brian fit into all this really good thinking?"

She moved her hand away from her mouth, swept it through her bangs, and looked away briefly. "Brian and I aren't seeing each other anymore. Not for a long time now. We didn't seem to want the same things."

"No? And what *do* you want, Kelly?"

She held his gaze as she stated, "I want you."

"And Brian didn't?"

Kelly laughed. "No."

Reis nodded his head again. "Well, I can understand how that presented a problem." His face grew serious as he wrestled with his thoughts. He picked up an old acorn cap and teased it between his fingers. She waited quietly beside him.

"My life," he finally said as he carefully studied the intricate pattern of the cap, "is not how I envisioned it. There are complications.... Issues...." His eyes left the cap and found hers. "There are flaws."

She looked back at him, a small smile playing on her lips. "Must you be perfect?"

"It would be nice." She laughed, as did he. He then became grave and insistent. "But there are serious deviations from perfection." He saw the uncertainly on her face.

"But you're doing well, here...." she said, a hint of a question mark. She glanced around the campus at this world he'd found for himself, then back to his eyes.

He nodded his head slightly with concurrence. "But there are no guarantees. Things could shift. Meds could fail. Stresses could arise."

The stress of opening himself up to the possibility of her....

She was closer now, and the soft redness of her lips was moist with possibilities.

"Yes," she said. "I suppose that's true.... But there's no guarantee that I won't, say, get hit by a bus, end up a paraplegic, and need someone to press straws to my lips." She looked at him. "There are *no* guarantees." She leaned yet closer, her words slower now. "Would you...press straws to my lips?"

And so he leaned in and kissed those lips because, after all, there are so many empty spaces in the universe that so desperately need to be filled, and if he could—if it were possible to—fill just one....

acknowledgments

My first order of thanks goes out to my readers. If not for the success of my debut novel, *Where Are the Cocoa Puffs?*, this second novel may not have existed! Heartfelt thanks to the people of Goodman Beck Publishing, especially David Michael Gettis, who has once again created an amazing cover and interior layout! (Where does he find such very cool fonts?) Also, thank you, David, for your anally accurate attention to editing detail, although your criticism regarding my use of semicolons was unfair, to say the least. Even though my dear friend and editor, Lorna Lynch, was not directly involved in the editing of this particular book, I must thank her for her support; she was always ready to tell me how wonderful I was, no matter how pathetic my needs. (David: do you approve of the semicolon use there?) I must thank my wonderful husband, Paul, for going way beyond the call of duty and reading this manuscript over and over and over again. Your help was invaluable! Known for his stupid puns, Paul's also directly responsible for coming up with the name *Reis* and thus the title! This leads me to thank all the many, many countless people who put up with me as I agonized obsessively for weeks over said title! Thanks to those who read this book in its very early phase (way before I could call myself a writer) and actually liked it: Wendy and Tom Brooks; my numerous family members (mom: Dot; sister: Sherri; brother: Doug Jr.; dad: Doug Sr.; his wife: Suzi; sister-in-laws: Debbie, Jane, Suzanne, and Mary; brother-in-law: Don; mother-in-law: Ruth; father-in-law: Chuck; his wife: Maggie); and anybody else I might have bothered with it. Special thanks to Sheila Le Gacy and Pat Hetrick for your input, support, and suggestions. Thanks also goes out to Dr. William Cross and Ellen Reynolds for your help in ironing out some final facts and details. And lastly, it would be remiss of me not to acknowledge the hugely positive influence that NAMI (National Alliance on Mental Illness) has had on my life. Thanks to all the thousands of wonderful people who keep that alliance strong.

about the author

Photograph by Reyna Stagnaro

Karen Winters Schwartz was born and raised in Mansfield, Ohio. She wrote her first truly good story at age seven. Her second-grade teacher, Mrs. Schneider, publicly and falsely accused her of plagiarism. She did not write again for forty years.

In-between, she moved to Columbus, Ohio, where she spent thirteen years of her life pursuing a seemingly endless education at The Ohio State University. She received her undergraduate degree in microbiology, her master of science in immunology, and a doctorate in optometry. Winters Schwartz met her future husband, Paul, at a student optometric conference in Chicago. They were both slightly drunk, and it was love at first sight. They married in 1987, moved to Central New York, and bought a house on the shores of Otisco Lake—the "pinky finger" of the Finger Lakes. There they began their lives together, their careers as optometrists, and raised two daughters, who are now off to change the world—hopefully in a good way.

Winters Schwartz is an active board member of NAMI Syracuse (National Alliance on Mental Illness), a sought-after speaker, and a strong advocate for mental illness awareness. This is her second novel and follow-up to her widely successful debut, *Where Are the Cocoa Puffs?.*

National Alliance on Mental Illness

For additional information and support:

nami.org

800-950-NAMI